PRAISE FOR
A ROOFTOP IN JERUSALEM

"In his beautiful book, *A Rooftop in Jerusalem*, theologian-turned-novelist Michael Kinnamon entwines a deeply moving love story with the Israeli–Palestinian conflict. Kinnamon's spirituality infuses his prose, and he comes as close as any outsider possibly can to understanding the inner reality of Israelis and Palestinians. A meditation on the persistence of love and the power of an open heart to transcend seemingly inviolate borders."

—**YOSSI KLEIN HALEVI**, author of
Letters to My Palestinian Neighbor

"*A Rooftop in Jerusalem* chronicles the turbulent spiritual growth of its main characters. By locating these inner journeys in Jerusalem, Michael Kinnamon offers a narrative of extraordinary spiritual depth. Among the novel's many charms—its humor, its deft characterizations, its skilled craftsmanship—the reader will most appreciate the central romance: a love story between two star-crossed lovers, but also between the characters and the sacred city, and the author and the twisty, ancient neighborhood with its fateful rooftop. Michael Kinnamon—a novelist, theologian, and scholar with a poetic soul—has produced a lyrical, evocative work of great transcendence and heartbreak."

—**PHILIP GRAUBART**, author of *Here There is No Why*
and *Women and God*

"As someone who spent many years living in Jerusalem, I was grateful for the way Michael Kinnamon's novel reawakened memories of that enigmatic, maddening, tragic, wonderful city. *A Rooftop in Jerusalem* is particularly relevant in these days when so many are embracing simplistic pronouncements about the seemingly eternal conflict between Israelis and Palestinians. The novel powerfully shows us the complexity of the situation: the grinding oppression that the occupation imposes on Palestinians, the way Israelis 'live with the nagging fear of losing everything, the way Jews have often lost everything.' It is a book that insists upon, and engages us with, the humanity of people in a place too often reduced to symbols and slogans."

—**WAYNE KARLIN**, author of *The Genizah* and *Memorial Days*

"Michael Kinnamon's novel, *A Rooftop in Jerusalem*, is an ode to the ancient, divided city of Jerusalem, a lamentation for the sadness and suffering to which it has borne witness, and a love story that breaks our hearts and restores our hope at the same time."

—**STEPHEN A. SECHE**, author of *The Silversmith's Secret*

"Rich with historical depth and political nuance, *A Rooftop in Jerusalem* movingly tells the story of an interfaith love affair while doubling as a tenderly written guide to Old City Jerusalem."

—**ROBERT KEHLMANN**, author of *The Rabbi's Suitcase*

"*A Rooftop in Jerusalem* is an insightful story for these current times. It weaves together Daniel's love for Jerusalem and for a woman he meets in Israel. These loves intertwine as Jerusalem evolves through the decades and Daniel collects the voices and questions of people from so many backgrounds. I highly recommend this novel."

—**BETH DOTSON BROWN**, author of *Rooted in Sunrise*

"There is nothing more evasive than memory, that fleeting period of time that memorializes itself in our minds but promises to never again emerge quite perfectly, a rejection of the way things once were. *A Rooftop in Jerusalem* is a love story that never quite takes off but still somehow soars—with a city and a person—evoking the true meaning of a first love that never escapes our whole being. Kinnamon reminds readers to view all perspectives, seek answers, and love with our whole hearts even from many miles away. *A Rooftop in Jerusalem* follows the growth of a man who constantly returns to himself to find new viewpoints from his favorite rooftop. "There are always things beneath what you see," Kinnamon writes, and he couldn't be more right. A masterpiece of fiction and a memorial to youth, love, and theology."

—**MIRANDA FAYE DILLON**, award-winning author of *The Unshatterables*

A Rooftop in Jerusalem

A Rooftop in Jerusalem

by Michael Kinnamon

© Copyright 2025 Michael Kinnamon

ISBN 979-8-88824-703-7

All rights reserved. No part of this publication may be reproduced, stored in a retrieval system, or transmitted in any form or by any means—electronic, mechanical, photocopy, recording, or any other—except for brief quotations in printed reviews, without the prior written permission of the author.

This is a work of fiction. All the characters in this book are fictitious, and any resemblance to actual persons, living or dead, is purely coincidental. The names, incidents, dialogue, and opinions expressed are products of the author's imagination and are not to be construed as real.

Cover art and design by Lauren Sheldon

Published by

köehlerbooks™

3705 Shore Drive
Virginia Beach, VA 23455
800-435-4811
www.koehlerbooks.com

a ROOFTOP *in* JERUSALEM

a novel

MICHAEL KINNAMON

VIRGINIA BEACH
CAPE CHARLES

For Trahan,
whose reemergence in my life has been a source of joy.

On a roof in the Old City
laundry hanging in the late afternoon sunlight:
the white sheet of a woman who is my enemy,
the towel of a man who is my enemy,
to wipe off the sweat of his brow.

In the sky of the Old City
a kite.
At the other end of the string,
a child
I can't see
because of the wall.

—Yehuda Amichai, from "Jerusalem"

In Jerusalem, and I mean within the ancient walls,
I walk from one epoch to another without a memory
to guide me. The prophets over there are sharing
the history of the holy . . . ascending to heaven
and returning less discouraged and melancholy, because love
and peace are holy and are coming to town.

—Mahmoud Darwish, from "In Jerusalem"

I say: How is this my concern? I'm a spectator
He says: No spectators at chasm's door . . . and no
one is neutral here. And you must choose
your part in the end
So I say: I'm missing the beginning, what's the beginning?

—Mahmoud Darwish, from "I Have a Seat in the Abandoned Theater"

Poets come in the evening into the Old City
and they emerge from it pockets stuffed with images
and metaphors and little well-constructed parables
and crepuscular similes from among columns and crypts,
from within darkening fruit
and delicate filigree of hammered hearts.

—Yehuda Amichai, from "Jerusalem, 1967"

Jerusalem's Old City

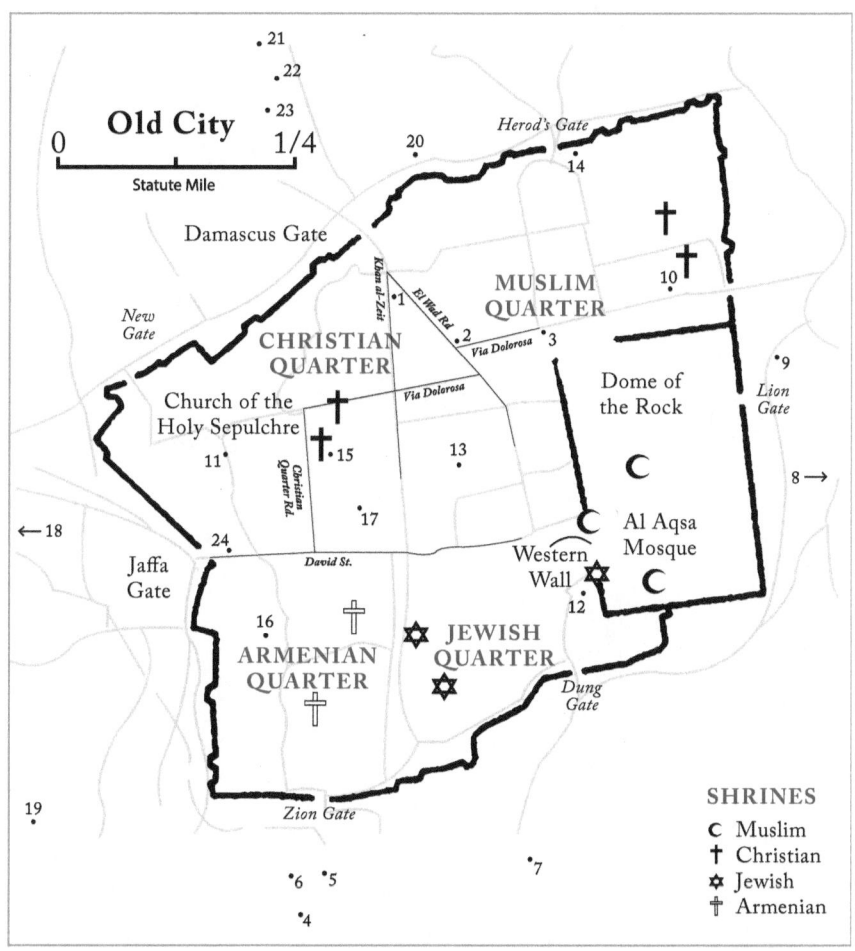

1. Al-Kamal Hotel
2. Austrian Hospice
3. Ecce Homo Convent
4. Mount Zion
5. The Rooftop (Room of the Last Supper, David's Tomb)
6. Dormitory Abbey
7. Village of Silwan (City of David)
8. Mount of Olives
9. Garden of Gethsemane
10. Church of Saint Anne
11. Casa Nova Guesthouse
12. Plaza in front of the Western Wall
13. Musa's Shop
14. Tea Shop at Herod's Gate
15. Samir's "Café"
16. Armenian Restaurant
17. The Muristan (rooftop restaurant)
18. New Jerusalem
19. Bloomfield Garden
20. Golden Walls Hotel
21. American Colony Hotel and Restaurant
22. Saint George's Cathedral and Guesthouse
23. Jerusalem Hotel and Restaurant
24. Polis Hotel

PART ONE

FIRES
(1969–70)

Chapter One

All the other men were up and moving about when Daniel opened his eyes for the second time. He had been initially awakened by the sounds of the Old City's competitive holiness—first the call to prayer shortly before sunrise, then the bells of the Holy Sepulchre—but drifted back to sleep until someone stumbled into the foot of his metal-frame bed.

Despite Bassam's assurance that the sheets were changed every few days, Daniel slept with most of his clothes on. He sensed that others in the room did the same, although he tried not to spy. Having stayed there for one night the previous week, he knew to bring his own towel, which he also used to cover the stained pillow.

Getting up after the others meant the hole-in-the-floor toilet was vacant, though well used, and that he didn't have to wait for space at the communal wash trough, located just off the back corner of what was generously called the "lobby." He brushed his teeth and splashed cold water on his face. The small mirror was placed too low for someone over six feet tall, but by squatting he could see that his hair stuck out in various directions. He splashed water on it as well and rummaged in his shaving kit until he found a comb. What would his mother, with her scrubbed and sanitized bathrooms, think of the Al-Kamal Hotel? Or his friends at Yale, for that matter? The thought made him smile.

Since the hotel opened directly onto the street, which in truth was an eight-foot-wide alleyway, he could hear plainly the sounds of Jerusalem's Old City coming to life: metal shutters being raised in front of shops, carts clattering on pavement stones, people calling out in languages he didn't speak. As Daniel walked back through the lobby, towel over his shoulder, Bassam greeted him from behind the small desk that sat near the open entrance. He was dressed, as he had been every time Daniel had seen him, in a brown suit coat and white skullcap, with a checkered *keffiyeh* wrapped like a scarf around his neck. On the wall behind him was the lobby's one adornment, a calendar with two sets of numbers beneath a picture of the Dome of the Rock and the nearby Al-Aqsa Mosque.

Bassam saw Daniel looking at the calendar and smiled. "Today is the eighth day of the sixth month in the year 1389, according to our calendar. August twenty-one for you." He moved from behind the desk. "Many tourists this time of year. Their buses will begin by nine o'clock, so now you can walk around without so many of them. You have a backpack? It is more safe to leave it with me."

When Daniel returned with his small pack, he said, "Last night was great. Do men gather like that every evening?"

"The old man with the cane, Mr. Khatib . . . you remember him? He is the owner of Al-Kamal. He and his friends, the old men, are here many nights. It is like their own café. Also the men who stay here like you, they sometimes come. We have many seats." He smiled and pointed to the folding metal chairs stacked against the stone wall. "The music player is the owner's friend, but he comes not so much."

The previous evening, Daniel had only intended to stop by the hotel to use the toilet, such as it was, and then wander longer in the fading light. But Mr. Khatib greeted him in Arabic and, when Daniel didn't know how to respond, pointed with his cane to an open chair. "When I say '*as salaam alaikum*,' you say '*wa alaikum as salaam.*' If you stay with us at Al-Kamal, you should know how to say 'peace be with you' like an Arab." Daniel repeated the response as the men around the small circle smiled and nodded.

He started to leave but then decided that might seem rude. And even though the conversation was mainly in Arabic, he found it was comfortable to sit there, absorbing the sounds, enjoying the occasional laughter. As night fell, a single uncovered light bulb hanging from the ceiling cast stark shadows of the men on the stone floor. Others joined the circle, and soon a tea vendor, the silver urn strapped to his back, stepped through the open doorway and served tea with mint and cubes of sugar all around. Daniel held the glass cup close to his nose, appreciating how, for a minute, the aroma of mint overpowered the odor of the toilet. Picking up on a gesture from Bassam, he paid for the tea, which seemed to be the cue to shift the conversation more into English.

"You have like me," said an old man, looking at Daniel while pointing to his own bushy mustache, "but not so white." The others laughed. He leaned forward in his chair. "Where are you home?"

"You mean," said the man to his left, "'Where is your home?'"

"I know English. I mean what I say: Where are you home?"

"You all are making me feel at home," said Daniel, although he wasn't quite sure that was true.

The old man frowned. "This is where we are home. Where are you home?"

"I was born in America, in the state of Ohio." When no one spoke, he added, "It's between Chicago and New York. I go to a university on the East Coast, so maybe—"

"My son, he has his work in Philadelphia," said the old man, now looking around the loose circle, "but here is where he is home." The others smiled and nodded, smoke from cigarettes drifting over the circle.

The musician arrived not long after the tea vendor, settling his large body into one of the squeaky metal chairs. After greeting the men all around, he began to play, and for Daniel the evening became magical. He closed his eyes, the instrument's resonant sound washing over him like Greek music he'd heard, only more exotic. In his mind, he could see pictures from his parents' leather-bound volume of *The Arabian Nights*.

When he opened his eyes, the musician was smiling at him. "You know what it is named?" he asked, holding up his pear-shaped, stringed instrument. Before Daniel could respond, he told him. "Its name is oud."

"Abu Yusef is a famous oud player," said Bassam. "People know of him in all Jerusalem."

His white keffiyeh swayed as Abu Yusef shook his head. "I am nobody. But Jerusalem, it once had great players of the oud; they played for kings. The greatest of them all, *Allah yarhamu*, was Wasif Jawhariyyeh." He closed his eyes as he said the name.

A younger man across the circle snorted. "Even as a man, he is like a girl."

"That may be," said Abu Yusef, "but back when he still played, he played like a *malak*."

"An angel," said Bassam, looking at Daniel.

"Yes, an angel. He comes from a family of Greek Christians. His father painted beautiful icons, some of the most beautiful ever in Al-Quds. When I see them, they make me, a Muslim, weep, though some Muslims say they are idols."

"You weep at nothing," said another man, and several of them chuckled. "Like your great Wasif, I think."

"Yes, he was born a Christian," said a man who until then had been quietly smoking, flicking ashes on the floor, "but some say when he played the oud he could be more a Jew than the Jews. And sometimes, when he played for the Husseinis, he was Muslim like we are. Now it is either this," he said, holding up his left hand, "or that," holding up his right. Others nodded, most of them smoking.

The younger man spoke again. "Why do we still talk of this Wasif? He left Jerusalem when the British were here."

Abu Yusef ran his fingers across the strings of his oud and the circle fell silent, expecting a song. Instead, he said softly, "King Abdullah, *Allah yarhamu*, he died in front of Al-Aqsa, that holy place, eighteen years ago. I was there that day on Haram al-Sharif with my sons. Now they are men with sons of their own, but do we forget the king?"

His voice rose. "Do we forget his murder? Do we take this picture of his blood on the stones of that holy place out of our minds? This is Jerusalem, where history is not ever dead."

While Abu Yusef played and occasionally sang, others joined the circle until there were no more chairs stacked against the wall. So when a man, older than the others, hobbled in, fingering prayer beads in a gnarled hand, Daniel instinctively stood to give him his seat.

"You sit," said the owner, lifting his cane. "You are a guest." But Daniel insisted he needed to stretch and then leaned against the stone wall, listening to the sounds of a conversation he once again couldn't understand. Although, from time to time, someone would ask him a question in English.

"Have you been to this wood stock?"

"Muslims are at your university?"

And finally, the most obvious one: "Why are you here?"

"Last week, I came to the Old City without a place to stay, and Bassam, standing right there in the entrance, invited me to stay here. And now I'm back."

"I told my young friend," said Bassam, "that he can be like all other tourists, or he can have real Arab hospitality—"

"For a few lira," said one of the men, and those who spoke English laughed.

The original questioner, however, wasn't satisfied. "I mean, why are you here from America?"

Daniel could feel his stomach tighten. "I'm here as a student." Expectant silence. "At the Tel Aviv University."

To his surprise, none of them seemed fazed or upset. After a pause, the questioner said, "But I don't think you are a Jew."

"No, I'm sort of a Christian, if I'm anything."

"Everyone is something," said Mr. Khatib while others nodded and smoked.

A group of young men passed by the hotel entrance, talking loudly. When they were gone, the man with the bushy white mustache said,

"I wish to know if you like Jerusalem . . ." He searched for a word.

"Better," said Bassam.

"Yes, if you like Jerusalem better. That is the question."

Daniel paused before saying, "The other students, the ones I've met, are my friends. But you are helping me feel more home in Jerusalem." *Is that really true?* he wondered. The old man smiled beneath his mustache.

Men had started to drift away, most saying "*tisbah ala khayr*" to the owner. One of them, however, turned to Daniel. "You come tomorrow for breakfast. I make you one of my pizzas."

"Ibrahim is a baker," said Bassam. "He has an oven made of bricks where people bring their bread for him to bake. You know, *pita*, bread that is open in the middle."

"And he makes *ka'ek*," said Mr. Khatib, his hands forming a ring, "with sesame seeds. You should eat them. They will make you not so thin."

"But if you eat there at breakfast," Bassam continued, "he lets the bread . . . get fat. How do you say that?"

"Puff up?"

"Yes, puff up." He savored the words. "Puff up. Then he takes off the top"—Ibrahim made a pinching motion with his fingers—"puts eggs and cheese in the middle, and puts it back in the oven until the eggs are cooked."

"That sounds great," Daniel told Ibrahim. "Where's your bakery? Do you have tables where I can eat?" There was laughter around the room, a couple of men whispering an Arabic translation to their neighbors.

"Don't look for a fine bakery with tables," said Bassam once the laughter had stopped. "You go right from here"—he motioned toward the opening—"in the direction of the gate to where the streets do this." He made a Y with his hands. "We are on this street," he held up his right hand, "but you take the other street," lifting up his left, "the one that goes toward the great mosque. But not far. Go left at the first alley and look for people taking bread to be baked. There is no sign, and you go down to get in the door."

Daniel was still smiling at the remembered conversation when he stepped out of Al-Kamal's open entrance, intent on finding the shop of Ibrahim the baker. The stones on this part of the narrow street were wet from someone's attempt at cleanliness, and he nearly slipped as he turned right toward the normally bustling Damascus Gate. Although not yet eight o'clock, the day had the promise of heat. A cart rolled past him loaded with boxes, the man pushing it already sweating. A spice merchant opened his shop, and Daniel stopped to savor the smell and colors of spices he couldn't yet name. He saw a juice vendor stacking oranges and stopped to have a glass, freshly squeezed.

He had reached the Y and begun heading back down the left-hand street, following a young boy with a tray of dough on his head, when he heard yelling from behind him and moved aside as several men rushed past. For a moment, the scene seemed frozen, people on the street standing and listening, a radio audible through someone's window. But then he heard screaming ahead of him—people around him now speaking, some loudly—and the street began to fill. *Where*, he wondered, *did all these people come from?* Did so many really live here?

He stepped quickly into a small tourist shop and asked the worried-looking owner, "What's happening?"

The man was quiet for a few seconds, straining to hear the voices outside. "They say the Jews are burning the *masjid* Al-Aqsa," he said, not taking his eyes off the street. "If you are a Jew, you should get out quickly."

The crowd had grown and was now streaming to the right, away from the gate and in the direction of the gray-domed mosque. Teenagers in T-shirts and jeans; men, some in work clothes, others in the traditional *thawb* under a jacket; a few women, one carrying a small child. Daniel glanced left where he could see what he supposed were Israeli soldiers moving along the crenulated wall that surrounds the Old City, and then, since there seemed little alternative, fell in step with the crowd. People were chanting, some crying. The man next to him stopped chanting in order to shout, his fist in the air, his face contorted in rage. He glanced briefly at Daniel before turning his eyes back to the alleyway.

Daniel could now see black smoke hanging in the air ahead of them, but when he stopped to look up, he was jostled from behind. His mind registered a shopkeeper who was wheeling in racks of merchandise and rolling down the metal shutter. He later recalled that a dog was barking, barely audible over the chanting and shouting of the crowd. He felt excitement tinged with fear, much as he had felt during an anti-war rally at Yale when word rippled through the crowd that police were beating students at the head of the march. Where was this march headed? What was happening ahead of him now?

As he neared the place where the street widens in front of the Austrian Hostel, a hand reached out and pulled him toward a shop entrance. Daniel recognized the man from the previous evening. "You should go back," the man was saying, loud enough to be heard over the crowd.

"How? It's not possible . . ." They both were looking back down the packed alleyway.

"Go to the right here at the Via Dolorosa. It will take you back to Khan al-Zeit, the *souk*, the market street. If you turn to the right there, you will go to the hotel. This street is not safe."

"What are they chanting?"

"They are saying 'Death to the Jews.' And some are calling for President Nasser to come with his army. The Israelis have stopped the water to the Old City, so our men cannot fight the fire at Al-Aqsa. That is what people are saying." There were tears in the corners of his eyes.

Daniel reached the intersection, shoved there by the crowd, and then walked quickly up the steps of the Via Dolorosa until he was back on the more familiar street of Al-Kamal. The distant sound of something crashing echoed off the stone walls and caused him to stop, but only momentarily. He turned right, back in the direction of the hotel and the Damascus Gate, his eyes adjusting to the dimness of this stretch of alley where direct rays of the sun had not yet penetrated. His friend had been correct, there were not nearly as many people on the Khan al-Zeit, probably because it didn't lead directly to the mosque.

He had only gone a few yards when he heard loud voices—*was that*

Hebrew?—and again the sound of people running behind him. He moved to the side, his back pressed against the metal shutter of an unopened shop, but was still bumped by a pack of young men—boys, really—in full flight, one of them slipping on the damp stones. While Daniel watched this unfold, another boy slammed into him, and when he recovered his balance, he discovered a folded newspaper at his feet. Without thinking, he picked it up, feeling something hard and sharp inside.

Most of the pursuing soldiers had rushed by, but before Daniel could discard the newspaper, three of them, submachine guns hanging from their shoulders, formed a semicircle around him. "You speak English?" asked the one who seemed in charge. Sweat trickled down the side of his face, and his tone was brusque.

"I'm an American," the words sticking in his throat.

"What," asked the soldier, "are you doing *here?*"

Daniel slid the newspaper under his arm, trying to seem nonchalant, desperately hoping the tip of the blade didn't show. Should he tell them that one of the young men had dropped it? Would they believe him? Why were they paying attention to him, an obvious foreigner? "I stayed last night at the Al-Kamal Hotel. It's just down—"

One of the others, perhaps thinking Daniel understood Hebrew, had whispered to the leader, who now interrupted. "Where did you walk this morning? The Har HaBayit?"

When Daniel's face showed he didn't understand, the whisperer said out loud, "The Temple Mount. Were you near the mosque this morning?"

Daniel shook his head several times, rapidly, like the beating of his heart. His back was beginning to hurt as he leaned more forcefully against the metal shutter. "I was going to get breakfast when the crowd . . . I didn't know what was going on, but a friend told me to come back to the hotel." It seemed to him that the whisperer had been eyeing the newspaper, but the three soldiers now turned in the direction of new shouting.

After listening for a few seconds, the leader looked back at Daniel. "Leave this Arab part of the city. Go to the Israeli side where it is safe." And they were gone.

Daniel waited nearly a minute, letting groups of people pass him before slipping the newspaper between the slats of the metal shutter. His stomach was churning as he made his way to Al-Kamal, where he told Bassam what had happened.

"Allah," said his friend, "protects the innocent and the foolish."

Chapter Two

Daniel Jacobs had arrived at the Tel Aviv University, along with nearly a planeload of other students, all Jewish, for his junior year abroad in June of 1969, two months before the fire at Al-Aqsa, and a month after he turned twenty. Regular courses didn't begin until late September, after the holidays of Rosh Hashanah and Yom Kippur, so the summer months were spent teaching Hebrew to the visiting students. Daniel soon discovered he was the only one starting from scratch.

Hebrew lessons continued during three weeks on a kibbutz in Galilee, and a week on an archaeology dig outside Beersheba. They were back at the university on July 20, but since there was no television in the dorms, most of the students, including Daniel, missed Neil Armstrong's famous "step for mankind," hearing about it after the fact. How easy it is, he marveled, to feel divorced from things that just months before would have seemed monumental. As a political science major, he was supposed to be interested in the space race or the latest developments in Vietnam, Biafra, and Belfast. But already, after little more than a month overseas, he was wondering: Did his old interests have to be his interests now? Did he still have to be who he had been? Here, six thousand miles from home in a place where no one knew him, wasn't he free to focus on new priorities, even try out new identities? He wrote about this to his mother, but when he reread the letter, it felt too adolescent, and so he tore it up. Besides, his mother, head of the local League of Women Voters, was the wrong person to confide in when it came to rethinking his major in political science.

Because the program kept the overseas students so busy, Daniel's first visit to Jerusalem didn't come until the beginning of August when two fellow students, Alan and Lenny, invited him to go there with them for the weekend. They arrived before sundown on Friday, stayed with a friend of Alan's at Hebrew University, and spent Saturday evening with a group of the friend's companions at a bar on Ben Yehuda Street.

It was from them that Daniel first heard of the Old City. "It always smells like urine," one told him. "It's where the tourists go."

"And the Orthodox," said another. "We sometimes go there on *Erev Shabbat* . . . I forgot, you aren't Jewish. We go there sometimes on Friday evenings, the beginning of the Sabbath, because there's usually something happening at the Western Wall. Well, the Orthodox are praying, it being our holiest place and all; but usually there's some dancing and people just hanging out. And having lots of Jews around makes it safer, even if they are Orthodox." This last comment made the others laugh, and Daniel laughed along, pretending to understand.

The trip was also significant because a young woman from the Hebrew University group, a visiting student from Canada, flirted so openly with Daniel that his friends teased him about it. "Maybe Sarah is into Christians," said Lenny. "Maybe she has a Christian boyfriend back in Toronto who is tall and has a mustache, and you're a stand-in." Was this, he wondered, another part of his new identity? Because he wasn't a Jew, was he now Daniel the Christian, even though he'd never set foot inside the chapel at Yale?

As they were leaving on Sunday, he asked Sarah, "What if I come back next week and we have dinner, just the two of us, maybe see a movie?"

She smiled. "If you want to spend money on bus fare," which he took as a yes. But when he arrived at the university the following Friday, Sarah's roommate passed on the message that something had come up. Something about relatives in town, although it all sounded pretty hazy.

Now what? It was nearly five o'clock, so he had to make some decision before buses stopped running for the Sabbath. It would be a waste just to turn around and go back to Tel Aviv. Besides, he might have to explain it to Alan and Lenny. Not knowing the city bus routes or even where he was in Jerusalem, he hailed a taxi, telling the driver in his broken Hebrew, "*Ha Ir Atikah, bevakasha.*"

"Where in the Old City?" the driver asked in English. "Dung Gate? Jaffa Gate?"

"Just someplace . . . wherever you think."

The driver shrugged and dropped him outside the Damascus Gate. Later when looking back, Daniel would regard it as a turning point in his life.

The first thing that struck him—amazed him—was the wall of limestone blocks, tinged pink by the setting sun, that stretched in both directions. Later, he would come to know that it was built by order of the Ottoman sultan, Suleiman the Magnificent, in the middle of the sixteenth century, but now he simply marveled that it was there at all in the twentieth.

Later, he would come to know the history associated with each of the eight gates, but now he only knew that stepping through the one called Damascus meant stepping into a world unlike any he had known or imagined. Yes, there was a whiff of urine, but there were also other smells that, much later, Valerie would identify as za'atar and cumin, saffron and sumac. Later, he would come to lament the divisiveness of the various sects that call the place sacred, but now he was simply entranced by the variety of robes and cassocks and headgear. Later, he would come to know nearly all the streets that branch like arteries and veins (Shoshana joked that he could be a tour guide), but now it felt as if he had entered a maze. Later, he would come to appreciate how challenging it could be to live in such a place, but now he was simply enchanted by the women, in long black dresses with colorful embroidery, squatting on the stones—herbs, vegetables, or fruit spread out in front of them. He was astonished by the professional porters who hauled crates, televisions, even refrigerators on their backs—a rope around the load and pressed to their foreheads—through the narrow alleys. Tel Aviv was a city foreign to him but comprehensible; Jerusalem, at least the Old City, was pure mystery. Tel Aviv was oriented to the West; Jerusalem, at least the Old City, was most definitely oriented to the East. This was Damascus and Baghdad, not New York or Paris. And certainly not New Haven or Columbus.

Daniel squeezed his way through the crowded gate, which zigzags as protection from invaders, and walked down the gradual steps to where the street divides, El-Wad (the valley) to the left, Khan al-Zeit (olive market) to the right. He went right, the street growing darker as the sun slipped below the top of the wall, past a merchant with mounds of colored spices, past a juice stand, past a jeweler. He paused at the side of the alleyway, trying to decide how he would ask for directions to a student hostel, mentioned by his Hebrew University friends, when he didn't even remember the name of it. And that's when a man in a white skullcap, a checkered keffiyeh wrapped around his neck like a scarf, spoke to him in English. "I can tell you where the hostel is," said Bassam, "or you can stay in the real Jerusalem and experience the hospitality of Palestinians."

The university took a month break from August 20 until after Yom Kippur, during which several trips were planned for the overseas students. Daniel had decided to skip the trip to the southern resort town of Eilat in order to return to the Old City, which is how he happened to be there the day of the fire at Al-Aqsa. He did take part in the trips to Sinai and the Golan Heights but was back in Jerusalem, with no thought of Sarah, on Tuesday, September 9, three days before Rosh Hashanah, the beginning of the Jewish year 5730.

He spent the afternoon wandering in parts of the wall-surrounded city that were new to him, including the Jewish Quarter where he had his first taste of pomegranate juice. But he was back that evening when Mr. Khatib gathered with friends in the lobby of Al-Kamal. The old man with the bushy white mustache was there, as was Fahad, the man who had told Daniel to get off El-Wad Street on the day of the fire. And there were others he recognized from the last time he sat in the smoke-filled circle.

"You are welcome here," said Mr. Khatib, pointing to a chair with his cane.

"*Shukran*," said Daniel, using one of his few Arabic words.

"*Afwan*," replied Mr. Khatib while the others smiled and nodded.

"I remember your name is Danyal. Danyal for Muslims is a great prophet who was not eaten by the lions. Have you come to sit again with these lions?" He gestured with his cane around the circle, and the men who knew English laughed while Bassam translated for the others.

"It seems," said Fahad, "you like our Al-Quds, even with the terrible fire."

"Al-Quds," Bassam added, "is our name for Jerusalem."

"Yes, I like Al-Quds," Daniel told them. "And I really like staying at the camel." The circle burst into laughter, an old man slapping his knee the way Daniel had seen his grandfather do in Tennessee.

"*Kamal* has not to do with camels," said Bassam, who was standing against the wall. "*Al-Kamal*, it means 'the perfect,' perfect hospitality like our ancestor Abraham, peace be upon him, gave to the angels. Our prophet, *salallahu alayhi wasallam*, was famous for not asking guests to leave."

"But here," said another man, "they must pay." More laughter.

"*Kamal* is a familiar word for Arabs," said Bassam. "Umm Kulthum received the *Nishan al-Kamal*, the highest of awards for her perfection of singing."

"Who," asked Daniel, "is Umm Kulthum?"—a question that caused several of the men to smile and shake their heads.

"You have much to learn," said one of them.

Mr. Khatib was the next to speak, the others listening intently. "Fahad talked of the fire. Today I finally saw for myself, and it made me cry out. Saladin's *minbar*, where the imam stands to give his sermons . . . gone. Who could imagine such a thing? It was *ibdae fanni*, a great work of art." He shook his head, and no one interrupted. "The fire, you have seen it, reached to the windows below the dome. The beautiful ceiling, we have all seen it many times, was made of wood." He looked at Daniel. "The sound we could hear everywhere in Al-Quds, you must have heard it, was the ceiling falling to the floor."

"Allah is merciful," said the man with the bushy mustache. "It is said that men on their way to prayer, including our friend Harun, carried out carpets and prayer books, or more would be destroyed. *Al-hamdu lillah*." The men nodded, three of them fingering prayer beads.

The circle expanded as some of the paying guests pulled folding chairs from the stack along the wall. One of them let it be known he was from Bethlehem, there in Jerusalem to help his uncle. He spoke in Arabic, Bassam translating for Daniel. "He says that Bethlehem sent trucks with equipment to fight the fire, but the Israelis would not let them near to Haram."

"How does he know that?" asked Daniel, and Bassam relayed the question.

"He says he has a friend, he is . . . do you say 'fire man'?"

Daniel nodded.

"His friend is a fire man in Bethlehem. It is not such a big town."

Fahad was now speaking, switching back to English once Bassam stopped his translation. "Why have the Arab nations not attacked?" He raised his arms to accentuate the question. "Israel must pay for this crime! The other Muslims must not forget us now."

Before he could think through the implications of speaking, Daniel said, "But Israel didn't set the fire." Now everyone was looking at him, the man from Bethlehem shaking his head. "Really. They caught the guy, I think his name is Rohan, who did it. A young guy from Australia. A Christian . . . like me, I guess. He was identified by the Muslim guards at the mosque." He looked at Bassam. "That must have been why the Israeli soldiers were giving me a hard time on the day of the fire. They already knew there was a young suspect who looked European. We even look a little alike: tall, pretty thin, fairly short, brown hair."

Three of the men were now muttering among themselves in Arabic. Mr. Khatib motioned for them to calm down before saying, "We have heard this also, but we have heard Israeli propaganda many times before, repeated in the international press."

"This man Rohan," said Bassam, "was brought here by the Jewish Agency to work for Israel. Even the international papers say this. No one could get inside Al-Aqsa early in the morning without the help of the Israelis."

Despite part of his brain telling him to be quiet, Daniel said, "But I've seen film of the Jerusalem fire department that shows Jews fighting the fire. They say some Palestinians tried to stop them, actually tried to shut off the hoses."

A man sitting across the circle from Daniel, obviously angry, started to speak, but Mr. Khatib cut him off. "Some say the Israelis were making the fire worse with their hoses. Some say the Israelis were the ones that shut off water to Haram al-Sharif." He leaned forward on his cane and looked around the circle before focusing on Daniel. "I do not know all that is true about that day, but my friends and I know that some Jews dream of destroying the great mosque and Qubbat al-Sakhra, what you call the Dome of the Rock. They think this is where their ancient temple stood, and they say many times they want to build it again."

"If your Vatican or your Notre Dame was burned, there would be great cries for vengeance. Great cries!" Fahad, who had spoken, leaned forward in his chair until it nearly tipped. "Al-Aqsa, where our prophet, *salallahu alayhi wasallam*, prayed before going to heaven, we cannot forget this! Other Muslims must not forget this!"

"And we cannot forget two years ago," said the man with the bushy mustache, "when they came through the Lions' Gate, with their tanks and their bombs, and then made a danger to the mosques."

The man from Bethlehem spoke, Bassam again translating. "He says they call it a war of six days, but it is a war of many years. His father fought the Jews and his father before him. And his grandson will be fighting them." Several of the men were nodding.

"Of course," said Mr. Khatib, pointing his cane at a man across the circle, "my friend Mr. Shawwa wants everything to be 'peace, peace' so he can make money from the tourists." Several of the men now smiled. "But after the fire, even he tells a different story." Mr. Shawwa smiled and nodded, flicking cigarette ashes on the stone floor.

The tea vendor arrived, but Daniel's offer to pay was brushed aside. "There is no need," said Mr. Khatib. "Tonight, Al-Kamal will buy the tea." Ibrahim the baker made an appearance and asked Daniel if he was coming tomorrow for breakfast, but he, too, was in a subdued mood.

Finally, the angry man spoke again, and this time no one interrupted. "Why," he asked, looking straight at Daniel, "are you here? Bassam says you are a Christian, but Daniel is the name of a Jew. He says you live in Tel Aviv. Why are you here, saying to us lies from the Israelis?"

Daniel was stunned, and it took him several seconds to respond. "I was just telling you what I read in the English newspaper and heard on BBC, that's all. I'm sorry if . . ." He looked at Bassam. "Maybe I shouldn't stay here tonight."

"Daniel is our guest," said Bassam firmly, looking at the angry man while Mr. Khatib nodded his agreement. He repeated it in Arabic. "He is staying here—*huwwa nazil hon*." But when the circle began to disperse, Bassam told Daniel to grab his pack and then led him to a separate room in the back of the hotel.

As he was closing the door, he said, "This man's brother is in an Israeli prison. That is why he is very angry. Not just because of you." He had told Daniel it was an extra room, but a shirt on a hanger and a checkered keffiyeh draped over the doorknob suggested it was where Bassam himself usually slept.

Chapter Three

Daniel had gone to Yale intent on majoring in political science (with the subtle encouragement of his mother) or history (following his father who taught history in high school) or some combination of the two, whatever that might look like. Where that would lead he wasn't sure, but something to do with politics. Maybe law or diplomatic work, possibly teaching. He did know he wanted to spend his junior year abroad, like an older friend he had met through his parents, and by January 1969 had been accepted for a year of study at the London School of Economics and Political Science.

At the beginning of February, however, he happened to see a two-inch advertisement in the university newspaper from the American Friends of Tel Aviv University, listing the address of their office near Times Square. As it happened, Daniel was going to New York the following Friday, and when he and a friend happened to be in the vicinity of Times Square, he decided to check it out.

An energetic woman with a large smile and frizzy, reddish-brown hair ushered him into a room with a table, two chairs, and the seal of the university on the wall. After writing down his name, she asked where he was from.

"I grew up in Columbus, Ohio—"

"Oh," she said, "I lived there for a while. You don't happen to attend Beth Tikvah, do you? I love that synagogue."

Daniel smiled. "Actually, I'm not Jewish. I just saw an ad and thought—"

"With a name like Daniel Jacobs? Is your father Jewish?"

"No, afraid not. He and my mother are both Christians."

Her smile disappeared. "Excuse me, but I need to ask. You're not one of these fundamentalist Christians looking for a way to get to Israel, are you?"

"No! God no! My family is, I guess you'd say, nominally Christian. I went to Sunday school sometimes when I was a kid, and one year to church camp, which I hated. But no. I'm a student at Yale, and I saw your ad and . . ." He paused. "Is your junior-year abroad program just for Jews?"

Her smile was back in place. "It's not, although almost everybody in the program *is* Jewish. We were just saying here in the office that it would be good to have some diversity on that score. A little diversity from the Ivy League would also be nice."

She asked more questions, looking occasionally at a sheet in front of her. Had he ever been to Israel? (No.) Had he spent much time abroad? (Two trips to Canada with his parents.) Did he have many Jewish friends growing up?

"Not that I know of. There are a couple of Jewish guys I hang out with at Yale, but we don't talk much about religion. We're all political science majors. That's why I've been thinking I would study for a year at the London School of Economics, because it's a good place—"

"—to learn *about* politics. But why not study in a place where major stuff is happening every day all around you? You can study in London whenever. That's like being at Yale East. Israel is a new, vibrant country. Lots to learn just by being there."

Daniel filled out the application, sitting beneath the seal of the university: a candle with the Hebrew letters for *t* and *a* at its base. The smiling woman identified the letters, which were foreign to Daniel. As he was preparing to leave, she told him he was accepted.

"That's it? No other papers to fill out?"

"You came on a good day. A couple of students have pulled out, so we happen to have spaces open."

He found his friend waiting in a café around the corner, and they discussed this unexpected turn of events over coffee.

"What would be easier?" asked his friend.

"Going to London, I suppose."

"Then do the other."

Daniel walked back to the office and, just as they were ready to close for Shabbat, told the woman he would commit to the program. He considered calling his parents before making such a commitment, but decided not to. A year in Tel Aviv, even with airfare, was a fraction of what it cost for a year at Yale. And besides, it was a decision *he* had made on his own, and that felt good.

When he got back to school, he immediately told his two Jewish friends, neither of whom seemed to have the slightest interest in going to Israel.

There was a sense in which Daniel was, from the start, the odd one out in the cohort of American students: the only one from Yale, the only one who hadn't studied Hebrew for a bar or bat mitzvah, the only non-Jew. As it turned out, however, he was regularly included in dorm parties or group outings, in part because he was easy to be around, a good listener, but also because others liked teaching him things. It wasn't long before he learned a whole playlist of Jewish folk songs and absorbed a new vocabulary of words, like *mezuzah* and *kippah* and *challah* and *Pesach* and *kiddush* and *sabra* and *Shoah*, while trying not to seem too ignorant. How, he wondered, had he lived twenty years without knowing this stuff?

Some of the other students knew one another from Jewish camps and youth organizations, even previous trips to Israel, which was an obvious advantage. And a few were astonishingly well prepared for the year. Like the classmate who, knowing it was hard to get tampons in the Holy Land, had her parents ship a large box of extras that she sold, one by one, out of her dorm room. Or the one who zipped around Tel Aviv on his motorcycle, shipped from New York.

He also learned what a *kibbutz* was firsthand since every student on the overseas program was sent, for three weeks, to one of these communal farms. Daniel was one of six assigned to a large, prosperous kibbutz just south of the Sea of Galilee, which he learned to call Kinneret, where he picked grapefruit in the mornings, studied Hebrew in the afternoons, and occasionally watched artillery shells bursting after sunset. "The PLO is active on the other side of the river," one kibbutz member told the Americans, "but army patrols stop them when they try to cross it. At least we hope they stop them." He did not write about this in his weekly letter to his mother, who was already convinced her son had taken up residence in a war zone.

When Daniel had imagined this year abroad, dating hadn't been a big part of his reveries. By the start of classes, however, it was clear, even to him, that a young woman in the program—Miriam, who went by Mya—was interested in spending time together. They had been sent to the same kibbutz where they were the two most reserved of the Americans. After a few days, she began helping him with his Hebrew, and several evenings they walked together on the grounds of the kibbutz, sharing their common interest in history and admiring the carefully tended roses. Once, as they watched artillery flashes over the river, Mya took his arm and briefly rested her head on his shoulder.

Back in Tel Aviv, as classes were beginning toward the end of September, Mya invited Daniel to go with her to the beach. Beach-going was not high on his list of favorite activities because he was more bones than muscles; but Mya, too, was thin, and he liked her. Before the afternoon was over, they had walked hand in hand along the shoreline and kissed, twice, as they sat drinking the juice he now called *mitz tapuzim*.

"Why," he asked, "did you decide to move out of the dorms?"

"I just thought it would be interesting to live with a family since we had that option. And I thought it would help me improve my Hebrew, although the Posners speak far better English than I do Hebrew, so most of the time it's easier to use English." They drank the orange juice for a minute, watching the horizon take on red tones and the water gradually darken. "Mrs. Posner wanted to have a student, I think, because she's lonely. She's very . . . gregarious. Her husband is a scientist who's gone most of the week to Haifa or Rehovot. Her daughter, Shuli, is married, and her son lives in the States. So now she can fuss over me, tell me to eat more so I'm not so skinny." They both smiled and slid closer. "Part of the deal is that I get breakfast. So the first week she fixed eggs, toast, and orange juice. I told her—big mistake—that I would just as soon have cereal or even grapefruit. So now I have eggs, toast, cereal, grapefruit, and orange juice. I'm afraid to tell her I'd actually prefer to just have oatmeal."

When they had finished laughing, Mya looked down and said, "Anyway, Mrs. P is planning a big *Sukkot* meal in the apartment on October third and said I could bring someone. So I'm wondering if you would come." She looked up and smiled. "I'm sure there'll be plenty of food."

Daniel added *Sukkot*, the Feast of Tabernacles, to his vocabulary list, and researched what to bring to a Sukkot meal in the university library. He arrived carrying a lemon and two oranges. Mrs. Posner, a short woman of around fifty, met him at the door to the apartment with a kiss on both cheeks, Mya standing behind her. Feeling awkward, he started to shake hands with Mya, who smiled and also kissed him on the cheek.

Mrs. P, as Mya called her, led them through the living room to the large balcony where palm branches were somehow attached to the ceiling and along the railing. Four people were seated around a table decorated with three vases of flowers and loose pieces of fruit.

"It is not a *sukkah* like we had in the old country," said Mrs. P, who was still standing, "but who cares? Am I right?" She turned and gestured toward Daniel. "This is Mya's friend Daniel. She told me she wanted to invite him because he is a Christian and has nowhere to go for Sukkot. But I think there's another reason. Am I right?" Daniel glanced at Mya, who was blushing. "And why not? We even had Christian friends, sometimes boyfriends, good-lookers like Daniel, in the old country. I remember—"

"Rivka," said the man at the head of the table, "why don't you tell Daniel who *we* are."

"This rude man—you say 'rude'?—this rude man is my husband."

"Yosef," said the man, standing to shake hands with Daniel.

Mrs. Posner pointed toward the far side of the table. "This is my daughter, Shulamit, who now calls herself Shuli. Why are these girls changing their names? This is her husband, Avi, who works on a pipeline he says we shouldn't know about. And this," she gestured toward an older man who was already standing, "is our family friend, Mr. Meltzer, whose wife died last year."

"Rivka was a good company to her," said Mr. Meltzer, extending his hand.

"You hear he sounds like he is from Germany?" asked Mrs. P, looking at Daniel. She turned back toward Mr. Meltzer who was still standing. "Tell him and Mya when you first came to Israel."

"My wife and me, we were in the famous five *aliyah*. You know what it is, *aliyah*?"

Daniel shook his head.

"It means immigration of Jews to Israel," said Shuli. "The fifth aliyah was Jews from Germany in the 1930s."

"Yes," said Mr. Meltzer, "we could see what was going to happen. Who could not see it? So we made aliyah. I owned a store; it was of my father who was in the first war as a German. But what is a store or a country compared to your life?"

They all settled around the table, which smelled of lemons—Daniel and Mya on one side, Mr. Meltzer, Shuli, and Avi squeezed together on the other. Within ten minutes, however, Mrs. P was in the kitchen, calling for Shuli and Avi to help her serve the soup, followed by roast chicken with vegetables, kugel, fruit salad, vegetable salad, challah with honey, and zucchini stuffed with rice and meat. Mrs. P held up the last dish for all to see. "This is made by Mya. I never hear of such a thing. We stuff cabbage but not these zucchini, but they do it in America." She set the dish on the table before sitting at the end opposite her husband.

"We say a prayer," said Yosef, looking at Daniel. "Like most Israelis, we aren't what you call religious, but on Sukkot we say it. *Baruch atah*—"

His wife interrupted. "Yosef, before you start with that, I will tell Mya and Daniel that Avi is terrible!" Mrs. P's son-in-law was smiling broadly. He glanced at Daniel and shrugged. "Named after Abraham, and he has never been to a *shul* in his life. Am I right? On Pesach, he goes to Jaffa to buy Arab bread and then brings it here! He, too, is very rude." They all now were smiling, even Yosef, who was shaking his head. "We are not religious Jews," Mrs. P concluded, "but Avi is very terrible."

"I saw a *mezuzah* on your doorframe," said Daniel, trying out one of his new words. "Isn't that a religious symbol?"

Mrs. P laughed loudly. "We didn't put it there. My scientist husband does not know how to use a screwdriver. It came with the apartment, like the doorknob."

During the dinner, Mya, in response to questions from Yosef and Mr. Meltzer, told about her family in Los Angeles. ("So now we can visit Hollywood," said Mrs. P.) Her family was originally from Romania but had been in the US since the late nineteenth century. Yes, she was going to a university in California, a history major who hoped to be a teacher. "I like Israel," said Mya, "but America is definitely my home."

"Daniel, what about you?" asked Yosef. "Mya says you study politics."

"Politics!" said Avi with a big smile. "If you ask me, we have too much politics, at least in Israel."

"Nobody asked you," said Mrs. P, "so—"

Her daughter cut her off. "You are too . . . nice to be in politics. In Israel, this is what Avi means, politics is very rough, not nice."

"So maybe we need more people like Daniel to study it," said Mrs. P.

"Well, I'm not exactly sure—"

But Daniel couldn't finish the sentence before Avi asked him, "What do you think of our—how do the papers say it?—our 'conflict' with the Arabs? Is there an answer in politics, or do we keep on this way until the whole world cries for the poor Palestinians and everybody hates us even more?" Why, Daniel wondered, had he not anticipated such questions? He could feel Mya put her hand on his knee beneath the table.

"I'm just here to learn," he said. "I don't have any answers." He paused. "But it does seem to me that people should spend more time talking *to* one another, not just *about* one another."

Yosef raised his wine glass, saying, "To a wise young man," and Mr. Meltzer nodded. Avi, however, was shaking his head.

"How can we talk to them when we look at the same thing and see different things? Like this fire at their *misgad*, their mosque. Some Christian sets a fire on a *dukhan* . . . How do you say it in English?"

"Pulpit," said his wife.

"A pulpit burns and they blame us and call for a *jihad*, when they're the ones that stop the *kabaim* from going there to put it out. And then, they try to kill the prime minister when she goes there to show she is . . ." He searched for the right word.

"To show her sympathy," said Shuli.

"Her sympathy. How can we talk with such people?"

Yosef, Shuli, and Mrs. P all seemed ready to speak, but it was Daniel who said, in a low voice, "I was there."

All eyes were now on him. "What do you mean?" asked Yosef. "You were where?"

"Staying in the Old City when Al-Aqsa was set on fire. It was a big deal, the same as if somebody tried to burn Notre Dame in Paris. And much of the ceiling fell in, so it wasn't just the pulpit. Which, by the way, was almost nine hundred years old. Muslims, when they talk about it, say it was a great work of art. And now it's lost."

"Like our Jewish *Kunstwerke*," said Mr. Meltzer, staring at his plate. "Like the paintings of my mother, *zikhronah livrakha*."

Even Mrs. P was quiet, traffic noise now audible on the balcony.

Daniel opened his mouth, beginning to say, *The Palestinians didn't do that*, but he could feel Mya tighten her grip and quickly stopped.

"Maybe," said Mya at last, "this is an example of what Daniel meant. It would be good to hear what the other side is saying." All but Avi nodded their agreement, and they spoke no more about it for the rest of the evening.

Daniel had actually expected, even looked forward to, conversations like this with Jewish students in his program, many of whom were gung ho for Israel. But as it turned out, his classmates generally appeared more interested in what was going on back home, especially whether they were likely to be drafted and sent to Vietnam. When the first lottery numbers for the draft were announced on December 1, a student read them from a dorm balcony to the loud groans or muted cheers of those gathered.

Or so Daniel was told, because he was in Jerusalem on that day. The Old City was now in his blood, and he went there as often as he could during the fall and early winter, which was the undoing of his relationship with Mya. Soon after the Sukkot dinner, he invited her to go with him for a weekend, which she did. But where could they stay? Since Al-Kamal obviously wasn't an option, they ended up in the apartment of a male friend of hers. This was awkward because the friend seemed more than a little interested in Mya, and frustrating for Daniel because he wanted to be inside the Old City walls.

No buses were running on the Sabbath, and it was a hike from the friend's apartment to the Old City, but Daniel convinced Mya to do it. They also managed to dissuade the friend from tagging along. Mya said little as they walked through the alleyways, but her body language made clear that she much preferred the new city to the old. On Sunday, she suggested they visit the Bloomfield Garden, the recommendation of another friend, but this only increased Daniel's frustration. Sitting on a bench near the garden's quirky modern fountain, he could easily see the Ottoman-built wall, the Tower of David, and buildings he knew were on Mount Zion.

The next weekend, she asked if he wanted to have dinner, maybe go to Jaffa, which, though close to Tel Aviv, "is a little bit like old Jerusalem." He was sorry, he told her, but friends at Al-Kamal would be expecting him. He couldn't say they broke up because they hadn't really been together. She simply stopped asking.

Chapter Four

It would be an exaggeration to say that Bassam had become a friend, but twice they ate falafel sandwiches together for lunch, seated on either side of Bassam's desk, watching the steady stream of foot traffic past Al-Kamal. And twice Bassam took Daniel to a tea shop near Herod's Gate, a grimy place with badly scarred tables, where he showed the young American how to smoke a *nargile*. On their second time there, news somehow spread that Israeli jets had bombed a school, maybe a hospital as well, on a raid over Egypt. As men in the café began to raise their voices, Bassam signaled they should leave.

"What are they saying?" Daniel asked him.

"One of them is saying we should have *jihad*. You know what it means?" Daniel nodded. "Dropping bombs on a school is war, not just this 'war of attrition' as your papers call it."

"Are they sure that's what happened? You remember the fire when Israel was blamed—"

"We go now," Bassam said and headed for the open entrance.

Daniel was now almost accepted as a regular at the evening conversations in the lobby of Al-Kamal. This meant less language accommodation, so he often had to guess at what was being said and rely on Bassam's occasional translation. But he loved the times when Abu Yusef, the oud player, was there, and he didn't even mind paying for the tea, which once again seemed to be his responsibility.

These were also opportunities, whenever the conversation switched to English, to hear the Palestinian perspective on the conflict, and this contributed to Daniel's growing sense that he was straddling disconnected worlds.

"Israel has been remarkably restrained in the way it responds to provocations." — "The Israelis overreact to every throwing of a stone."

"Israel is surrounded by hostile nations poised to attack." — "The Muslim nations talk big and set up organizations, but then do nothing to help us Palestinians."

"Israel has provided services that improve the standard of living on the West Bank." — "We are living in an open-air prison."

He didn't contribute much to the discussions at Al-Kamal, except when the men asked him questions about the United States. But one evening he did suggest that Palestinians and Israelis should talk more with one another and less about one another. No one, however, picked up this conversational thread.

It was no surprise that Daniel savored the history of the walled city and its environs: a water tunnel dug seven hundred years before Jesus, a pile of limestone blocks left over from Herod's temple, paving stones put in place by Crusaders. He returned several times to a newly opened site, the ruins of a house burned by the Romans when they destroyed Jerusalem nineteen hundred years before—including scorched beams, layers of ash, and the skeletal forearm of a no doubt desperate woman.

What he hadn't expected was the fascination he now felt with religion. In Jerusalem, history and religion are inextricable, but increasingly it was the religious dimension of what he was seeing that sparked his imagination. Pilgrims braved bandits and armies, crossed mountains and oceans, to be *here*. What drove them? What made it all worth such risk, such sacrifice? What did they experience once they got to the places deemed holy?

Such questions, however, were still academic. The big surprise came when he realized that something more personal was going on.

It was clear to him that, for all his interest in them, he didn't belong to Islam or Judaism, and he never would. But if he was by default a Christian, what did that mean? What was he supposed to believe?

Having not read much of the Bible, his knowledge of the city in the time of Jesus came from a guidebook, *Ten New Testament Walks in Jerusalem*, purchased at a shop in Tel Aviv. But it was a start. He hiked to the top of the Mount of Olives, and then slowly followed the path that tradition says Jesus took on Palm Sunday, letting his imagination stand in for knowledge of the biblical account. He went to Mount Zion, where, according to tradition, Jesus ate a last meal with his disciples before walking down the hill to the ancient olive trees in the Garden of Gethsemane. This time Daniel had the foresight to bring the pocket-sized New Testament he had picked up in a Christian bookstore, reading in the garden how Jesus prayed there amid followers who couldn't stay awake. He walked the Via Dolorosa, the traditional journey made by Jesus while dragging his cross—starting at the Ecce Homo arch, turning left at the Austrian Hospice, right, up the steps where he'd hurried on the morning of the fire, left on Christian Quarter Road, and left again to the Church of the Holy Sepulchre. The second time he walked it, he stopped at every station of the cross, reading about them in his guidebook. The third time, he stopped again, trying without much practice to pray.

Various friends at the university hinted that they would like to go with him on one of his trips to the Old City; and he did meet a group of them one Friday evening at the Western Wall where they mainly stood around, watching the Orthodox and making fun of the tourists. But something in him resisted sharing Bassam and Al-Kamal. And the thought that others might glimpse his newfound passion felt somehow embarrassing. What if his friends joked about how he was becoming religious, "like the Orthodox"?

It felt less embarrassing, however, to *study* religion, so halfway through the fall he changed part of his spring semester schedule from "Political Developments in the Middle East" and "Israeli Government and Politics" to "Archaeology and the Bible" and, since there was no course on Christianity, "Judaism in the Twentieth Century." He could study politics, he told himself, back at Yale.

Daniel's favorite sacred site, during these early explorations, was the Holy Sepulchre, where, tradition has it, Jesus was crucified and buried. Later, he would read scholars who vented their disappointment at the drab exterior and dim, cramped, often chaotic interior. Tourists, he would discover, generally expected a soaring church, one that stands alone like Westminster or Chartres. By contrast, the Church of the Holy Sepulchre looked squeezed, other buildings clinging to it haphazardly. But to Daniel, unburdened by aesthetic or historical expectations, this was how it was supposed to be. The sounds of workers hammering, sawing, and drilling made it feel more alive. The chaos of competing chapels added to the sense of veneration. The dimness enhanced the glow of candles on the ancient stones.

The interior light became especially mysterious, he found, in the hour before the great door was locked for the night. He made it his practice to go there as daylight was fading, until one chilly late-November evening, instead of leaving for Al-Kamal, he decided to stay, hidden on a bench in the crypt where Saint Helena is said to have found the True Cross. He loved the smell, mustiness mixed with incense. He loved the feel of the damp stone wall. He loved the tiny crosses carved in the stone by generations of pilgrims.

Eventually he dozed, but was awakened by chanting in the chapels above him, which he later learned came from Greeks at two o'clock and Armenians at four: *Pater hemon ho en toes ouranoes . . . Hayr mer vor hergeens yes . . .* The words reverberated down the steps and off the rough, rocky surfaces. It was uncanny, from a world he hadn't known existed. It thrilled him at a level deeper than intellect, deeper even than emotion. Was this the level people meant when they talked about your soul?

Sitting there in the darkness, with only a faint light from the stairway, he told himself he should pray. It was surely the perfect time, alone in a place where he could practically feel the prayers of a thousand years embedded in the stone. But he didn't even know what it was he would be doing if he did. He couldn't imagine his parents praying, but his grandmother had. What words went through her head? To whom or what were they aimed? What did she expect to happen when she prayed? He spent part of the night trying to formulate prayerful words, hoping she would have approved.

When Daniel returned to the Old City two weeks later, Al-Kamal, much to his surprise, had no available beds. He hoped Bassam would offer him the private room, but when that didn't happen, he was in need of a place to stay. To make matters worse, it was beginning to rain. He cut over to El-Wad, thinking he would take a room at the Austrian Hospice—until he heard the price. It was the woman at the reception desk who recommended the guesthouse run by the Sisters of Zion. "It is just down the street," she told him, "at the Ecce Homo arch." He was silently offended when she asked if he thought he could find it.

It rained heavily the next day. In the morning, Daniel stayed dry by exploring the ancient cistern and the pavement of a Roman fortress buried beneath the sisters' convent. When it was still raining, he borrowed an umbrella in order to dash outside for lunch. Still raining. He tried reading in his cramped room, with its single bed under a crucifix, but by three o'clock, feeling claustrophobic, he wandered down to the common area where a nun in a simple black-and-white habit was fixing a cup of tea. "You look," she said, "like you could use one, too."

At her invitation, they settled into chairs in a corner of the room, Sister Mary introducing herself and telling him she was from England. Her tone was gentle, inviting, and without having planned it, he asked, "Can I talk to you, Sister Mary, about . . . I don't know how to say it. I guess, about being religious?"

She smiled. "The other sisters say I have a gift for listening."

How, he asked to begin with, had she decided to become a nun? Had she grown up in the church, or had she come to it later, say, when she was twenty or so? She answered that the church had always been her home, practically the air she breathed. Her uncle was a priest, and she had a cousin who was also a nun.

"But there are lots of ways to become religious," she told him, as if intuiting what was behind his question. "I know I shouldn't, but sometimes I envy people whose journey to God is more difficult. Of course, I also envy those for whom the skies seem to open, and they have a great moment of clarity. I just muddle along as I always have, believing as best I can. Maybe God needs those of us who are muddlers, somewhere between the difficult and the easy." She finished her tea. "But we shouldn't be talking about me. Tell me what brings *you* here."

And so he told her about his not-very-religious parents, about his interest in politics, about his program in Tel Aviv, and about his trips to Jerusalem and his love for the Old City. When he finished, her first question caught him off guard: Was he lonely?

"I wouldn't say lonely . . ."

She sat patiently.

"It's more like I don't quite fit in anywhere. I'm obviously not really 'one of the guys' at the Al-Kamal, and there are a million things I don't know that others take for granted at the university. I'm not at home in Israel, but being here makes home back in Ohio seem less appealing. And now what I thought was my great academic interest doesn't feel so interesting. At least not interesting enough to spend my life teaching it." Without much transition, he found himself telling her about the girlfriend he'd had at Yale and how they'd gone separate ways. He told her how he didn't hear much from his parents, maybe because he seldom wrote to them. He mentioned Mya.

Perhaps because this monologue was beginning to feel self-indulgent, he asked, "Why did you come to Jerusalem?"

"Oh, I was a teacher at one of our Catholic schools, in Worthing on the south coast of England. When I got too old, the order sent me here, three years ago, to help oversee the guesthouse. Sometimes I just feel like a tour guide, but maybe that's a kind of teaching." She paused.

"You're not the only one, you see, who has vocational questions."

After Sister Mary had gotten them both a cookie, which she called a "biscuit," Daniel asked, "What's your favorite spot in Jerusalem? You must have done a lot of exploring in three years. What place speaks to your . . . soul?"

She smiled while considering the question, eating her cookie in small bites. "I guess I don't think of Jerusalem as a city of holy places. The entire city is holy, at least that's the way I see it."

"There's not some spot that really speaks to you?"

She thought for a moment. "I guess I'd have to say the Room of the Last Supper."

"But it's just a plain room. Nothing—"

"Oh, I know it's not the real place, and there's certainly nothing special about the room. That's true. For some reason, though, my imagination takes over, and I can practically see the disciples there with Jesus around a table. Maybe I like things on Mount Zion because of our name." She took the last bite of her cookie. "If you go there, you might want to climb up the stairs on the outside of the building. They look as if they might collapse at any minute, but so far they haven't. And from the rooftop, you can see a corner, just a little part, of the Western Wall. Someone told me that was as close as Jews could come to it while Jordanians controlled the eastern part of the city."

Daniel went there the next evening. After climbing the rickety staircase, he stumbled across the uneven stones of the mostly flat rooftop toward a modest-sized dome, squeezing past it to a railing looking east. He could see the wall of the Old City not far to his left, the silhouette of the Mount of Olives ahead of him, lights dotting the village at its base like scattered glitter. The sky was still cloudy from the recent rain, so though he knew they were there, he couldn't see the stars, just intense darkness. It felt to him that the city was on the edge of a great something, now hidden. What Bedouin camped there beyond the mount? What mystics had wandered there? What fervent prayers had been cast into this blackness?

He put his hands together on the damp railing and rested his forehead against them, his mind a muddle of thoughts and emotions. There was no sudden insight, no parting of the veil, but after a minute he simply *knew* that he was a particle of an existence, a mix of history and nature and psyche, far greater than he could grasp. He was part of it, and it was part of him. All this worry about who he was and what he should do with his life felt, at the same moment, both trivial and monumentally important.

Daniel closed his eyes while the call to prayer rang out from minarets across the city, as it had for more than thirteen centuries. "*Allahu akbar,*" the first word drawn out, followed quickly by the second. Intoned testimony, in a language he didn't know, to something welling up inside him.

Chapter Five

In the third week of January, Daniel met Shoshana. After Bassam had no room in his inn, Daniel decided it was for the best. He had been spending too much time at Al-Kamal. So when friends at the university—a group that included Alan, Lenny, and Mya—invited him to go with them to Jerusalem for Tu B'Shvat, he agreed after only a little convincing.

"What," he asked Lenny, "is Tu B'Shvat? I've never heard of it."

"The New Year for Trees. Are you into ecology?"

"Yeah, I guess."

"It's a celebration of nature, that sort of thing. We're going up on Wednesday after classes to meet some Israelis. I think they're with the Jewish National Fund. Mya made the connection. Then on Thursday, which is the actual holiday, we'll help them plant a few trees in the Jerusalem Forest and come back that evening."

"Jerusalem has a forest?"

"It's on the edge of the city in the valley below Yad Vashem, if you know where that is. So, you in?"

"We have classes, at least I do, on Thursday morning. What—"

"Come on, man, it's a year abroad program! Classes are just part of the experience, as you know better than anyone with all your trips to Arab land."

They met at a campground in a national park, ten miles west of Al-Kamal, seven American students from Tel Aviv and nine Israelis. There was a campfire and the obligatory folk songs, most of which Daniel knew. He had envisioned staying close to Mya, whom he still thought of as a good friend, but the leader of the Israelis urged them to mix it up, and after a bit of milling, he ended up sitting on a log next to an Israeli woman. She had been wearing a hat but now took it off, and dark hair cascaded down her back—beautifully, he thought.

Various people with official-looking badges were talking about the tree planting, how important it was and how it brought American Jews and Israeli Jews together. But no matter how hard he tried to pay attention, Daniel couldn't help glancing at her. Twice. Three times. Four times. Finally, the speeches ended and she turned to face him, straddling the log, and extended her hand.

"I'm Shoshana."

"Daniel."

"So, tell me about yourself, Daniel. You're not the Ivy Leaguer, are you?"

He smiled.

"So you are! My friend at your school told me there was a guy from Harvard . . ."

"Yale, actually." He mentally kicked himself for saying something so stupidly irrelevant.

"Okay, from Yale, who isn't Jewish and is the smartest guy in their group. That doesn't speak well for us Jews, does it?" Half her face was highlighted by the fire, and he could now see that her hair wasn't the only beautiful thing about her—at least to him. Very dark eyes and eyebrows, the shadows accentuating her cheekbones and partially hiding a birthmark on the right side of her neck. Her teeth made her upper lip protrude slightly, but this only enhanced her smile—at least to him.

"Are you really an Israeli? You have no accent, none at all."

"Good. A straightforward question like an Israeli would ask." Her smile widened. "If I have an accent, it's when I speak Hebrew. But then half of Israel is from somewhere else and speaks Hebrew with an accent."

The next hour flew by. The two of them sat talking while the others mingled and danced the *hora*, only occasionally trying to pull them in. Her mother, he learned, was American, and the family had lived in Boston until Shoshana was eight. But then her mother, who was nearly forty when Shoshana was born, had died of breast cancer. "It was pretty awful. I hope no daughter of mine has to see me die like that." She paused. "Anyway, after she died, my dad and sister and I moved to Israel, and an aunt lived with us." She adjusted her seat on the log. "Why am I telling you all this? I just met you!"

He started to reply but stopped, watching the light flicker across her face. "Maybe," he said after the pause, "because you can tell I want to know."

"Well, to quickly finish the story, I went back to study at BU where we were always told to stay away from Harvard boys." That beautiful smile. "It was clear though, really, as soon as I got there, that Israel is home. In the US, I was Susan. I didn't feel like a Susan! So after graduation, I came back and did my two years of military service. There are lots of Jews in Boston, but here I can be a Jew without even thinking about it. I even keep kosher, most of the time. And now I'm working for the Jewish National Fund, at least until something better comes along. End of story." Such a smile.

"You've graduated and been in the military . . . how old are you?"

"Another Israeli question! I'm sure I am older than you. Twenty-three."

"Okay, I'll ask another one. Do you always wear a hat?"

"Most of the time."

"Why is that? You have terrific hair."

She smiled, seemed to hesitate, and then turned the left side of her head toward the fire, pulling back her hair to reveal a prominent scar near the hairline. "But you would have to know me a lot better before I'd tell you how I got it."

Others were already headed for the cars when Daniel and Shoshana finally abandoned the log. In the shadows away from the fire, he told her how great it was to meet her and gave her a hug—which he wasn't sure should include a kiss—until she kissed him, quickly, on the lips.

"Have fun planting."

"Won't you be there?"

"I've got other work I need to do, so you're on your own."

Daniel could hear friends from Tel Aviv calling for him to hurry up. "What if I came back to Jerusalem this weekend? Actually, I come here a lot, and if I came on the weekend, which I think should work, maybe we could, you know, have dinner."

"Are you always so definite?"

He could feel himself blushing, which he was glad she couldn't see in the dark.

"Meet me on Saturday at the Sabra Restaurant," she told him. "It's near Ben Yehuda, everyone will know it. But don't show up before sundown and look like a goy!"

Even in the shadows, he could see her smile. He wanted to kiss her again, but she had turned, and soon they were with the rest of the group.

The restaurant, it turned out, was crowded and noisy, so they ate faster than Daniel had pictured in his fantasies. Once outside, he suggested they walk to the Old City; it would only take fifteen minutes. But Shoshana just laughed. "And do what? Have a cup of tea and smoke a water pipe?" She led him to a bar where they talked about ecology (he had spent Friday reading up) and politics and his family and her sister, who lived near Haifa, and his plans for graduate school and her hopes for the future.

"If I stay with JNF, I might be able to travel from time to time to the US. But to be honest, I'm not big on travel, and all I have left in the States is an aunt and a couple of cousins." She took a drink of her wine. "Israel's where my heart is. I'd rather do social work here, though that'll mean more study."

At some point, he took her hand, sliding his chair closer. He wanted her to invite him to her apartment, even formulated in his head the words he hoped she would say. This time he would be more definite! Although the idea also made him nervous.

In any case, she didn't. He spent the night at Al-Kamal, tossing and turning until one of the others in the room muttered something in Arabic.

But the next weekend she did.

Chapter Six

For Daniel, the next four months were like nothing he had ever known, full of anticipation of their next meeting, which was nearly every weekend. None of this was lost on his Tel Aviv friends, including Mya. "I never should have left the two of you alone," she teased him, a clear indication that she was the one who'd told Shoshana about "the Ivy Leaguer."

Even though she hadn't been raised in a particularly religious household, Shoshana had decided, once she returned to Israel, not only to keep kosher but to observe the Sabbath rituals. This meant they usually ate the Friday-evening meal in her three-room apartment, with photographs of nature looming over the small sofa and a print of Chagall's *The Praying Jew* hanging near the table she used for every meal. Shoshana would cover the challah, light two candles, wave her hands over the flames to welcome the Sabbath, and, closing her eyes, recite "*Baruch atah Adonai, Eloheinu melech haolam, asher kid'shanu b'mitzvotav v'zivanu l'hadlik ner shel Shabbat.*"

After a couple of weeks, Daniel was participating fully in meal preparation and the ritual. Once, when friends were present, she invited him to light the candles and start the prayer. "I have the most Jewish Christian boyfriend in all of Jerusalem," she told her friends. "He even has a Jewish name." Which made them laugh and him feel great for more than one reason.

Since his new interest in Christian identity hadn't yet translated into church attendance, these Friday evenings with Shoshana were the most worshipful moments of his week. They touched that sense of tradition, of mystery, of being part of something larger that he'd felt in the crypt of the Holy Sepulchre and, especially, on the Rooftop. Only now he wasn't being religious alone.

Of course, the weekends included other activities. "It's a good thing that sex is permitted on the Sabbath," she told him, smiling. "In fact, it's encouraged, if you read the right commentaries." Sometimes, they would linger in bed, drinking wine and listening to Israeli hits like "Al Kapav Yavi" and "Yerushalayim Shel Zahav," which even Daniel could sing along to.

When they weren't praying, eating, or making love, Shoshana showed Daniel her Jerusalem: the Hadassah Hospital, with stained glass windows of the twelve tribes, by Chagall; the Israel Museum, where she skipped the Dead Sea Scrolls in favor of drawings, by Chagall; her favorite shops on King George Street and Jaffa Road, including the one where she bought her hats. Being into nature, she took him to see the trees in Bloomfield Garden, which he now enjoyed, and to walk in the Ramot Forest, a mere six miles north of Al-Kamal. He marveled at her knowledge of the natural world; she congratulated him, a man whose natural habitat was cities, on being a good sport. "If my experience is any guide, most Israeli men see the outdoors as a place to do macho things, not admire trees."

"So, you do this often . . . ?"

"Go ahead, ask like an Israeli. Do I go hiking with other guys? I have, but I like doing it with you. You want to know what I'm thinking, not just show me what you know or how tough you are."

Then, on their sixth time together, she took him to Yad Vashem where the names of her father's family murdered in the Holocaust are recorded. They walked through galleries filled with photographs and objects that gave witness to the horror, Daniel not sure what to say, Shoshana apparently lost in her thoughts. It wasn't until they were seated on a bench, under a sign identifying the Hall of Remembrance, that she asked him, "Are your grandparents alive?"

"One of my grandmothers died, but the others . . ." They looked at each other in silence before he asked, almost in a whisper, what, if anything, she knew about hers.

Whenever Shoshana had other obligations, Daniel would slip over to the Old City, about a thirty-minute walk or a ten-minute bus ride, where he roamed the by-now-familiar alleyways. It was already March, however, before they went there together. "Now I see," said Bassam when Daniel introduced him to Shoshana, "why you have not been staying with us," and summoned one of the ubiquitous runners to bring them tea.

Later, when they were seated in Daniel's favorite Old City restaurant eating hummus and tabbouleh, Shoshana said, "I can't believe you actually stayed there!" That beautiful smile.

"The Al-Kamal's not so bad once you get used to having six strangers in the room."

Even as he was speaking, she was shaking her head. "It's a dump! One common toilet and a trough to wash in. No wonder you like my apartment."

"That's hardly the main—"

"I'm serious. I don't get it. You say all the time that you love the Old City. What do you love about it? It's dirty. It seems like everywhere you go you're either walking up steps or down them. The merchants are pushy. The 'famous places,' from what I've read, are generally fakes. It's often crowded with tourists. And for a Jew, it can be dangerous."

"The Palestinians say the same, about it being dangerous. They're not the ones here with the guns."

Their chicken shashlik arrived, and they ate for a minute before he said, "I went to New York City with my parents when I was ten or eleven, and I remember loving Manhattan because everywhere you looked there was something new. Just walking outside the hotel was an adventure." He took a bite. "That's how I feel here. The sites may not be authentic, probably aren't, but *something* was there that people thought was special. It makes me feel part of something bigger and older . . . and sacred. I guess that's the word. It's hard to explain."

She put her hand on his arm. "I think you explained it just fine." She smiled, as much with her eyes as her mouth. "Actually, it's one of the things that I love"—she paused—"that I appreciate about you. But haven't you ever felt threatened here?"

That's when he told her more about being in the Old City on the morning Al-Aqsa was set on fire. He had talked some about it during their many conversations, but now he told her in detail about being questioned by the Israeli soldiers. Yes, he had felt threatened within these walls, he told her, and it was then.

Since he'd said that much, he also told her about the anger of his friends at Al-Kamal. Her response took him by surprise.

"What did they have to be angry about? Palestinians attacked the firemen when they tried to put it out. I read that they even broke the fire hydrant on the Temple Mount. That's why so much of the mosque burned. Then, when Golda went there, they almost overran her bodyguards." She lifted her hands in a gesture of disbelief. "So I don't get why they would be angry, at least why they'd be angry at us. Jews didn't start the fire."

Daniel smiled until she said, "What? What did I say that's so funny?"

He shook his head. "Sometimes I just forget that you are a real Israeli."

Shoshana clearly saw their relationship as something substantial. Hadn't she called him her "boyfriend" in public? He was sure she wasn't seeing another guy. When would she have the time? There was, however, always a hint of reserve. When he apologized that he couldn't come to Jerusalem one weekend, her response was abrupt. "Why are you apologizing? You have things to do besides see me. And I have things to do that don't involve you."

"What does that mean?"

"What does what mean? For one thing, I have a job. People at the JNF have been covering for me on Sunday the past couple of months. You do know we work on Sundays?" Her tone softened. "Look, Daniel, do what you need to do. I'll be around. And if I can't be, I'll tell you."

Several times he suggested she meet him in Tel Aviv, but she only came once—for Purim, because she liked the big city's more Carnival-like atmosphere. The evening was great fun, full of bopping others on the head with squeaky plastic hammers (although he wasn't sure what this had to do with Esther's saving the Jews in ancient Persia).

"You are too gentle!" she told him as they bopped their way around the crowded Kings of Israel Square. "Israelis really whack each other, take out their aggression."

But then things got awkward. "I can't spend the night in your dorm," she told him. "You share a bathroom and showers with a bunch of guys. How's that supposed to work?" Maybe, he said without much conviction, they could stay at a hotel. Shoshana just laughed, assured him that hotels in Tel Aviv cost a lot more than the Al-Kamal, and stayed with Mya at Mrs. P's.

The following week was Holy Week for Catholics and Protestants. Daniel arrived at Shoshana's apartment on Thursday evening so he could experience Good Friday, when local Christians, joined by pilgrims, carried a cross through the Old City's streets. And he wanted Shoshana to go with him.

"You know," she told him, "this is not high on the Jewish list of favorite holidays."

"Well, I went to Purim, so—"

"That's hardly the same! There aren't any ancient Persians around for us to pick on."

"People today, at least educated people, know it was the Romans who killed Jesus. They know it wasn't the Jews."

"Good. You keep saying that loud and clear when you get back home, because the wrong people, and that often means us, have been blamed throughout history for things we didn't do."

She ended up going, but the alleyways were so jammed they could barely move, let alone get close to the Holy Sepulchre, the terminus of the procession. After an hour of jostling, she whispered in his ear, "Let's go to the apartment and do something more enjoyable," and he readily agreed.

This wasn't their only attempt to do religious things together in public. Early in April, after the Easter crowds were gone, they were back in the Old City for Erev Shabbat at the Western Wall, another of his suggestions. Even standing outside the area designated for worshippers, they could see the prayers written on slips of paper and stuffed in cracks between the massive stones. As they stood looking, Daniel could feel Shoshana rubbing her leg against his, almost inviting disapproving stares.

"Are you going to write a prayer?" he asked her.

"Never have and don't intend to."

They were now facing one another, the wind gently blowing the hair that flowed from under her wide-brimmed hat. "We could do it together—"

"No we can't!" Her voice was loud enough for others to hear. "That's my point. The Orthodox control this place—men here, women over there—and it makes me feel like I'm less of a Jew. That's how they're *trying* to make me feel!" She lowered her voice. "It wasn't this way when my dad and I came right after the Six-Day War, but after that the Orthodox just took over. These people are nuts, living in the past. Even being here makes me tense."

Daniel nodded. "I get it. But isn't there something in between, something between crazy religion and no religion?"

"I don't have 'no religion'! Is what we do on Friday evenings in the apartment 'no religion'? I pray, but I'm not going to be told where and how to do it by these people."

"No, you're right. Sorry."

After a few seconds, she smiled—that beautiful smile—and ran her fingers along his temple. "You are a good man, Daniel Jacobs. If it's what you want to do, go put one in the Wall for both of us."

The next day, Daniel insisted—"to balance things out"—that they visit the Holy Sepulchre. This, he let her know, was the church where he had felt closest to God, whatever that meant. In the daytime, however, it just looked dingy, even to him. And crowded. A large tour group stood around the Stone of Unction, listening to the drone of their guide, apparently oblivious that they were blocking others from entering the church. As he and Shoshana stood there—unable to move forward, being pushed from behind—he could see the dust that coated the great doors, one of them bricked shut. The grime that encrusted the hinges, and the sandwich wrapper discarded in a corner, made him wince.

Once inside, he led her quickly down two flights of worn stone steps to the Saint Helena crypt. But in the noisy swirl of tourists, it was impossible to communicate what he had felt on that night in November. They even sat on the bench where he had sat—after candy-bar-eating tourists had vacated it—but the frustration of trying to recapture something so singular left him nearly in tears.

Once they were outside, Shoshana took his hand and told him she had enjoyed it. She could see why spending the night in this church had moved him so deeply. He was sure that couldn't be true, which made him love her all the more for saying it.

As Daniel was leaving her apartment that weekend, Shoshana invited him to go with her to her sister's home north of Haifa for the Seder meal on the first night of Passover. Of course he said yes, but with some trepidation. It would be a chance to meet her family, including her father, Ira. But what if they didn't like him?

"It'll be fun," Shoshana told him, as if reading his mind. "I've never brought a male friend to a big family meal like this, so they'll be as uncertain about it as you are."

She picked him up in her rust-spotted, Israeli-made sedan in the early afternoon of April 20, and they arrived in time to help her sister, Rahel, set the festive table. Ira showed up not long after, complaining about the traffic, but the conversation soon became pleasantly superficial. The men—especially Rahel's husband, Yaron—carried on about the Israeli national soccer team that, miracle of miracles, was going to the finals of the World Cup in Mexico. Daniel, mercifully, knew that Israel had defeated New Zealand in a big match played in Tel Aviv; exuberant fans had been all over the streets. Then, stretching the bounds of his knowledge, he mentioned the goal Mordechai Spiegler scored against Australia that got Israel to the finals. But unfortunately, he called him "Spangler," to the amusement of the others.

The teasing, however, was gentle. "It's tough to get inside another society," said Ira. "It took me a while when we lived in Boston. The whole time, I thought the Detroit Lions was a baseball team." He shook his head at the memory. "And I think it took Shoshana a while when we moved back to Israel. Of course, she was only eight or nine and it's easier then. Now she's more Israeli than me."

The meal was also fun, sort of. Since Rahel and Yaron's son was too young to read, Daniel, the youngest adult, was designated to ask the ritual questions. Their Hagaddah booklets included an English translation, but Daniel, again straying beyond his limits, decided to try the first question—"Why is this night different from all other nights?"—in Hebrew. When he had struggled through the sentence, Rahel said, "*Todah rabah*, Daniel. Now let's do the rest in English." The others were smiling as Shoshana kissed him on the cheek.

They did sing in Hebrew, teaching Daniel "Dayenu" and "Echad Mi Yodea." Wine flowed freely, and no one complained when a few lines were omitted here and there. "We all know how it ends," said Yaron as he urged them to skip pages sixteen through twenty.

Rahel had seated her father at the head of the table, with Daniel and Shoshana to his left. At first the dinner conversation took in all of them, but gradually it broke into pairs, Ira shifting in his chair to look more directly at Daniel.

"My younger daughter tells me you are interested in religion."

She had spoken with her father about him! "She did? My major is actually political science, but yes, I'm getting more interested in religion, certainly more than I expected to be."

"Examining your Christian roots, I think she said."

Daniel nodded. "Maybe there's something in the water in Jerusalem."

They both smiled. "Maybe that's so, because I hear that even my daughter is lighting candles for Shabbat." He took a drink of wine. "How does that work, you becoming more Christian and her becoming more Jewish?"

She had told her father the relationship was serious! He could now sense that Shoshana was listening with one ear. "We don't talk about it that way very much," Daniel told him. "It just . . . is what it is."

Ira nodded. "I'm sure you two have plenty of things to talk about." He took another sip of wine. "But it might be useful to consider that a little more." They ate for a minute before he asked, "Are you involved back home in these war protests we read so much about?"

How to answer? "I've taken part in a couple of marches, but I guess I'm not . . . I mean, I don't support the war, at all, but I try to see different points of view, if I can." He could feel his ears turning red.

Ira nodded again. "Will you be going into the military?"

Daniel shook his head. "I got a high lottery number, and I'm in school. So, thankfully, no."

"You know, Shoshana was in the IDF."

Shoshana now turned in their direction. "I've told him about all that, *Abba*."

Ira continued as if she hadn't spoken. "She finished her service just before the Six-Day War and then was called back. We're all in the reserves—as you know, or maybe you don't—until you're as old as I am. She was stationed here in the north."

"Not right here, and I was hardly 'stationed' anywhere during the war," said Shoshana, looking at Daniel. "I was sent to the Golan Heights after the Syrians tried to capture the water plants around

Kibbutz Dan. But the Women's Corps wasn't in combat. I was basically a driver, and did some things in communications."

"So you haven't told him about it," said Ira.

"Yes I have!" It was clear Shoshana was trying to keep her voice low but also that others were already listening.

"That you carried a gun?"

"Why would I need to talk about that when I never fired it, except in training? I never had any reason to fire it."

Daniel felt he should be part of this conversation, but what to say? "I appreciate Israel's need for defense," he said, looking first at Shoshana, then at her father. "It's just not my experience, so I need to listen to yours."

Ira smiled and put his hand on Daniel's shoulder. "Good. I have experience myself with Americans, as you know, and it is my experience that they don't understand. Even Shoshana's mother didn't completely understand. You can't know unless you were here in '67 when we painted over our car headlights so they wouldn't attract enemy planes. You have to see your country digging mass graves and holding mass blood drives in case your enemies make good on their threat to push you into the sea. If you haven't done such things, it is good to be a listener."

They had to stay overnight—Rahel simply pointing them to the guest bedroom without comment—but were back in Tel Aviv in time for his Tuesday-morning class. "It's a good thing you are smart," Shoshana said as she dropped him off, "because you do a lot of things other than study."

Naturally, Daniel was back in Jerusalem that Friday, but this time he insisted that after dinner they walk to Mount Zion. During the bus ride from Tel Aviv, he had mulled over the conversation with her father. Ira was right: they *should* share with one another what they were feeling about religion, and that meant taking Shoshana, finally, to the Rooftop. This was important, he told himself, as they made their way there—she taking her time, he attempting to move her along—on a beautiful spring evening. But he was also getting nervous. What if she didn't feel anything? What if this visit was as disappointing as the one to the Holy Sepulchre? On the Rooftop, there were no candles to light, no special words to recite, no slips of paper for writing prayers. Should something be called "holy" if it's only one person's experience?

Up the rusted staircase, the flat rooftop barely illuminated by the lights from the nearby Dormition Abbey. This time, however, the sky was clear, and the stars more than mirrored the lights from the village at the foot of the hill. They squeezed past the dome to the railing facing east.

Daniel wasn't sure what he wanted to say, if anything. But in any case, it was Shoshana who spoke first. "This place is famous. Though why the Orthodox thought there was something sacred about looking at the Wall from . . ." She glanced at Daniel and then stopped abruptly.

"Yeah, I know," he said, an edge to his voice. "I didn't discover this spot. I just . . . like it."

She was now facing him directly and put her finger to his lips. "Daniel, *neshama sheli*, I'm glad you brought me here, but I can't in a million years experience what you experienced. To me, it's just a rooftop with a good view." She ran her fingers, the way she did, along his temple. "I can tell it's more than that to you, a lot more, and that's great." When he said nothing, she turned back to the railing, her voice barely audible. "I'm glad you have a Rooftop . . . Sometimes I wish I had one."

Chapter Seven

On May 4, the beginning of Daniel's last month in Israel, an event back home sent shock waves through the overseas program. The American students, at least those who were aware of the world, had been following the protests against the war in Vietnam; but the killing of students at Kent State University made it all immediate as nothing else had.

This was still on Daniel's mind when he met Shoshana that Friday. "My mother always ends her letters by telling me to stay safe. I think I feel safer in Israel than in the US."

"Don't be silly. The war in Vietnam will end, eventually, and American campuses will go back to being as boring as ever. But here it will always be war. Sometimes shooting, sometimes not, but never really peace. That's just how it is." She was slicing fresh tomatoes for their Shabbat meal, and suddenly he was overwhelmed, yet again, by her beauty. By how she spoke and how she moved and how she thought. By everything about her. It made his chest feel full, as if it would overflow.

"You know, I can't help wishing that I had studied in Jerusalem instead of Tel Aviv. Then we—"

"Then you wouldn't have stayed at the Al-Kamal and had all those adventures in the Old City you love so much. It seems to me that things have worked out pretty well for you."

"And for you?"

She dried her hands, looking at the towel. "And for me."

Daniel busied himself setting the table, trying to sound nonchalant as he said, "If there's always war here and you haven't found the perfect job . . . maybe you should move back to the States."

That smile. "I already tried that. This is where I belong, peace or no peace."

"Then maybe I should"—he paused—"move here."

He could feel his stomach tightening and his ears turning red as Shoshana stopped her chopping and stared at him, no longer smiling. "What are you saying?"

"Well, I'm just . . . If you won't—"

"Daniel, *motek*!" She put down the knife and spread her arms. "These months have been *nehedar* . . . *nifla*. You know what that means?"

He shook his head.

"I think you know. They have been wonderful, like nothing before, at least for me." As he started to speak, she cut him off. "But you have to go back! You have a year of college left—at Yale, no less. And you have plans. Look, we'll keep in touch, and who knows what might happen? But for now, it is what it is. You have to go home."

That was the most direct conversation they had on the subject. He did assure her, many times, that he would write every day, and would return to Israel next year, as soon as he graduated. Shoshana promised to write, though probably not every day. "If you come back," she teased him, "it's because you're in love with Jerusalem."

Daniel wasn't sure she remembered his birthday, but when he arrived the following Friday, there was a cake. And on top of it, along with twenty-one candles, she had drawn an outline of the Old City with frosting.

"I was going to put a dot to mark your favorite hotel, but then I realized I have no idea where to put it. That's your special world."

"When I come back, you can be sure my first stop won't be the Al-Kamal Hotel."

"Well," she said, after they had kissed, "you know where to find me. I'm not going anywhere." Words he turned over in his mind all the way back to Tel Aviv.

On his last full day in Jerusalem, Daniel made a quick trip to the Old City in order to see Bassam. As he stepped through the shadowy entrance of Al-Kamal, he could see that his friend was in conversation with three other men. Finally, after several minutes, he decided to interrupt.

"I'm leaving for America in a couple of days, so I thought I'd say goodbye and thanks, *shukran*, for inviting me to stay here way back in the fall. Please say goodbye to Mr. Khatib for me." Bassam, dressed in his usual skullcap and keffiyeh scarf, smiled and bowed slightly. "I'll see you," Daniel added, "maybe spend a night at Al-Kamal when I'm in Jerusalem again."

"*Inshallah*. We always say '*inshallah*' because such things are in the hands of the One who is merciful and compassionate."

Daniel also stopped by the Sisters of Zion convent, hoping to say goodbye to Sister Mary. "She's resting," he was told, "and it would not be good to bother her."

That night, after he and Shoshana had made love, he rested on one elbow, running his free hand over her body—the shape of her neck and shoulders, the curve of her breasts, the softness of her stomach, the contour of her hips, the sensuous tapering of her legs. Gently, he brushed the hair off her face, kissing the scar that ran along her hairline and, then, the birthmark on the side of her neck. In the moonlight, he could see her watching, her eyes blurry, as he kissed other parts of her he had never before kissed, trying to imprint it all in his memory. They made love again and then lay there, his arm around her, her head on his chest.

"You never have told me how you got the scar."

There was a long silence before she asked, "Has anyone ever hurt you, physically? Really hurt you?"

"No, not really."

"Maybe that's why I knew you would never hurt me." She said no more, and although he wanted to, he didn't ask.

Shoshana had told him she wouldn't see him off at the airport. "I don't like goodbyes in public places, especially with all your friends around. Besides, I have a job, you know." But, in fact, she was there.

On that last night in the apartment, he had given her a tote bag, adorned with a picture of an angel by Chagall, and a silver kiddush cup he had purchased in the Jewish Quarter of the Old City. "To remember me on Shabbat."

At the airport, she gave him a T-shirt with "Jewish National Fund" and the drawing of a tree on the front. Folded inside the shirt was a small box, which he opened to reveal a key chain decorated with an Eilat stone, the Hebrew letter *shin*—the English *sh*—affixed to it in silver. "This," she told him, "is the national stone of Israel, so it's a way of carrying a piece of the country with you."

"And to remind me of you."

She nodded slightly. "And to remind you of me."

PART TWO

WALLS
(1975)

Chapter Eight

Outside the Old City wall, things had changed dramatically in five years. There were even plans for a shopping mall not far from the Jaffa Gate. A shopping mall where kings and prophets and apostles had walked! To Daniel, it seemed almost sacrilegious.

Inside the wall, however, change was less apparent. Or maybe that's just what he hoped would be the case when he arrived in Jerusalem on Wednesday, May 21. The rest of that day and the next were spent in orientation at the Gutmann Institute, where he would be participating in seminars and doing research for his dissertation. He circled Friday the 23rd on his mental calendar as the day he would reacquaint himself with the Old City: have his breakfast of egg and cheese on pita, cooked in Ibrahim's open-flame oven near the Damascus Gate; smell the spices and fruit in the souk; wander past shops on El-Wad, remembering how crowded it had been on the day of the fire. He wanted to walk the Via Dolorosa and sit in the crypt of the Holy Sepulchre where he had once spent the night, leaning against the slightly damp stone walls; savor tea with mint in the café he had gone to with Bassam near Herod's Gate; and, of course, drop by Al-Kamal. He deliberately did not include the Western Wall in his daytime itinerary, saving that for the evening. Erev Shabbat at the Wall. It was one of the many things he associated with Shoshana.

That evening, lights were coming on as Daniel left the Casa Nova guesthouse in the Christian Quarter and made his way to the open area inside the Jaffa Gate. From there, he turned left, away from the coral sunset, down the gradual steps of David Street toward the Wall and Al-Aqsa. Since it was the cusp of the summer tourist season, several shops were still open, and he greeted some of the merchants, two who invited him "just to look."

"Maybe later," he told them. "I'll be here for a month."

He walked past the small vegetable market, now closed, moving aside to allow a cart to squeeze by on the narrow ramps connecting one stone step to the next. Past a stall he remembered for its excellent freshly squeezed orange juice, again moving aside, this time for a group of Orthodox Jewish men in long silk robes and round fur hats—also, no doubt, on their way to the Wall. Past the jog in the street where it intersects with the butcher and goldsmith markets.

Even after five years, Daniel could mentally picture his location, as if looking at a map: the Damascus Gate to his left, the heart of the Jewish Quarter to his right. In the tangle of narrow streets, some covered like tunnels, a newcomer could easily become disoriented; but he took pride in not being a newcomer. Standing there in the fading light, he could see in his mind the Rooftop on Mount Zion (behind to the right), the Al-Kamal (to the left), the Dome of the Rock (straight ahead).

In another sense, however, Daniel felt completely lost. What in the world was going on with Shoshana? When would he hear from her? *Would* he hear from her? Why would moving to a new place keep her from seeing him right away? Okay, it was too much to expect things to be as they were. Her letters made that clear. But once they saw one another again, who knew what they might feel?

He turned right, up several steps to where there was now a military checkpoint, a sure indication that things had, in fact, changed. More security, more tension. Israel had "won" the Yom Kippur War two years earlier, but from all he read, ended up feeling even more vulnerable. As he passed through the metal detector, he resolved not to expect that anything here would be the same as it was in 1970. Including himself. Including Shoshana.

Daniel stood for several minutes at the top of the long flight of steps leading to the expansive plaza, taking in the sight. Beyond the Wall, which rose more than sixty feet above the plaza, were the distinctive domes of Al-Aqsa and the Dome of the Rock. Clustered at its base were people praying—diminutive figures, from where he stood—who produced a surprisingly loud drone.

Again his thoughts drifted to Shoshana. "I came here with my father and Rahel," she had told him years before, "still in my uniform, in the first month after the Old City was liberated." She described the experience, a time when her hopes for Israel were at their peak, in almost-religious terms.

"When you were here, had they already started bulldozing homes to make way for this plaza?" he'd asked.

He could picture her expression—disappointment? resignation?—as she said, "Yes, but they had to do it. You know that, don't you? Before that, the space for Jews to pray was nothing but a narrow street. I think it was ten- or twelve-feet wide. The Muslims used to herd mules through there just to ruin it for the Jews who were praying. And this entire area was ramshackle. Israel did them a favor."

"I doubt the people who lived there saw it that way. Arab leaders still call it a war crime."

"Of course they do! They always say things like that! They destroyed the Jewish Quarter, tore down our synagogues, ran people out, and then they blame us." She had said no more, and neither had he.

Standing there now, Daniel regretted how he had wrung the joy out of her recollection, even though what he said was true. Abu Yusef, the oud player, had declared that in Jerusalem history is never dead. He could have added that it's also never unambiguous.

Daniel walked slowly down the stone stairway leading to the plaza and for a while simply wandered, paying particular attention to various groups he had seen from the top of the steps, some talking among themselves, others listening as a guide explained what they were seeing. One group was singing, their sound mixing with the background of murmured prayer. As he moved closer, he felt the excitement of the singers and realized he envied how Jews experience holiness in a particular place. Even Shoshana had experienced it, right here, at one time in her life. He had wanted the Holy Sepulchre to be such a place, but it had been ruined for him by insensitive tourists and squabbling priests, just as the Wall had been ruined for Shoshana by the Orthodox who now acted, in her opinion, as if it were their possession. The Rooftop came closest for him, but he now thought of that as a one-time event, shaped by circumstances. And wasn't sharing such experience with others part of the point?

As the plaza began to fill with new arrivals, he walked toward the Wall until he was standing just outside the chain that separated onlookers from those intent on worship. Surely, he told himself, it didn't make it any less sacred for faithful Jews to have a Christian join them. He, too, wanted to write a prayer on a slip of paper and stick it in a space between the stones, as he had done when he was with Shoshana. That's what religious people did, and he was now one of them, wasn't he?

There were pieces of paper and stubby pencils on a small table beside the opening in the chain, but what to write? Finally, he wrote his prayer, just six words, and picked up a black paper yarmulke from a box on the table since he didn't have one of his own. But were those young Orthodox men, with their wide-brimmed black hats and sidelocks, staring at him as he stepped inside the chain? Was their laughter at his expense? Was such suspicion merely an extension of how Shoshana felt about them?

There seemed to be fewer men near the barrier that separated male and female worshippers, so he made his way there, eventually getting close enough to rest his hand on the cool limestone and place his prayer in a crevice next to a wad of others. He looked up at one of the plants that somehow grew from cracks in the Wall, then leaned his forehead against the stone, searching for the words he wanted to say. But was he really being elbowed aside? Were those muttered phrases directed at him? Did his paper yarmulke, which kept slipping off, give him away as an impostor? He stepped back, looking for another opening in the throng, finally mumbling the six-word prayer where he stood.

As he turned from the Wall, irritated and self-conscious, his eyes fell on the group he had heard singing. They looked like students, some in a circle dancing the hora, while an older man, with a beard and curly hair that poked out around his skullcap, sang and played the guitar. There seemed to be about fifteen in the basic group, although others stopped to listen to the singer and, at times, to sing along to the folk melodies.

But while others gradually moved on, Daniel lingered at the edge of the circle, as if he belonged there, as if he weren't an outsider. Some of the songs were new to him, but others were familiar, including one, "Vehaer Eynenu," that was popular when he was a student in Tel Aviv. He could picture Shoshana singing it, leaning against him in her bed or fixing food in her tiny kitchen. He looked down, feeling tears forming, and when he looked up, the man they were calling Reb Shlomo seemed to be smiling kindly in his direction. He returned it, thinking of Abu Yusef and that first evening at Al-Kamal.

When the singer took a break, Daniel decided it was time to wander back to the guesthouse, his home for the next twenty-seven days. As he turned to go, however, a breeze caught his paper yarmulke and sent it flying. Did that man in his long silk robe actually step on it on purpose? Was that a smile he saw on the faces of the young men with him?

"Do you know why they dress that way, like eighteenth-century Polish aristocrats?" Daniel turned to see that the singer had come up behind him. He shook his head. "It was imposed on them by the Ottomans who required religious minorities to wear an identifying costume. And the Orthodox just kept doing it. Think of it as a kind of protest." He smiled. "It's the same reason we sing here in front of this bare wall. The Ottomans and the British wouldn't allow Jews to sing here, on the edge of where our holy temple once stood, so we do it as both a celebration and a protest."

"Thank you. I wasn't feeling very charitable toward the Orthodox."

The singer smiled again and strummed once on his guitar. "Never mind that paper *kippah*. I have something better for you." While the students looked on, the singer rummaged in a satchel that had been resting on his guitar case and pulled out a large yarmulke in dark red velvet. "I have a feeling you aren't Jewish," he said as he handed it to Daniel.

"I have—or, at least, I had—a girlfriend who used to say I was the most Jewish Christian in all of Jerusalem, if that counts."

This time the singer laughed. "Be whatever you are," he said, "but may you also be a good friend to Jews. As we say at Passover, *dayenu*. It will be enough."

Chapter Nine

Daniel had wanted, and intended, to return to Jerusalem practically from the minute he left it, but life dictated otherwise. For the first two or three months back at Yale, his overseas experience continued to be in the forefront of his mind. He talked about his experiences incessantly, until it was apparent that friends were losing interest. He spoke about it in two local churches where questions from the audience made him realize how much he didn't know. He even wrote a lengthy paper on the "sublime," trying to explain his Rooftop experience in aesthetic terms. "The intense emotional experience associated with the sublime," he wrote, "can be evoked by natural scenes that are both pleasurable and frightening in their mystery and grandeur. In most cases, the experience of sublimity is made more powerful by its association with ideas of God."

"A discerning, analytical treatment of the topic," wrote his professor, who gave him an A.

Gradually, however, his focus shifted to his future, which began to take on more definite shape. He would pursue a PhD, having something to do with Jewish-Christian relations, in order to teach at a university or even a seminary, although he wasn't yet a member of a church. This meant applying to graduate schools, and for two months his dorm room was littered with catalogues. Finally, after dithering over choices, he decided to stay at Yale for a master's in theological studies. After all, he had been a political science major. When it came to theology or religion, he was a novice.

It was possible to finish this degree in two years, but it took Daniel two and a half because, as his father made clear, he was on his own financially for graduate school. This meant a part-time job during the academic year and a full-time job during the summer. No time or money for overseas travel.

So it wasn't until January of 1974 that Daniel began his doctoral study at Temple University in Philadelphia. That summer he not only had to work, but he had to take an intensive German course in order to prepare for a required language exam. "I'm never going to get back to Israel!" he groused to a somewhat sympathetic friend.

But then, in the fall of that year, his grandfather died, leaving money earmarked for "the further education of my grandson, Daniel Jacobs." Part of this modest windfall he used to register for a two-week seminar at the Gutmann Institute in Jerusalem, with plans to stay another two weeks for "research." And part of it he used to buy the airplane ticket to Israel. He departed the day after his last class in May of 1975, almost five years to the day after he had last set foot in the Holy City.

The Gutmann Institute had rooms for most of its seminar participants, and it wasn't far from Mount Zion. Daniel, however, knew he wanted to be right in the Old City, so he used yet another part of his grandfather's money to reserve a room at the Franciscan guesthouse, Casa Nova. He had briefly considered staying at Al-Kamal, but quickly decided it was a little too basic, especially for a month-long residence. And he was no longer twenty, when it was okay to sleep on used sheets with a towel over a stained pillow.

He had, of course, kept in touch with Shoshana, at first sending aerograms every other day, then twice a week, then every week, or at least every other. From the start, his letters were more effusive than hers, in which she told what she was doing—some of it, anyway—but little of what she was feeling or thinking. "I'm not as good as you are at expressing things on paper," she told him when he complained. Eventually, this led him to dial back his own language, to invest less emotional energy in their correspondence. Besides, it was just too painful to keep wondering if she was with some other guy.

Without quite knowing how it happened, he had a passionate fling with a woman who worked in the Yale library. This was followed by a steadier relationship with a woman named Susan. But she had a good job in New Haven, and once he moved to Philadelphia, they drifted apart. He never wrote to Shoshana about his love life, which reinforced his assumption that she wasn't writing to him about hers.

Naturally, he did write to her about his return to Israel as soon as he got his ticket, even fantasized about her running to greet him as he emerged from customs. But her response—"It will be good to see you"—was not what he had hoped for. And when, in late March, he dared ask if she would meet him at the airport, he got no response at all.

Finally, after he had sent two more letters and was beginning to despair of ever hearing from her, he got what looked like a hastily scribbled note:

Dear Daniel,

I'm sorry for not replying sooner. Things have been hectic around here for reasons I can share with you when we get together. But that can't be when you arrive because I will be right in the middle of moving. I'm not even sure of my new address, so it will be hard to contact me. I will send a note to Casa Nova as soon as I'm settled. Don't worry, we will see each other while you are in Jerusalem. Have a safe trip!

Shoshana

Of course he worried! What did moving have to do with not seeing him right away? He could help her move, break the five-year ice by doing something like that together. And why wouldn't she know the address? Unless . . .

Daniel soon realized it was a waste of time to keep parsing Shoshana's note, and once he arrived in Jerusalem there was plenty to fill his calendar. For one thing, the seminars were more interesting and demanding than he had expected. The overall topic was provocative: "Can Israel be a Jewish state, a democratic state, *and* include land captured in 1967?" As expected, it generated heated discussions, starting when one of the early presenters, a professor from Hebrew University, contended that Israel's occupation of Palestinian land was "draining the nation's soul." Israel had gone off track, he argued, when it rejected Martin Buber's "greater realism" of a country based on power-sharing and a commitment to dialogue.

The first question, loaded with sarcasm, was asked by a young rabbi from New Jersey: "How do you dialogue with people whose purpose, stated right there in their documents, is to wipe you out of existence?"

"How do you know there are no dialogue partners?" the professor asked in return. "Israel hasn't tried to find them or done anything to encourage them."

A retired Jewish dentist from Long Island said he thought this was incredibly naive. Had the professor really forgotten that Jews have to protect themselves because it's certain no one else will?

It was Abby, a woman about Daniel's age, who came to the professor's defense. "As Buber said, Zionism was meant to promote the spiritual and cultural renewal of the Jewish people, not turn us into a carbon copy of every other nation. Just because the United States sees every conflict as 'us versus them' doesn't mean Israel has to. In fact, it *should* be different. Jews should be showing others the possibility of dialogue."

This provoked an uproar and more charges of naivete, until the seminar moderator intervened. "We have two participants who aren't Jewish. Let's hear from them." When neither volunteered, the moderator called directly on Daniel. "You're a Christian who has studied at an Israeli university. How do you see this? By occupying the West Bank and Gaza, is Israel legitimately promoting security or losing its soul?"

Daniel could see Abby watching him closely as he said, "I can see merit in both points of view. Israel needs security, but it comes at a high cost, not just to Palestinians but to Israelis."

"You can't get off that easy!" said the young rabbi, smiling.

Daniel could feel his ears turning red. "Well, I think it's fair for outsiders to comment on, even criticize, Israeli government policy. But"—he paused—"it seems to me that Abby was pushing the discussion to a deeper level, really talking about Jewish identity. And I know enough not to wade into that." This drew a chuckle from the professor.

When the session ended, Daniel was surprised to find Abby waiting for him in the building's courtyard. "I liked what you said," she told him simply. "I appreciate trying to see both sides of something, and I *was* talking about identity." Her tone was direct but not off-putting. "I'm interested, why did you study in Israel, and why did you sign up for this program?"

It was the first of numerous conversations over the course of the next week and a half. The day after the contentious seminar, they sat together on the bus that took their group on a field trip to Bethlehem, Hebron, and a new Israeli settlement built on land seized in 1967. As they bumped along an unfinished road into the settlement, Abby steadied herself by taking hold of his arm in a way that reminded him of Shoshana. The following evening, they managed, without attracting too much attention, to eat dinner by themselves in the institute's dining hall, talking about Buber and dialogue, about their favorite places in Israel and the US, about how they both liked Steely Dan, even though not all of their friends did. When Daniel confessed that he also liked classical music, Abby said, "Me, too. Now all we need is a stereo, a candle, and a bottle of wine." Her smile wasn't Shoshana's, but it was warm, even lovely.

Daniel learned she was a graduate student at NYU, her first time living in New York, and that she had been pleased to discover how easy it is to travel to other East Coast cities, like Boston and Philadelphia. He learned she had grown up in a predominantly Jewish community but was ready to explore others, even eager to find out more about Christians. He learned she had a grandmother who lived in Cleveland—"so I occasionally get back to Ohio." He also learned she had found it hard to date anyone this past year—"but my schedule should ease up next semester." And he learned she worried about being too short and having hair that was too frizzy. After a pause, he assured her that he thought she looked just fine.

Naturally, he told Abby about his own graduate study, including how he was struggling to focus his dissertation. Over tea on the institute's patio, she asked, "Why not narrow it down to 'Jerusalem as an issue in Jewish-Christian relations'?"—the aptness of which was immediately apparent. He told her about the kibbutz he'd been on and seeing artillery fire across the Jordan, about Al-Kamal and the day of the fire at Al-Aqsa, even about Sukkot with Mrs. P and how he felt when he first saw Yad Vashem. He did not tell her about Shoshana.

Several afternoons, during the two weeks of seminars, were left free for reading and exploring. So on Friday the 30th, Daniel invited Abby to go with him into the Old City, where, at her urging, he introduced her to some of his favorite Christian sites. At one point he wondered how he would feel if they happened—most unlikely!—to run into Shoshana. Did he want her to see him with another woman? Would she be with another man?

That evening, they joined a group of Gutmann friends at the Western Wall, and Daniel, much to the envy of the others, recounted the story of how he was given his velvet yarmulke.

"You know, don't you, that the guy they were calling Reb Shlomo is famous?" said one of the students. Daniel added it to the list of things about which he was clueless.

Most of the group found taxis at the Jaffa Gate for the trip back to the institute, but Daniel, seeing Abby hesitate, said he would be pleased to walk her back, and she immediately agreed. In a small park along the way, they kissed, the embrace longer than he expected.

Reb Shlomo had not been at the Wall that evening, and, to Daniel's disappointment, he also wasn't there the following week on Erev Shabbat when Daniel and Abby went alone, as he once had with Shoshana. He considered taking her to the Rooftop, as he once had Shoshana, but something, a feeling that something just wasn't right, kept him from it. This same something kept him from inviting her back to his room in Casa Nova, an invitation he was pretty sure she would have accepted. It wasn't a guilty sense that he would be leading her on; she knew what she was doing. And it wasn't that he didn't like her; he liked Abby a lot. Just not in that way. Especially not here in the other's backyard.

After wandering for a while inside the walls, he found a taxi for her outside the Damascus Gate. "I would like to stay in touch," she told him through the window, looking sad.

The next evening, when she and the others departed, that same something kept him from seeing them off.

Chapter Ten

Even in the midst of the institute's program, Daniel found time to revisit favorite spots in the Old City, like the Sisters of Zion convent where he hoped to have a conversation with Sister Mary. But Sister Mary, he learned, had suffered a stroke—"not a major one, but major enough"—and had been moved to a retirement community near London.

"Sister Mary had a real impact on me," he told the brusque nun at the reception desk. Silence. "That's why I was hoping to see her again."

"She could be a talker, all right. It's what she did best."

"She had a hand in what was for me a life-changing experience." Pause. "I'm sorry I never told her that. I got busy with things and never told her." Silence. "Maybe I could send her a note."

"I doubt," said the nun, "she would remember you. We get lots of visitors."

After this less-than-satisfying encounter, Daniel wandered back to the souk, passing by Al-Kamal. When he had stopped there three days before, a young man told him Bassam was out of town, probably for a week. But, in fact, Bassam was now behind his rickety desk near the open entrance. His greeting was not effusive, but cordial. "I was told an American asked for me. Now that I see you, I remember who you are."

It took several seconds for Daniel's eyes to adjust as he stepped into the dim lobby. The odor of urine and cigarette smoke was just as he remembered. "I thought you were going to be gone for a while."

"My sister lives near to Haifa, and I want to see her because she is sick. But Israel did not give me a permit to stay over a night." Daniel could hear the anger in Bassam's voice. After a few awkward words of sympathy, he asked if the men still gathered in the evenings as they had back in 1969.

Bassam nodded. "Mr. Odeh, the one with the fat white mustache, he is dead, and Mr. Khatib, the owner, is very old. But some still come here."

"Is it okay if I show up this evening?" Daniel smiled. "I'll be happy to buy the tea."

Bassam neither smiled nor nodded. "There are not many now who come all the time. And there are no jobs, so not many men stay here." Pause. "But yes, you are welcome."

He went, just after Maghrib prayer, joining six men in their circle of well-used metal chairs. Mr. Khatib welcomed him but didn't seem to recall seeing him before, and Bassam did not jump in to refresh the older man's memory.

Daniel was sure he would remember the tea vendor, but it turned out to be a different man. While the vendor served the tea—in thick glasses, with mint and sugar—the men sat silently, some of them smoking, one thumbing his black prayer beads. After Daniel had paid, Mr. Khatib said, "Now we speak in English for some minutes." This led one man to leave the circle with a few parting words in Arabic. Mr. Khatib simply shrugged.

"I was in Sheikh Jarrah this very morning," said a man who looked vaguely familiar to Daniel, "and saw them with my own eyes tear down the house of Hatem. With a bulldozer from America."

Although none of the men looked at him directly, Daniel felt as if all eyes were on him. Finally, since no one spoke, he said, "Not all Americans agree . . . There are lots of Americans who hope Palestinians will also have their own country."

"Then," Mr. Khatib began, "you must speak—"

But before he could finish, a man who was clearly not one of the regulars interrupted. "What does it mean, 'a Palestinian country'? We are Arabs! We are Muslims! America and Europe cut up the map like pieces of a chicken, then tell us what piece we can have. We are to say '*shukran ktir, shukran jazilan*'"—he made a caustic bow—"'thank you, thank you, O great Masters,' and forget we are all Arabs and Muslims together." He had been looking around the circle, but his gaze now focused on Daniel. "They should only leave us alone so we can make a little money, have a real life, have a family. Israel . . . Jordan . . . it matters not so much, if they leave us alone."

For the first time Daniel could remember, Bassam offered his own opinion, and not gently. "You talk nonsense!" he told the newcomer. "Drive from here to Nablus and then tell us it does not matter who has control."

"I do not like Israel," said the man, "but my son now has a job building houses in the Jewish part of Jerusalem. What did the Jordanians do for him? Nothing!"

"Is he the boss?" Bassam asked sharply. "Is he respected like a man should be respected?"

"His family eats. He has work, and his family eats!"

Mr. Khatib raised his cane. "This is enough." He turned toward Daniel. "What," he asked, "are you doing in Jerusalem?"

So Daniel explained about the seminars, not giving the name of the Gutmann Institute, and about his dissertation. "I would like to be a bridge, help people in America listen to other voices."

He intended to say more, but the newcomer didn't let him. "Do you speak Arabic?" Without waiting for a reply, the man continued. "Since you do not speak the language of Muslims, how can you write about Al-Quds? We are the *ruh* . . . How do you say it?"

"Soul," Bassam told him curtly.

"We are the soul of this city, not the Jews with their Wall, not the Christians with their churches. How can you write about us if you do not speak our language?"

Daniel left as soon as the conversation switched back to Arabic, saying farewell to Bassam and Mr. Khatib, who acknowledged it by lifting his cane with its silver handle. His route to Casa Nova took him near the Holy Sepulchre, which was already locked for the night. On the spur of the moment, though it was getting late, he turned south toward Mount Zion. The Rooftop, he decided, would be a good place to sort through his thoughts.

Once he had climbed the steps, he squeezed past the dome, plastered now with pictures of a famous Orthodox rabbi, until he was standing at the railing looking east toward the outline of the Mount of Olives. He had intended to pray and think about God, but instead, his mind gravitated to Shoshana. Where was she now? Why hadn't she contacted him? Was it possible he wouldn't see her at all?

Because of where he was looking, he remembered the time he suggested they splurge, have dinner at the InterContinental Hotel, with its distinctive seven arches and great views, perched on top of the Mount of Olives.

"Are you kidding?" she had responded. "It's a monstrosity! I guess you just take it as part of the landscape, but I remember when the Jordanians built it. You have an ancient Jewish cemetery, sacred ground for many Jews, and there above it is this modern eyesore. I can't believe you want to go there!"

Daniel smiled at the memory. A woman of strong opinions, at least about some things.

He hadn't been on the Rooftop ten minutes when he heard voices behind him, loud voices, speaking Hebrew. His presence, appearing from behind the dome, clearly surprised the group of young Israelis, but they quickly recovered and, in English, offered him a beer. Daniel was ready to say no, feeling irritated by the interruption, but they persisted. And they seemed so happy, in a place that was so often tragic, that he changed his mind and accepted the bottle of Goldstar thrust at him by a woman he guessed to be in her early twenties. She asked if he was a tourist. He told her he was a student, there for a month.

He started to ask why she and her friends were on this rooftop, but then decided it was theirs as much as it was his. More, actually. Still, when he saw a couple making out, leaning on the railing facing east, he couldn't help feeling that something personal and sacred was being slightly profaned.

Chapter Eleven

When the two weeks of seminars were finished, and the participants, including Abby, had departed, Daniel thought seriously about making a quick trip to Tel Aviv to check out the university, look up a professor or two, maybe even say hello to Mrs. P. But since he only had a month, he decided to spend all of it in Jerusalem. Now that he had settled, with Abby's help, on his dissertation topic, he had all the more reason to stay put. This city itself was the subject of his research. The more he could learn about it—the more he could commit its sights and sounds and smells and tastes to memory—the richer his dissertation would be.

With that in mind, he also thought about hiring a private tour guide, something he never would have considered if it hadn't been for his grandfather's money. He certainly knew the highlights of an Old City tour, but he also realized there was so much more to Jerusalem, hidden treasures he didn't even know he didn't know. A tour guide, however, didn't seem quite the answer. He needed a friend who could introduce him to the walled city as a place where people actually lived.

And, as if providentially arranged, that's when he met Musa. It was fairly late in the afternoon, and Daniel was just wandering—thinking about how many days he had left, about how he was going to pay for the next semester, about Shoshana—when he happened on an out-of-the-way street in the Muslim Quarter. If he had walked there before, he couldn't remember it, and he definitely couldn't remember seeing the display of handmade earrings resting on a foot-pedal sewing machine. This was next to an open door and a hand-lettered sign: *Welcome To Look. No Charge!*

Musa greeted him exuberantly from his worktable behind a dusty counter that was littered with bowls of beads, rolls of wire, and a stack of used books. He was wearing a rumpled long-sleeve T-shirt, despite the heat, and a newsboy cap.

"You look like an American. Right?" This said with a wide smile.

"Is it that obvious?"

"I can tell. I am good at telling Americans because I lived there, not a long time, with my uncle in Detroit—he is from Jerusalem but moved to Detroit to start a business, very successful—but I traveled many places in America, sometimes with my uncle, sometimes not. My name is Musa—*M . . . USA!*" He laughed loudly. "I think you are from . . . not New York . . . not Texas. I think you are from the middle, from Missouri."

"Pretty close. Ohio." Before Musa could respond, Daniel asked, "Do you sell jewelry?"

"I *make* jewelry. If I want to sell more jewelry, I should move to Khan al-Zeit instead of stay here in my family home." He laughed again. "Anything you want, I can make it. Or maybe I *have* made it. Look around. Like it says on my sign: Welcome to look. No charge!"

Daniel turned slowly, surveying the trays of earrings and bracelets, piles of yellowed newspapers, books in cases that leaned precariously, and dishes filled with coins and beads. On the rough stone walls were old prints of Jerusalem and a worn map labeled *Filastin*.

"I might be interested in jewelry," he said, turning back toward Musa, "but I'm actually more interested in books or pictures of Jerusalem, as long as they're not in Arabic."

"How can a picture be in Arabic?" More laughing.

It was the beginning of their friendship. Musa, it turned out, not only made jewelry, but collected artifacts from Palestine prior to 1948:

stamps with the word *Palestine* and a picture of the Dome of the Rock; five- and ten-pound notes with Western and Eastern numerals, from the Palestine Currency Board; a passport from the period of the British Mandate marked *Palestine* under the royal coat of arms; a map from 1947 showing the proposed UN partition, with the entire area labeled *Palestine*.

"Look at this," he told Daniel, holding a heavy book filled with black-and-white photos. "They are pictures of Wilhelm's visit to Jerusalem in 1898, and you see the title, *Unser Kaiser in Palästina*. There was a place called Palestine long before there was a nation called Israel."

"Well, yes, it's an ancient name," said Daniel, "but that doesn't mean people here thought of themselves as a nation."

"I know. I know. You are right. We have been under the rule of outsiders, like the Turks and the British, that is true, for centuries, that is true. We are now learning to be Palestinians, like the Israelis are learning to be Israelis. But we were learning this before there was Israel. *That* is the message of my pictures and coins and stamps. Israel must see this if we are to live together."

When Daniel returned the next day, Musa closed his shop early and showed him where to find a staircase that lets people walk on the rooftops, from the Armenian Quarter to the Jewish Quarter. He pointed out the spot on the roofs where the four quarters meet in a kind of architectural armistice. He also took him to a fabric store in the area of the Old City known as the Muristan, near the Holy Sepulchre, where the merchant pulled aside a display case to reveal the top of a Crusader church buried beneath. On the way there, Musa taught Daniel how to recognize the massive grooved paving stones used by the Romans.

That evening, they ate dinner together in a restaurant just outside the Damascus Gate because, according to Musa, it had the best *makloubeh* and *musakhan* in Al-Quds. "I would say they are like my mother's, only my mother was not such a good cook. Even my uncle in Detroit says so, and he was in love with my mother. So maybe I should say like my grandmother's." The by-now-familiar laugh. "The house I live in, it was the house of my grandfather, and his father before him, and his father before him, and his father before him. It is in our bones. The stones are in our bones!" More laughter.

The next day, they had tea and *ma'amoul* in a small bakery, after which the owner took them in back to see an old battered sign. It had been painted over, but the newer paint was fading and peeling so that the old lettering—*Halwayat Bakery, Jerusalem, Palestine*—was now showing through.

Most importantly, Musa introduced Daniel to the Old City as a place where people live day-to-day: where to buy eggs and soap, where to go if you need laundry done, where to get a lamp or typewriter repaired, where to find a lawyer or a notary public, where to watch boys practicing soccer, where to see the best trees in a city made mostly of stones. He took him to a market Daniel had passed numerous times but hardly seen, with huge cabbages, mounds of garlic, and towers of vine leaves. How had he missed all this? It was as if the alleyways were becoming three-dimensional.

Along the way, Musa also introduced him to people who lived there. Like the owner of a smoke-filled tea shop near Herod's Gate in the Muslim Quarter. "I have been here," Daniel told Mr. Jaradat, "with my friend Bassam from the Al-Kamal Hotel."

"Yes, I know Bassam. He wears his keffiyeh around his neck like a scarf."

Daniel smiled. "That's Bassam. We were here once when someone had a television on and the announcers said Israeli bombers had destroyed a school in Egypt. This was 1969 or '70. The men in here were very angry, I remember that!"

"Allah protect us from such bombings," said Mr. Jaradat.

Musa asked, "Were you worried?"

"A little," said Daniel, "but I was with Bassam so—"

"That's good, that's good. My uncle, the one in Detroit I lived with, says every American should feel a little worried sometime, because it is how we feel all the time."

Mr. Jaradat nodded before bringing them a cup of tea.

On Christian Quarter Road, they ate falafel at what Musa called the "café" of his friend Samir. The café was, in truth, three small tables under an arched stone ceiling, behind the cart where Samir stuffed the deep-fried chickpea patties and salad into pita. After making each sandwich, he wiped his hands on his UCLA T-shirt.

"Samir," said Musa between bites, "is a Christian like you. He thinks a Muslim like me is going to his hell because I don't believe in Jesus. Well, I do believe in Jesus, all Muslims do. But not the way he does, so he thinks I am going to hell." The friends both smiled, and Musa pointed to the shop on the other side of Christian Quarter Road. "Look at this window, crosses next to menorahs next to pictures of Al-Aqsa. That is Jerusalem, but Christians like my friend Samir want to make us all one thing."

Samir nodded, still smiling.

"What church do you go to?" Daniel asked.

"It is called Christ Church, by the Jaffa Gate. Lots of young people and Americans, so I practice my English while I worship." He brought them each a glass of pomegranate juice before adding, "I was an Orthodox, but too much funny business. It doesn't matter because God is in charge, but too much funny business."

Later that week, they met for dinner at an Armenian restaurant, on the street between the Jaffa and Zion gates, where Musa introduced Daniel to the owner. When they were seated waiting for their food, Musa leaned close and said, "Hayk's family has been in Jerusalem for hundreds of years, like mine. His brother has a ceramic shop in the Christian Quarter, and his . . . well, there are so many in his family, I cannot tell you all of them. But he says they are still outsiders. The Armenians are not Arabs or Muslims, and they are not like other Christians, so they are always outsiders. I tell him not to worry so much. In Jerusalem, everybody is an outsider to somebody."

Musa leaned back and took a drink of water while Daniel said, "You've helped me feel less like an outsider. I always loved Jerusalem, but now even more."

"My uncle in Detroit, he likes America, but he doesn't love it because here is his home. He says Americans live—how does he say it?—on the top of things without going deep."

"On the surface?"

"Yes, and so special Americans like you want to love places where history is long and there are things below the top . . . the surface."

Their food arrived, and they ate for several minutes before Daniel, without intending to, began to talk about his other real attraction to Jerusalem.

Musa listened carefully, surprising Daniel with his response: "This is a city, not only of history, but of dreams. Maybe you have dreamed her."

"No, I guarantee you she's real."

"Yes, I am sure she is alive. I mean that the Shoshana in your mind is more of a dream. The dream and the real, they can be close in Jerusalem, but also different." Seeing Daniel's raised eyebrows, he added, "It is a good thing, what I am saying. Jerusalem survived because people who did not live here still dreamed of her. Like you dream of your Shoshana."

Daniel considered this idea while the owner cleared their plates and offered them *vozni* or *baklava* for dessert, "as my gift." When the owner had returned to the kitchen, Daniel showed Musa his key chain.

"Can you make me one like it, an Eilat stone but with a *dalet*"—he traced the Hebrew letter for *d* with his finger—"instead of a *shin*?"

"Of course!" exclaimed Musa. "I can make anything. Anything you can say to me, I can make. But will you give it to her, that I think is the question."

On the morning of Saturday, June 14, two 107mm rockets were fired at Jerusalem, leaving craters near the botanical gardens, two miles west of the Old City and much closer than that to Shoshana's former apartment. Daniel learned of the attack while having coffee in Musa's cluttered shop. Musa's neighbor urged him to turn on his radio because "the Jews are now feeling the fury of Arab nations." So Musa blew the dust off his old Victrola and turned the dial to a Jordanian broadcast, which said rockets were hitting the grounds of the Israeli Knesset. At Daniel's suggestion, Musa tuned to the BBC, which gave a substantially different account.

"I'm going to go into the new city," Daniel told his friend. "See if I can find out what's happening."

Musa shook his head. "That may be not a good idea. There could be more rockets, and the buses may be not running in that area. When I was in Detroit—"

"The BBC report said they hit near the botanical gardens. I can walk there if I need to."

Musa shrugged and then rummaged behind the dirt-streaked counter, bringing out a small set of prayer beads, black with silver tassels. "I have saved this to give to you sometime, but maybe now is the good time. We call them *misbaha*. You have seen the long ones, ninety-nine beads for the ninety-nine names of Allah, but this is short, only thirty-three beads. First, you say *subhan Allah*, 'glorious is Allah,' thirty-three times, then *al-hamdu lillah*, 'praise be to Allah,' then you say *Allahu akbar*, 'God is greater.' Or say what you want. Your God and Allah are the same."

"Musa, this is a wonderful gift! Thank you. I'll carry them with me, along with my key chain." He paused before saying, "I think I believe in prayer but often forget to do it. You're helping me be a better Christian." Musa had turned back to his worktable, but Daniel could tell he was smiling.

As it turned out, the buses were still running. The area around the botanical gardens was cordoned off, but the city did not seem to be on highest alert. Daniel picked out a man who looked as if he might speak English and asked if he'd heard anything from the police. Was anyone killed?

"No one," said the man. "No one hurt. These were not big rockets. They don't have big rockets, *baruch ha Shem*."

Later that afternoon, the BBC confirmed the man's statement. The "rockets" were forty pounds, the size of mortar shells, the kind fired from the back of a truck. Still, the US secretary of state declared, "This is more than terrorism. It is a war crime to fire indiscriminately at civilian populations." The Israeli government vowed to hunt down the "cowardly perpetrators," while at the same time minimizing the attack. "The life of Jerusalem continues as normal. Our people do not live in fear."

A different verbal picture was being painted that evening when Daniel joined the conversation circle at Al-Kamal. "They hide the damage from the cameras," said an old man he didn't know. "It is said that homes were destroyed and there will be more rockets soon."

Mr. Khatib shook his head. "Who says this? Who can trust the news, our news or their news? Who can trust it?"

"Maybe no, but I heard with my ears what the Americans say. They *want* to be blind, not see what is happening. The Israelis steal our land, put us in prison, kill our boys, and say we are terrorists when we fight back."

Daniel, having learned his lesson five years before, kept quiet, thankful that no one seemed to associate him with American foreign policy. He could feel his anger rising, however, when Ibrahim the baker—the gentle baker!—declared his hope that Israelis would suffer as Palestinians had. Shouldn't the hope be for no one to suffer? Shouldn't the goal be mutual understanding, not mutual suffering? And why did they have to put all Israelis in the same basket? "Israelis" included someone he knew and loved—or, at least, once had loved.

But where the hell was she?

Chapter Twelve

Two days later, on Monday, June 16, the beginning of Daniel's last week in Jerusalem, he finally received a note from Shoshana. The night clerk at the guesthouse handed it to him as he came down to breakfast. "A woman with a big hat, very pretty, left this one hour back." He pointed to the clock. "I said I can get you, but she said no."

Daniel poured a cup of American coffee before settling at a corner table of the breakfast room, staring at the envelope with its familiar handwriting. Why had she not wanted to see him, talk to him directly? Why had he let his expectations get so overblown? Finally, using a knife meant for bread and butter, he slit open the envelope and read:

Dear Daniel,

I should have been in touch with you before now, but it is more complicated than you know. I almost decided not to write at all. That would have been easier, but not fair to you. I am married, the wedding was two months ago, to a man named Yossi (Joseph when he was growing up in New York). It's true that I've been moving because we moved to Neve Ya'akov about the time you arrived. I'm sure you have heard of it, not too far from your beloved Old City. People sometimes call Neve Ya'akov a settlement, but I don't think of it that way because we moved here for cheaper housing and so I could have a big garden. Yes, I still love nature! I told Yossi that a good friend was coming from the States and I was hoping to see you, but I think he thought there was more between us than there may have been. Maybe I said too much. Anyway, I brought it up again and told him I could meet you in Jerusalem, but he said it was better for you to come here. So I hope it's still possible for you to come, maybe for dinner. Call me please and we can set a day.

Shoshana

Daniel sat for several minutes with her letter in his hand. Hadn't he really, in his heart of hearts, expected something like this? Especially when he hadn't heard from her. She was almost thirty, for God's sake, so what did he think was going to happen? A rekindled romance after five years? What was he thinking? But why hadn't she said something before now about this Yossi? And what did she mean "more between us than there may have been"? Had she never felt what he had felt? Why had he been so goddamn stupid!

Rather than stew over it further, he immediately called the number included with her note, using the telephone in the guesthouse lobby, and they quickly arranged for him to come to Neve Ya'akov on Wednesday, the day before his departure from Israel. Hearing her voice was exhilarating, but the call struck him as perfunctory ("I can only talk for a minute"). And when he arrived, although she met his taxi at the side of the street, her hug was quick, like that between friends. But then, what else did he expect?

"Yossi just got home from work and is taking a shower," Shoshana told him once the taxi was gone, "so let me show you around our neighborhood for a few minutes."

"And your garden."

"The garden may not happen, but . . . who knows."

They walked to an open area at the end of her block, Shoshana talking rapidly about Neve Ya'akov. "Doesn't it look more like a suburb than a settlement, at least as settlements are portrayed in the media? There are lots of good people here, people who just want a nice place to live." She had already met another couple, Americans, and that would help with the transition . . .

As they turned to walk back, Daniel put his hand on her arm and interrupted the monologue. "Why didn't you tell me about Yossi? Why didn't you tell me? All this time, I've been . . ." He stopped, trying to keep the anger out of his voice. "At least tell me how long you've known him. You've been married two months?"

"Daniel, what difference does it make?" She stopped and turned to face him, without the familiar smile. "What did you think, that I would just be available after four, no, five years? That you could just drop back in? To be honest, you were pretty clueless about relationships when you were a student here and apparently still are." She stared at him, lips pursed. "Don't tell me you haven't had a serious relationship in five years."

He knew he should respond, but say what? "I thought we had . . . at least enough that you could be straight with me." He paused, and they stood staring at one another until he said, "No, you're right. I shouldn't have expected . . . I tried to get back sooner, but, like I told you in my letters, things kept happening. It's just that being with you was—"

She interrupted his rambling, but now her anger had also passed. "I could tell from your letters that you were remembering me—imagining me—as some sort of ideal woman, which I'm not, obviously. And that there was a future . . . and that made everything awkward." She smiled for the first time that evening. "It's partly my fault. I liked writing to you, Daniel. I guess I liked being the person you imagined." She started walking again toward the apartment. "At first, when Yossi and I decided to get married, which was just in December or January, I thought it would be easier, or better, to tell you in person since you were coming back. And to be honest, I still wasn't certain things would work out with Yossi. It has been complicated. I've already said that, haven't I? So, I don't know why I didn't, lots of reasons. But now I am sorry I didn't tell you."

They entered the ground-floor apartment where a table in the combination living and dining room was already set for three. Daniel noticed that Chagall's rabbi was nowhere to be seen. There were photographs on one wall, but not the ones he remembered from her apartment in Jerusalem.

For some reason, Daniel had expected that Yossi would be large, burly; but the man who now got up from a living room chair was rather slight, with glasses, his short hair wet from the shower. "Sit," he said to Daniel without shaking hands. "Shani tells me the food is ready." He walked slowly to his wife and made a show of kissing her.

Shoshana talked nearly nonstop as she served the chicken with rice and eggplant salad. Daniel complimented her cooking, making no mention of the times she had fixed this very meal in the spring of 1970, and that led Shoshana to talk about the problem of finding new places to shop now that they had moved. Yossi said almost nothing, except to remind Shoshana that a supermarket was planned for Neve Ya'akov.

Daniel took that as an opening to address him. "I understand you're from New York."

"Yes, my wife apparently likes men from America," this said without looking up from his plate.

Daniel tried again. "Shoshana said you moved here, to Neve Ya'akov, because the housing's cheaper."

"And the good tax breaks," said Shoshana, looking at Yossi. He, however, looked directly at Daniel.

"That's what she tells people, but the truth is that I always wanted to live in Judea and Samaria." Shoshana was frowning, and he now smiled but without humor. "Oops, I forgot, I'm not supposed to say that because Americans don't like it. Especially if they aren't even Jewish."

"It's your home," said Daniel. "Say what you want, I guess."

They ate for a minute in silence before Shoshana began to fill the void with questions about Daniel's dissertation and about the program that had brought him back to Jerusalem. Yossi ate steadily, eyes on his food, as Daniel told Shoshana about the folk singer on Erev Shabbat and the gift of the yarmulke. He stopped himself before mentioning how the songs that evening had reminded him of times with her.

The conversation continued between the two of them—Would she still work for the Jewish National Fund now that she was married? How was her sister?—until Yossi said abruptly, "My wife, Shani, tells me you spend a lot of time in East Jerusalem."

"Yes, Shoshana accuses me of being in love with the Old City."

"The Arab part of the city."

Daniel put down his fork. "The Old City belongs to everyone."

"Only when Jews control it," said Yossi. "You saw, everyone should have seen, the whole world should have seen, what happened when the Jordanians were in charge. They destroyed our synagogues and wouldn't let Jews anywhere near what I suppose you call the Wailing Wall."

"Why are you being like this?" Shoshana asked him, her cheeks red. "Daniel is my guest, *our* guest! You don't know what he believes. For the record, I have never heard him call it the Wailing Wall. He knows more about Jews—"

"Is that why he stayed in Arab hotels . . . when he wasn't staying with you?" He now looked directly at Daniel. "What do your friends in these hotels say about us settlers?"

Whatever embarrassment Daniel had felt at witnessing this domestic spat was now turning to anger. "They say you are illegally building on land that doesn't belong to Israel."

"Well, if they say that, then they've conveniently forgotten that Neve Ya'akov has been here since 1924 when it was purchased, legally purchased, by Jews. I bet you didn't know that, did you? A lot of Israel was swamp or desert. We bought it, made it bloom, and now they conveniently want it back."

It was Shoshana who answered, looking at Daniel. "That's true what he says about Neve Ya'akov, but Yossi knows this place was abandoned in 1948." She turned to her husband. "And when it was restarted five years ago, you know it was also on land that belonged to Palestinian villages."

"There is no 'Palestinian'!"—his voice loud enough to be heard outside. "That makes it sound like we invaded a country. There was and is no country of Palestine." He took Shoshana's hand but looked at Daniel. "I love this woman, but she hasn't seen what I've seen, how we are at war."

"Your war," said Daniel, louder than he intended, "seems to include shooting boys throwing rocks."

Yossi stood up quickly, his face now red. "Were they boys with rocks that took children hostage and killed them at Ma'alot and Kiryat Shmona? Or killed those hostages at the Savoy Hotel? The missiles that were supposed to hit the center of Jerusalem, if they could aim straight, were those rocks? Or what about the terrorists that murdered Israelis at Kfar Yuval just this past weekend? Were these boys with rocks! They push children to the front of their phony protests and then accuse us of brutality."

Shoshana slid her chair back but stayed seated. "Really, Yossi, you are too much! Acting like this just because you are jealous of someone I haven't even seen for five years."

It was Daniel who broke the ensuing silence. "What's funny about this is that I'm one who has stood up for Israel, taken Israel's side a lot of the time. But there is another side to the story. Both sides need to listen to the other. That's all I'm saying."

Yossi was not appeased. "You obviously understand nothing about what's going on here. Palestinians, many of them, *like* the settlements. We give them jobs. Making an appearance back here because you once had a thing with my wife . . . You know *nothing* about Jews or Israel!"

Yossi sat back down but soon left the table to have a cigarette. Shoshana quietly began to clear the dishes.

"There are a million things I want to ask you and tell you," Daniel said as he stood to help, "but I suppose it would be better if I left before he comes back."

She nodded. "I would drive you into the city," she lowered her voice, "but you can see that Yossi wouldn't like it." She called a taxi and then walked him to the curb of the new well-lit street. "He's a good man, you know, and I do love him, although there are times when he can make me furious."

"Thanks for dinner," said Daniel, "and the conversation wasn't that terrible. At least he didn't say God gave this land to the Jews."

"Oh, I've heard him say it all right, and he really isn't the slightest bit religious. He probably didn't want to get into religion with a religion scholar." That smile.

Daniel stepped off the curb so they were looking eye to eye. "You talked earlier about what I imagined. Well, I have imagined, a million times, kissing you. Though I guess that's out of the question."

She nodded and then turned her head. "On the cheek." But the hug that followed was not perfunctory, and he felt a familiar thrill as he breathed in the scent of her hair and felt her breasts against his chest. She took his hand. "I didn't mean those things I said earlier. Daniel, I loved our time together . . . But life moves on."

As he was getting in the taxi, he asked, "If I come back to Jerusalem, can I see you, maybe have a cup of coffee together?"

"Not if, but when." They both smiled. She leaned in the window. "Yossi doesn't really love this place, this settlement. He loves the idea of it. Like you love the idea of the Old City. In any case, I am sure you'll be back."

As the taxi pulled away, Daniel suddenly remembered the key chain Musa had made. But by the time he yanked it from his pocket, the taxi was down the block, and Shoshana had turned back toward her apartment.

PART THREE

BRIDGES
(1992)

Chapter Thirteen

The hallway, longer than two football fields, is shaped like a triangle—wider where people walk, a narrow skylight far above them—and it ends with a spectacular view of the Jerusalem Forest on the slope of Mount Herzl. The group moved toward this distant triangle of light in somber silence, passing in and out of galleries filled with artifacts, testimonies, and black-and-white photographs that, once someone sees them, are forever imprinted on their brain.

At first, Daniel tried to stay with various members of the group, but eventually proceeded at his own pace, past the pictures of skeletal survivors and piles of shoes and eyeglasses, lingering in front of the photo of a boy dressed in shorts and winter coat, hands raised in pointless surrender above his anxious face. He thought back to the first time he had seen these displays.

"I can't believe you've been in Israel nearly nine months and haven't gone to Yad Vashem!" He couldn't tell at that point in their relationship whether Shoshana had been truly outraged or was only pretending, but in any case, they went the next day. As he remembered it, she spent more time in the first galleries—life before the *Shoah*—than in the ones filled with images of horror preserved behind glass. Though he realized that may be more assumption than recollection. Memory, he knew, isn't always trustworthy.

When Daniel reached the circular Hall of Names, near the end of the lengthy corridor, he saw that most of the group were ahead of him. Three of the Jews were gathered on one side of the room, speaking in hushed voices. As he stepped closer, he could hear Devorah say, "I'm named after her. Deborah is actually what my parents named me, but I changed it when I was old enough, so coming here and seeing her name . . ." Batya slid her arm around Devorah's shoulders, and they leaned on one another. One of the Christian couples, perhaps seeing Devorah's tears, joined the little cluster.

Daniel walked slowly around the room, his eyes scanning the pictures that covered the inner surface of the large hanging cone: smiling families, some with four generations; bearded rabbis; men in peasant dress; women in stylish wide-brimmed hats; couples on their wedding day; students, perhaps on the day of graduation; young men in military uniforms; a woman with her arms full of flowers; a small girl, her face resting bashfully on clasped hands. The names of Shoshana's murdered ancestors were recorded in this hall. Was it possible he was looking at her great-grandfather or great-aunt or distant cousin without knowing it? His mind flashed back to the Passover with Shoshana and her family, and he wondered with a mixture of sadness and rage how many Passovers had been forever lost, roots of the future ripped up before lives had a chance to grow and blossom. He mumbled a prayer for these ancestors, for Ira, and, of course, for Shoshana.

By the time Daniel stepped back into the hallway, most of the group had gathered by the opening at the end of it, and he walked toward them.

"You see this valley?" Layla was saying, pointing to the north. "On the other side of it, past the pine trees, is Deir Yassin, or what used to be Deir Yassin."

"Where?" someone asked.

"Across the valley." Vigorous pointing. "See those buildings straight across? That's a Jewish mental hospital where the village used to be. They bulldozed what was left of it."

"What," asked Alan, one of the Christians in the group, "is Deir Yassin?"

Layla started to respond, but Daniel now saw that most of the Jews had slipped away from the opening, whispering among themselves, and so he interrupted. "Let's talk about all this when we get to the courtyard." He nodded toward the exit. "As I recall, there are benches where at least a few of us can sit, especially Liz with her sprained ankle."

After some milling about, all twenty-five of them—eight Jews, seven Muslims, nine Christians, plus their leader, Daniel—congregated around two backless stone benches in the center of what a placard identified as the Square of Hope. Liz sat on one, her husband, Jim, standing behind her. Next to her sat Ghazala and Saeed, an older couple, both born in Pakistan. By now, the whole group seemed aware of the tension, although Daniel could tell that not all of them knew what caused it.

Batya spoke first, staring directly at Layla. "Why did you have to bring that up in there, of all places?"

"I don't understand. Why wouldn't I bring it up? You remember a tragedy that happened to Jews, why shouldn't we remember—"

Batya threw her hands in the air, but it was Jon, Devorah's husband, who spoke. "Because this was genocide and that was . . . well, one incident, and historians aren't quite sure what happened." Now it was Layla and her sister, Jamila, who were shaking their heads, lips pursed.

"For heaven's sake," said Jo, one of the Christians, "will someone explain what we're talking about!"

"Deir Yassin," said Daniel, looking around the group, "was an Arab village. Layla's right, it's not far, although I didn't know you could see it from here. It was attacked by a Jewish paramilitary group during the war of . . . the war in 1948."

"Destroyed," said Layla, "not just attacked."

"The people who did it were extremists," said Ben. "Most Jews, like me, don't support the people who did that."

Daniel nodded. "That may be true, but that doesn't mean we

shouldn't remember what they did. More than a hundred Arabs were killed, some of them women and children."

"Executed," said Layla. "Paraded some of them around in Jerusalem and then shot them."

"Some of those stories are just propaganda," said Jon. "Besides, the village was obviously armed because several of the Jews died, too. Probably had Arab League fighters hiding there." His voice grew louder and higher. "And then, a few days later, they ambushed a convoy of Jewish ambulances—"

"Doctors and nurses," said Devorah.

"Killed eighty or ninety of them and made postcards of it that they sold in the Old City, for God's sake!"

"Have you ever seen one of these famous postcards?" asked Layla. Before Jon could answer, she added, "Neither has anybody else. Talk about propaganda!"

Jon turned toward Daniel. "This is what I meant by not being sure what happened."

"There were survivors," said Jamila, her cheeks red. "You think they didn't know what happened? You tell us to believe Holocaust survivors."

"I would like to say something." It was Layla's husband, Amir, who was standing at the back of the cluster. People now turned in his direction, some of them whispering to their neighbors. "Let's all agree, my wife included, that it was good for us to come here to Yad Vashem." He cleared his throat. "Daniel was right to bring us here to see these things. No one should ever say this isn't important or real or horrible. We just hope you agree that Deir Yassin is an important and real memory for us as well."

"We can talk about Deir Yassin, should talk about it," said Ben, who was seated on the other bench with his wife, Sarah. "But why now? Here, just for an hour or so, why can't we Jews mourn our dead without having it mixed up with something else? Why does the Holocaust have to be compared to what happened to the Armenians or what's happening to the Palestinians? Why? Those are terrible things, but they're all different. Let *us* have *this*."

There was a sob—Daniel couldn't tell from whom—and then the group fell silent. One part of him wanted to speak, knew others were expecting him to speak. But say what exactly? And why did he feel compelled to "fix it" every time people were at odds? These questions were mixed up with another more personal one. When he and his friends from Tel Aviv had planted trees in the Jerusalem Forest back in 1969, had they been planting on a destroyed Arab village? Does every positive action have downsides attached? The prayer beads Musa had given him all those years ago were in the pocket of his lightweight jacket, and he found he was now fingering them, his stomach churning.

Finally, Liz, her ankle resting on part of the bench, said, "This whole Israel-Palestine business just seems to bring out the worst in people. I don't mean people in our group, but—"

Now Daniel interrupted. "I appreciate that, Liz, but to be honest, I think the Christians in our group would be wise not to jump into this conversation. It's very emotional, as you can tell." Another silence while he wondered if he had sounded rude. Well, so be it. He was the leader. And now, several minutes after being caught off guard, he finally knew what he wanted to say, what *needed* to be said.

"We've talked about trying to see through others' eyes. Well, this is a great chance to do it. Surely we all can understand why Muslims in our group want atrocities like Deir Yassin to be remembered. People died; it was a tragedy. But all of us can also understand—can't we?—why Jewish members of our group resist comparisons. The Holocaust was genocide, the systematic murder of Jews, just because they were Jews." He cleared his throat, and no one spoke. "We're at Yad Vashem today. Let's be here as a group, let all of this sink in. We'll have other opportunities to reflect on Muslim deaths. And Christian ones, for that matter. Agreed?"

He looked around the cluster of folks, all from Columbus, most of whom he had known for years through interfaith activities. People he liked. People he respected. "As we all said back in Columbus, the idea behind this trip is to look over each other's shoulders, experience what others experience." Some nods. "We knew this wouldn't always be easy, didn't we?" More nods. "Besides, nearly everyone here except me is old enough to be a grandparent, so surely we know how to deal with a little disagreement." A few smiles.

Daniel pointed to a squat building, designed to resemble a tent, just off a corner of the square where they were gathered. "This is the Hall of Remembrance where there's a memorial flame and ashes of victims. I want to go in, and I imagine . . ." He paused. "If for some reason you don't want to, it's fine just to wait here."

Those who were seated stood up, and the group began slowly to move in the direction of the hall, with its memorial flame, when Devorah stopped them. "Now I need to say something. It will ruin it for me if we all aren't in the same . . ." She searched for a word. ". . . spiritual space. Oh, I'll just say it. If this is simply another stop on the tour, then please don't go in. Okay?"

"First you want us to mourn," said Saeed, "and then you don't—"

But his wife, Ghazala, had already edged near Devorah and taken her hand. "All these people"—she swept her free hand around in a way that took everything in—"are people, and they should be remembered and prayed over."

Devorah smiled faintly, and the two of them headed toward the tentlike building together.

Chapter Fourteen

After Daniel's month in Jerusalem in 1975, his life picked up momentum. In rapid succession, he completed his PhD, with a dissertation on "The Problem and Promise of Jerusalem: A Study in Jewish-Christian Relations," and was hired as an assistant professor at Green Mountain State University in Vermont. His appointment was in the humanities department, with an understanding that he could teach courses in Judaism and other world religions. As it turned out, however, he taught mostly general introductions because there wasn't much demand for courses in religion. So when a position opened at United School of Theology in Columbus, he immediately applied. Are you willing, the search committee wanted to know, to teach a course on Jewish-Christian dialogue with a local rabbi? The question made him smile.

The course that Daniel and Rabbi Eisen put together, which became a perennial favorite of seminary students, explored a number of challenging questions, including: How should Christians understand Jewish attachment to the Land of Israel? Ironically, this meant he had to do more reading than ever about Palestinians and their own claims to this sliver of territory at the eastern end of the Mediterranean. When Jews and Christians talk about Israel, they must keep in mind that there is a third party in the room. He had always known this. Now he insisted on it.

Another theme of the course was the history of Christian anti-Semitism. This legacy of persecution, Daniel told students, means that Christian treatment of Jews is a central justice issue for the contemporary church. Among other things, that means taking seriously what our Jewish neighbors take seriously, including the survival of Israel. As the years passed, students increasingly wanted to know, "Does this mean we shouldn't criticize Jews who support a state that persecutes others?"

He also began to teach courses that emphasized the intersection of religion and politics. At some point during his year in Tel Aviv, his own focus had shifted from politics to religion, or so he told himself. This had become his new identity, one *he* chose. Now, however, the old interests were coming to the surface, like the original message on the bakery sign Musa had shown him. With the dean's blessing, he taught such courses as "Peace and Justice in Interfaith Perspective." His message to students was unequivocal: In the Middle East, every political decision bears the mark of religion, and all religions are shaped to some degree by political decisions. This conviction led him to support organizations like Churches for Middle East Peace and to become more involved in the Franklin County Interreligious Council.

Daniel also got married. Peg, like Daniel, was a new professor at Green Mountain State. Her field was botany not religion, but being new teachers on campus still brought them together. It started with comparing notes on students and administrators and poking fun at small-town life, followed by romantic weekends in the "big city" of Burlington. She was smart and pretty and had a confidence, a resolute sense of who she was, that he found very attractive. For Daniel, their relationship lacked the euphoria, the all-consuming passion, he had experienced in Jerusalem; but maybe, he decided, such feelings only happen once.

And being with Peg was good. They had many fine times together, especially in the early years of marriage: hiking in the Berkshire Hills (although nature was more her thing than his), going to Boston to visit museums and watch the Red Sox (although baseball was more his thing than hers), visiting her parents in Hartford (although there was tension when Peg's father, a small businessman, let slip his disdain for "Jewish bankers"), enjoying evenings with friends (although, right from the beginning, they tended to run in somewhat different circles).

Peg agreed to the move to Ohio, at least on a trial basis, or they wouldn't have gone. But she was from New England and clearly preferred it to the Midwest, just as she preferred her old teaching position to her new one at a community college in Columbus, and preferred being nearer her parents than his. She didn't take part in Daniel's church activities or show much interest in anything religious. He once joked at a gathering of friends that if Peg ever saw the Western Wall her sole focus would be on the plants growing in its crevices, which she did not find very funny.

She also did not share his fascination with the Middle East. When he suggested they visit Israel, she asked, "What for? Haven't you spent enough time there? Why go back to a place you've been?" Once, when she was particularly angry, she told him he was like a high school football player who lived on memories of past glory and excitement. "Branch out," she urged him. "Become interested in other places." So they traveled to the Lake District in England, the fjords in Norway, and, since Peg was fairly conversant in the language, various parts of the French countryside. They should at least spend part of his sabbatical in Jerusalem, he had argued, so he could do more research. Peg's viewpoint, however, had no flexibility, so he spent the sabbatical in Columbus. They did interrupt his library research with two weeks in Costa Rica, where Daniel saw more birds than he knew existed. Or cared to know.

Eventually, all of this took an irreparable toll on their relationship, exacerbated by two failed pregnancies. They cried together as Peg recovered from the miscarriages, but Daniel suspected that neither of them revealed the depth of their feelings. It was simply less painful not to rehash with each other what they had lost.

Increasingly, they lived in parallel worlds. She went hiking with friends at Caesar Creek State Park and the nature preserve at Clifton Gorge, he went with friends to see the Columbus Clippers, as well as

Major League baseball games in Cincinnati and Cleveland. She was active in programs of the Wilderness Center, he in programs of his church and the interfaith community. She traveled several times a year to Hartford, he made it a point to spend time with his mother after his father's fatal heart attack. They did make an effort to have dinner together, but often it was eaten in front of the television.

As he and Peg drifted apart, Daniel considered going to Jerusalem on his own. He even mentioned this to Jewish friends, which may have been why several of them invited him to dinner in November of 1991. We would like to organize an interfaith group from Columbus that would travel to Israel and the Palestinian areas, they told him, and you are the obvious person to lead it. Let's put together a group with an equal number of Jews, Muslims, and Christians and go places where each of us alone might not go. Try to see the situation through one another's eyes, tell each other why that part of the world is important to our communities. After all, we get along here in Columbus. Surely we can find common ground there as well.

"It's a great idea. Are you positive you want me to lead it?"

"Of course," said the rabbi. "Who else? You've been president of the Interreligious Council, you've lived in the Middle East, you teach courses on dialogue, everybody sees you as a bridge builder. You're the right person for this, no doubt about it."

Naturally, Daniel accepted the invitation, jumped at it. Possible participants, which meant people with some interfaith experience who could afford to pay their own way, were soon lined up, and they began making plans for September of 1992. That would be after the crush of tour groups in the Holy Land but before the seminary was in full swing. Ramadan was in March that year, so that wouldn't be a conflict. And since Rosh Hashanah was particularly late, the Jews would be back for the High Holy Days. Temple Emanuel told Daniel they would pay all his expenses and offered to pay for Peg as well, but she declined. She had a professional meeting in October, and that, along with a trip to Hartford, would be enough travel for her. Her husband didn't press the issue.

The group, twenty-four plus Daniel, met four times during the spring and summer to get better acquainted and hear background on what they would encounter. At the last of these meetings, Barbara, one of the Christians, recommended they give their group a name. She had read about friends who traveled together to someplace, calling themselves "Birds of a Feather." Others liked the idea, or at least didn't object to it out loud.

"I know," said Sarah. "We should call ourselves 'Shalom Seekers.' That's what we're doing, isn't it? We're a group from religious traditions that have sometimes been at war with each other, and we are seeking peace."

"*Shalom* is a Jewish term," said Amir. "I know everybody now uses it, but it's really not very inclusive when you get right down to it. You'd have to say 'Shalom/Salaam Seekers,'" which they all agreed was awkward.

Barbara wasn't ready to give up. "What about 'Wall Busters'? We are breaking down walls."

"That doesn't sound very pleasing, not to me anyway," said Sandra.

"I know you didn't mean this, Barbara, but I'm afraid it sounds a little anti-Jewish," said Batya. "When someone says 'wall,' I think of the Western Wall, our most sacred site. And unfortunately, there are lots of people who would like to bust it."

In the end, they settled on "Bridge Builders."

"I've heard Daniel call himself a 'bridge builder,'" said Ghazala, "and it is a good thing to be." Someone proposed having T-shirts made with the name, even drew a picture with the words over the famous outline of Golden Gate. But Ghazala, Layla, and Sandra said they never wore T-shirts, and several others thought it sounded hokey, so the idea was shelved.

Chapter Fifteen

Daniel had stayed in touch with Shoshana through occasional letters and cards at holidays. He told her of his teaching and his marriage and sent her a copy of his book on how to feel at home in an unfamiliar religious setting. A note taped to the book read, *Even if you don't have time to read all of this, be sure to read the acknowledgments*, in which he mentioned *Shoshana, who taught me about the Sabbath and other things*. She told him of her social work degree, which was a struggle after her daughter, Ofra, was born in 1976. Several times she included pictures, but only of Ofra. One of them showed a small girl in a pool. On the back was written, *Sometimes I think I gave birth to a fish*.

Then, eight years after their difficult dinner at Neve Ya'akov, he saw her again. Daniel accepted an invitation to speak at a conference at Hebrew University in Jerusalem even though it wasn't a good time of year for a seminary professor to be gone. His speech was scheduled for March 29, and no matter how he tried to shift his calendar, the result was the same: he would have to arrive on the morning of Sunday the 28th and leave early on the 31st. They arranged to meet on Sunday afternoon, although she told him she couldn't stay long. Seven-year-old Ofra would need to be picked up by four.

At her suggestion, they met on the terrace of the King David Hotel, with its postcard view of the Jaffa Gate and the Tower of David. Daniel had been mentally preparing for this encounter almost more than he'd been preparing for his speech at the conference, but the first minutes were still awkward. He started to kiss her on the cheek but bumped into the brim of her hat so hard he knocked it off. They both laughed as she picked it up and kissed him quickly. "I suppose there's no need for this," she said, looking at the hat. "You've seen my ugly scar."

Once they were seated and ordered coffee, he said, "So, should I be calling you Shani?"

"Why would you ask that? You've never called me Shani."

"That's what Yossi—"

"Oh, he just does that sometimes to tick me off. When I was eight and we moved to Israel, my aunt started calling me Shoshi, but I hated it. I'm very stubborn, as you may remember, and it's been Shoshana ever since. Well, except when I went back to Boston for college and people decided it was easier to call me Susan. Whoever I am, I'm not a Susan. That confirmed where my home is, but I think I've already told you that." The familiar smile. "Maybe I should be calling you Professor Jacobs."

"Only if you want to get kicked under the table."

"Did you expect to be a professor back in . . . was it 1970?"

Daniel took a drink of his coffee. "To be honest, back then I didn't know what in the world I wanted . . . except to be with you."

While he worried over that remark, Shoshana changed the subject, first telling him how difficult it now was to live in Israel "with prices completely out of control, through the roof" and then, hardly taking a breath, saying she would like to hear him speak at the conference but had to work. Which led to questions about whether she had envisioned being a social worker back in 1970, and whether her work included Palestinians.

"I'm surprised you haven't asked me that in your letters. Yes, it does. In fact, we even protested when the Haredi, the crazy Orthodox who always manage to control the interior ministry, held up housing permits in East Jerusalem. I hope you teach your students that nothing here is this or that, black or white."

"Like this war in Lebanon?"

Shoshana finished her coffee before she replied. "I want Ofra to be safe, but also not afraid. Last year she was afraid of PLO attacks from Lebanon. Now she's not."

The terrace was beginning to fill up, the waiter hovering anxiously, so they both ordered a pastry to go with more coffee. "I know I should be crashing from jet lag," said Daniel, "but I feel wide awake. It must be your effect on me."

Shoshana smiled and began talking about Ofra, who was, naturally, top of her class in English. "With an American accent."

"Isn't Ofra the name of one of the new settlements? I read something about it being built on . . ." Seeing the look on Shoshana's face, he stopped. "Did Yossi give her—"

"Ofra is an Israeli name, lots of women have it. It means deer, young deer. *I* named her," these last words said sharply. Daniel started to speak, but she continued, her tone back to normal. "Our daughter is not only good at English, she's excellent in math, too. *That* she gets from her father the accountant."

This seemed like an invitation to ask about Yossi, but Daniel had barely begun his question when Shoshana checked her watch. "Sorry, but I need to keep an eye on the time. Ofra has a swimming lesson that ends at four o'clock. She really is a good swimmer, but I guess I have fifteen minutes before I have to leave to pick her up." This led her to recount the first time she brought Ofra to the King David Hotel and how her daughter immediately wanted to see where people went swimming.

She had been looking toward the hotel's pool but now turned back to Daniel. "You haven't told me how Peg is doing. You know, you really haven't said much about her in your letters." But as Daniel began to describe his wife's current botany project, involving students at the community college, the waiter asked, unsubtly, if they were ready for the bill, and Daniel used their final minutes to speak about his most recent publication, an article on Jewish-Christian collaboration in combating poverty.

As they moved into the ornate art deco lobby, Daniel said, "I have something for you. I meant to give this to you in 1975, but the time got away from me." He pulled from his pocket the key chain Musa had made and, as she turned to face him, put it in her hand. Shoshana ran her finger over the *dalet*, the Hebrew letter *d* that was affixed to the Eilat stone, then leaned forward and kissed him gently on the lips.

"Thank you, Daniel."

"Shoshana, do you think about me, every now and then? I think about—"

She put her finger to his lips. "Of course, Daniel. But it is what it is."

"Well, I can still tell you that you're as beautiful as ever."

That smile. "Goodbye, Daniel. Please don't walk me to my car. It has been good, very good, to see you, and I don't want it to get awkward." He watched her head toward the hotel entrance, where she turned back. "It makes me happy whenever I get your letters."

And so he wrote more often, in the years that followed their brief meeting in 1983, telling her about his teaching and his speaking, especially when his presentations were to Jewish audiences. He told her about the little congregation to which he belonged and their efforts to fight the stigma associated with AIDS, especially after one of their members contracted it. And he talked, occasionally, about Peg and their marriage, especially when he needed a safe place to vent.

Her letters, too, came more frequently. At first they were basically informational—their move to a larger apartment with a view of nearby Jerusalem (she was sure he would like it), Ofra's progress at her school in Neve Ya'akov (which now felt like any other suburb). But, gradually, they became more personal. Her father was dying of cancer, and she felt guilty that most of his care had fallen to Rahel. Her best friend, a neighbor, died by suicide, which made her aware of how dangerous it is to keep emotions buried. Yossi was often gone because of work, and twice she implied there may be other reasons. Her letters often included pictures of Ofra and, from time to time, of Ofra and her.

For years, they had ended their letters "*L'shalom*" or "*B'yedidut*," but by the late '80s, "with peace" or "with friendship" didn't seem adequate. Finally, he signed one *Love, Daniel*, and added a PS: *I do love you, although it's at a distance.* Shoshana didn't comment, but followed suit. And one of her letters had its own PS: *I really wish you lived closer. There is so much we could do together.* He kept that one in a file in his office.

Daniel sent her the interfaith group's itinerary even before he shared it with Peg. The trip would include obligatory stops in Haifa, to see the Baha'i Temple; Nazareth, to meet with Israeli Arabs and visit the Church of the Annunciation; Safed, to learn about Jewish *kabbalah* and drop by a few artists' studios; and the Sea of Galilee, where they would eat Saint Peter's fish at a kibbutz. But he convinced the group to spend only a day or two in Tel Aviv and skip an excursion to Eilat in order to spend six days in Jerusalem and the West Bank. "After all," he told them, "that's what this group is going there to experience. If you want mainly to see religious sites or tourist places, there are plenty of other tours."

He promised Shoshana he would call as soon as he got to Jerusalem so they could arrange where and when to meet. And he was pleased at how pleased she seemed by the prospect.

Chapter Sixteen

Daniel had proposed staying at a hotel in the Old City, but two Jewish couples who had been to Israel vetoed the idea. They compromised on the Baruch Haba, a moderately priced hotel within walking distance of both the Jaffa Gate and Ben Yehuda Street, in the heart of downtown new Jerusalem. They had planned to arrive in their thirty-passenger minibus by six p.m. on Sunday the 13th, but it was after seven by the time they got there and checked in.

Daniel quickly phoned Shoshana from his room. He was free Tuesday evening and all day on Thursday. Could she meet him both times? Tuesday dinner won't be possible, she told him, but she might be able to get free later in the evening. She had to work Thursday morning, no way around it, but she would definitely meet him as soon as she could. They should keep in touch by phone during the week.

When the group met back in the lobby, Devorah and Jon suggested they all go to a restaurant not far from the hotel in the new part of the city. "It has a big menu," said Jon, "at least it did when we were there the last time. Something for everyone." Sarah, Ben, and Batya supported this plan, but to everyone's surprise, Ghazala, the most accommodating of all the travelers, demurred.

"I would like . . ." She looked at Daniel. "If it's okay to go into old Jerusalem at night, I would like to go there this evening." After a brief conversation, the Bridge Builders agreed that, since Devorah and Jon knew where they were going, they would take whoever wanted to go with them to the Israeli restaurant. Daniel would go with Ghazala and the rest to see what was open inside the Old City walls. Seventeen members of the group, including Adam, one of the Jews, went with Daniel.

They entered through the Jaffa Gate, the only place where the wall has been broken. To their right was the brightly illuminated Tower of David, part of the ancient fortified compound called the Citadel. There were people where the street widened inside the gate, but by no means a crowd. They moved easily down David Street, then left to the Muristan, an area in the Christian Quarter with a fountain in the middle of converging alleyways. There the owner of a small café pulled together enough tables and chairs, some borrowed from a café nearby. Without asking, he began bringing plates of hummus and tabbouleh followed by kebabs and fries.

"How did you know what we wanted?" Daniel asked him.

The owner smiled. "It is all I have left from the day, and some comes from my friend." He pointed to the café of the borrowed tables.

While they were eating outdoors, the area illuminated by strings of lights that ran from shops to the top of the fountain, Ghazala asked, "Can we see Al-Aqsa?"

"Yes," said Daniel. "It's on our itinerary. We may all try to go to the Temple Mount"—he smiled—"to Haram al-Sharif, on Wednesday. But you can go there on your own, as well, later in the week."

Ghazala pulled her scarf up over her head. "I mean to see it from a distance, just to look at it . . . tonight."

Daniel consulted with the owner, who in turn spoke with his friend from the neighboring café. His café's building had access to the roof.

"He says it is not possible for so many," said the owner.

"What about three of us?"

But Ghazala's husband, Saeed, shook his head. "My knees are too old for stairs."

"Okay," said Daniel, looking at the owner, "what about two of us, and we all get baklava from your friend?"

Ten minutes later, while dessert was being served, Daniel and Ghazala stood on the rooftop looking east. The Dome of the Rock, its gold top shining in spotlights, dominated the scene. Next to it, with its modest gray dome, was the profile of Al-Aqsa.

Ghazala adjusted her scarf and then stood quietly, her eyes on the mosque. It was Daniel who broke the silence. "I was staying in the Old City the day a Christian set fire to Al-Aqsa. I'm sure you remember that incident, that tragedy."

Ghazala nodded. "May Allah show him mercy." After a pause, she added, "It is wonderful that you have spent so much time in this city."

"Not as much as I would like, but yes, I have been fortunate to be here, even make some friends." He pulled the prayer beads from his pocket. "One of them gave me these. I don't carry them in the US, but it seems right to have them with me in Jerusalem. He's a Muslim friend, although we don't talk much about religion."

More silence, Ghazala still looking toward the mosque. When she began to speak, it was so softly that Daniel had to strain to hear her. "I was raised in Pakistan, as you know. Saeed and I both were, in Lahore. He studied there to be a doctor, but we moved to America so I could go to medical school." He could feel the emotion in her voice. "Sometimes I miss Pakistan, but if I lived there, I couldn't be here. This is a big reason why I wanted a US passport, so I could come to Jerusalem and see Al-Aqsa."

The next day, Monday, was the tour of new Jerusalem, including Yad Vashem. Daniel was gratefully amazed at how the verbal wounds of the afternoon seemed basically healed, or at least buried, when they met for dinner at the hotel. Devorah did talk at length about how moving it is to be in Israel and see everyone—well, every Jew—stand still while the sirens wail on Yom HaShoah, the day for remembering the Holocaust.

"People stop their cars wherever they are, right downtown on busy streets—I've seen them—and get out and stand there. The country just stops. It's very emotional."

"I can see doing that," said Layla, "but I hope you, all of us, will also say a prayer for the dead on April ninth when Palestinians remember the . . . remember Deir Yassin." Daniel was sure she had started to say "massacre," and he made a mental note to tell her he appreciated the restraint.

"April ninth," Sarah repeated. "That's right around when Yom HaShoah is every year."

"Maybe that's a sign of something," said her husband, Ben, which made Sarah laugh.

"As if you ever stop playing golf long enough to remember either one!" And the whole group, Ben included, joined in her laughter.

On Tuesday, however, things again got testy. In the morning, they visited Bethlehem, their first time encountering the "flying checkpoints," temporary roadblocks set up by the Israeli military. It took them nearly an hour to travel the six miles from Jerusalem to Bethlehem, and the group was silent—*sullen?* Daniel wondered—when their bus was finally parked near Manger Square. There was overt grumbling, however, as they stooped to fit through the door to the Church of the Nativity. "This can't be four-feet high!" one of them exclaimed.

"The Ottomans made it this way," Daniel explained to them, "to keep people from riding their horses and camels inside."

"To keep me from getting inside," said Alan, who was the oldest member of the group.

After the church visit, in order to lighten the mood Daniel suggested they stop by an olive wood shop, talk to the owner, watch them carve the wood, perhaps buy some gifts. But once they were there, the first question—from Ron, one of the Christians—had nothing to do with wood. "The name on your shop is Giacomini's. That's not an Arab name, is it?"

"I see you are a very smart man!" The proprietor's ingratiating tone made Daniel cringe. "I can assure you I am Arab, one hundred percent plus. The name, it goes back to the Crusaders. My family has deeds to land around Bethlehem for a thousand years. They are there in the great church. You have been there already?" Lots of nods. "Go back and you can see for yourself, there on the deeds: Giacomini." Since people seemed interested, he added, "Come, I show you something."

He led the way to the back of the building, the fruity aroma of olive wood growing more intense as they approached the workroom. But instead of showing them carvers at work, he headed up a narrow flight of stairs. That ruled out Saeed, Alan, and Liz with her still-wrapped ankle, but the rest of the group trouped behind him until they were standing shoulder to shoulder on the roof. In front of them, to the east and north, were buildings of Bethlehem and the neighboring town of Beit Sahour, crowned by three steeples and a minaret.

"You see that land of farming," said Mr. Giacomini with a sweep of his hand. "Much of that belongs to my family. But now, because of checkpoints and troubles from the army, my uncles and cousins many days cannot get there to do farming. And when we cannot get there, the Israelis say there is no farming, so they can take the land."

"That's terrible," said Jo. "That's stealing!"

"Wait a minute! Wait a minute!" Devorah seemed ready to explode. "Excuse me, Mr. Gacomi, but Jo, we don't know that this is accurate. And besides, people seem to forget that Israel has reason to worry about security. Don't forget this *intifada* business—"

Batya interrupted: "Knifing people, throwing Molotov cocktails."

"Yes," said Devorah. "All of that and more. The only reason we can travel here now is because Israel clamped down on the violence."

"You know as well as I do," said Jamila, "that fifty Palestinians have been killed or wounded for every Israeli."

Devorah started to respond, but it was her husband, Jon, who said, "That's an exaggeration." He shook his head as if in dismay, or disgust.

Daniel had been biting his tongue, hoping the group would resolve their dispute, as they eventually had after the blow up at Yad Vashem. But now he intervened.

"Come on, friends. We're here as guests of Mr. Giacomini. Let's allow him to show us what he wants to show us and then go down and spend a few minutes, and maybe a few dollars, in his shop." He looked at the line of friends from Columbus: Batya, with whom he had organized interfaith Seders; Amir and Layla, who sponsored an overseas student at the seminary; Barbara and Hamza and Adam, persons who said little but were always present at interfaith events; Sarah and Ben, Ron and Cynthia, generous financial supporters of interfaith activities in the city. He spoke often with students about how to deal with conflict, in the abstract. It's different, he now reflected, when confronted with the emotions of real people—good people, good friends. "Mr. Giacomini is not a politician. He's just telling us his family's story, the same as you would if he came to visit you."

The shop owner had looked distressed by the earlier conversation, but now recovered quickly, his smile back in place. "I like the Israeli security," he said, looking at Devorah and Jon. "During the worst times of the intifada, business was very bad. Nobody coming, all of Bethlehem suffering. But look here." It seemed for a second that he would take Devorah by the arm. Instead he pointed to a cluster of white buildings on a not-too-distant hill. "You see that? It is an Israeli settlement. If Israel wants to protect its settlement, let it put its checkpoints up there next to the settlement, not down here around Bethlehem so it is hard to get to our farming. That is what our people are saying."

After a few more minutes in the shop—part of the group buying a lot, the other part very little—they ate lunch in a restaurant on Manger Square. The conversation seemed normal, but Daniel noticed that Devorah and Layla sat on opposite ends of the long table.

Their next stop was Hebron, which, Daniel informed them, is the largest city in the West Bank. "It is almost entirely Palestinian, and that's one reason I thought we should go there. I've arranged a discussion with two community leaders, one Muslim and one Christian."

This, however, would come after a visit to the Tomb of the Patriarchs. The tomb—which, according to tradition, is the burial site of Abraham and Sarah, Isaac and Rebecca, Jacob and Leah—is actually a place for Jewish prayer alongside the Ibrahimi Mosque, each with its own entrance. "This fortlike structure that encloses both," Daniel told the Bridge Builders, "was constructed by King Herod—well, on order of King Herod—above a series of caves. Of course, we don't know if Abraham is really buried in the caves, if there even was an Abraham, for that matter. But it seems that people revered the place long before Herod. It's part of the stories we all tell about ourselves." After this introduction, the group moved with appropriate reverence through both worship spaces, the Jewish women not hesitating to don the well-used *abayas*, body and head coverings, kept for visitors at the mosque.

Daniel stayed in the building until he was sure all of the group was out, his usual practice, and by the time he reached the spot where they had agreed to gather, Layla and Devorah were again butting heads.

"I didn't say all Jews are a threat," said Layla, her voice growing louder as she spoke. "I said the *settlers* are a threat. They have attacked Muslims worshipping here several times, and there's going to be a real disaster, mark my words, if something isn't done about it!"

"What about the hand grenade thrown at Israeli Jews? Right here. That was sure a threat. And—what was it? ten years ago?—Jewish worshippers killed, right here. You can't just blame one group." Devorah now spoke quickly, perhaps so no one would interrupt. "What gets me—I'm not talking about our group, or just our group—but what gets me is that people go to Yad Vashem and then forget this is how Jews have been treated. No memory of it. And I'm not talking Middle Ages. In our century, this is how Jews have been treated."

"Why do you keep bringing that up?" asked Jamila. "We all agree the Holocaust was beyond awful, we know what happened. But the Palestinians didn't do it. Muslims aren't responsible for it."

Daniel, furiously fingering his prayer beads, now cut in. "Abraham," he pointed out, "is a common ancestor for all of us—Jews, Muslims, Christians—*all* of us. You all talk about being bridge builders, about finding common ground. Well, here it is! The single root of our traditions. According to scripture, Isaac and Ishmael overcame their hostility in order to bury Abraham here in these caves, *together*. His tomb should be a place of common prayer, of shared history. Don't let the actions of a few others divide us." This was all said at greater volume, and with more passion, than he had intended, and it felt good.

His remarks calmed things down, at least until the group gathered over tea and coffee in a room at Al-Bishara Church for a conversation with the two community leaders. It was obvious that Mr. Khoury and Mr. Shehadeh were friends, each dressed in a suit coat, shirts buttoned to the collar. They sat next to each other smiling as Daniel introduced them.

"This is the first time I have met these gentlemen," he told the friends from Columbus, "but they come highly recommended by people I know in Jerusalem. Their English is excellent. In fact, Mr. Khoury taught English in a local Christian school. And they say that you can ask them anything."

The first question, however, was directed at Daniel. "Why," asked Jon, perhaps at the urging of Devorah, "is there no Jewish leader present?"

Since Daniel had anticipated this question, his reply was immediate. "Because, as I said earlier, this is a Palestinian city. The Jews here are almost all settlers—"

"Who throw garbage on the heads of Muslims," said Amir, perhaps at the urging of Layla.

"Muslim children," added Jamila. She looked around the group. "You saw those nets over the walkways going to Abraham's tomb? The old cans and bottles and trash on them? Daniel didn't make a big deal of it because he's trying to keep us on the same page, but you need to know that settlers throw that stuff there on purpose."

"Okay," said Batya, "but give the whole picture. There was a terrorist threat against Jews here in Hebron just last week. It was in the paper while we've been in Israel."

Jamila shook her head so vigorously that her scarf nearly fell off. "Why do only Muslims get that label? Throwing garbage on the heads of children, that's terrorism in my book."

"Stop!" Daniel was surprised at how loud his word sounded in the large church hall. "We are here today to listen to our guests."

He turned toward the two older gentlemen, but it was Jo, looking ready to cry, who now spoke. "Why," her voice quavering, "does religion always have to be something we fight about? We didn't fight with each other back home."

Before Daniel could respond, Mr. Khoury said, "The problem is extremists. All of us have extremists." Mr. Shehadeh silently nodded his agreement. "*Hebron*, it means 'friend.' In Arabic, we call this city *Khalil al-Rahman*, 'the friend of God.' But extremists, they believe they should hate other people to the glory of their God. One group of them does something, and then the other does something back. Instead of being friends, they make enemies." He paused, and no one interrupted. "I think—and I know Mr. Shehadeh, he agrees with me—that most Palestinians want what most Israelis want: to earn a living, raise their children, celebrate their holidays—"

"Take a trip, do some shopping," added Mr. Shehadeh, and they both smiled and nodded.

Later, when the group was back at the hotel, Daniel called Shoshana. "It has been a hell of a day," he told her, "so I hope we can get together."

But she couldn't. "I'll explain," she said, "when we see each other on Thursday."

Chapter Seventeen

The next morning, Daniel was still irritated about not seeing Shoshana, which may be why he lectured his Columbus friends over breakfast on the need to listen, not only to their invited speakers, but to one another. "We should be a sign of what can be, not an example of the tensions we all read about." The Bridge Builders seemed to take this homily to heart because they listened attentively, apart from an occasional yawn, as a young staffer from the Ministry of Agriculture droned on about water projects and new kinds of crops that were making Israel flourish. "And Palestinian areas, too. We have improved life for everyone," she insisted.

She was followed in their hotel conference room by a representative of B'Tselem, a Jewish organization whose mission is to document Israeli government abuses of Palestinians. "Our name means 'in the image,'" the bearded speaker told them. "We believe that all persons, Israelis and Palestinians, are created in the divine image. Even Americans"—the last words said with a smile.

Every member of the American group received a map of the West Bank, and tensions could have been rekindled when Ghazala noted that the checkpoints, settlements, and Israeli-only roads made Palestinian territory look like Swiss cheese. "You can't make a country out of Swiss cheese." But since it was gentle Ghazala who said it, no one openly objected. Ben did note, tongue in cheek, that Daniel was trying to give them whiplash by putting such speakers back-to-back.

That left time before lunch for a quick stop at what was called the Global Christian Embassy. One of the Jewish couples, David and Rebecca, had heard about this "embassy" from someone and proposed adding it to the itinerary. "We have scheduled a lot of Jews," they argued at one of the travelers' preliminary meetings, "and this sounds like a chance to get another Christian perspective."

"I don't know much about the place," Daniel admitted, "but I know it was started by Christian Zionists. Are you sure that's something we want to include?"

"What's wrong with Christians supporting Israel?" asked Jon. Since no one spoke in opposition, Daniel ended up agreeing to the proposal.

The Bridge Builders arrived at the GCE—an old mansion with a large portico and an array of Israeli flags, located in the new part of Jerusalem—shortly before eleven and were ushered into a modern conference room. A young man named Tim, dressed in jeans and tennis shoes, introduced himself as an embassy "host," while looking around the room at the two yarmulkes and three headscarves. "You are, of course, welcome," he said, "but there may have been a misunderstanding. I was told this was a Christian group."

"Nope," said Daniel. "We are Muslims, Jews, and Christians traveling together, from Ohio. You will have to give your spiel to all of us."

Tim frowned. "'Spiel' sounds a little negative. The people who support the embassy are simply Christians from many countries, not just the United States, who believe in biblical prophecy. The Bible says that God will return the Jewish people to the Land of Israel, and who can deny that today we see this being fulfilled right before our eyes?"

"Why an embassy?" asked Ron, the one lawyer in the group. "Christians aren't a nation."

"Because various countries moved their embassies to Tel Aviv, so this is a way for Christians to show our disagreement with those decisions, show our support for Israel." He smiled, apparently feeling back on track. "Jerusalem has been Israel's capital for three thousand years. That is a crucial part of God's plan."

He started to say more, but most of the group had turned their attention to Batya, who was now standing. "I understand," she said, "why Rebecca and David suggested coming here, I really do. But after we agreed to it, I ran across an article about this place that has me worried. The article said you want Jews to return to Israel as a prerequisite for Jesus coming back. It made it sound like you don't really value us as Jews. Is that true?"

Tim was again frowning. "The second coming of Jesus is also part of God's plan in scripture."

Ben chuckled loudly. "Not in our scripture it isn't."

"I think we should let him speak," said Batya, looking at her friends. "I just wanted to tell you my worry. I was going to make this little speech at breakfast, but then Daniel had things he needed to tell us . . . about listening." She sat down, and for the next ten minutes they listened to how the restoration of Israel demonstrates God's faithfulness to the covenant made with Abraham.

"Our *common* ancestor," said Amir, but softly.

"This is not a fringe belief," Tim assured them in closing. "This is what biblical, evangelical Christians believe. It is what the church has always believed until liberalism tried to take the Bible out of the church."

Daniel had heard enough, but before he could speak, Ghazala said calmly, "You haven't talked about Muslims. Where do we fit in this plan of your God?" Her scarf had been on her neck, and she now pulled it over her hair.

Tim hesitated. "I can only say what I know is true, that God's work of salvation began with the Jews and culminates in Jesus Christ, who was a Jew."

"Well, I'm a Jew," said Ben, less calmly, "and I love Israel. But I know damn well that Zionism is a political movement. We heard what worried Batya. What worries *me* is when people like you mix up politics and religion."

Daniel couldn't tell how many members of the Bridge Builders were clapping, but he could certainly see Tim's facing turning red. Definitely time to say something. "We appreciate, Tim, that you took time to share with us, give us the perspective of the Christian Embassy. But as you can hear, we have some reservations. One of mine is very personal. You may remember back in 1969 when a Christian named Rohan tried to burn the Al-Aqsa Mosque. I was here, so I sure remember it. And as I recall, he wanted to clear the way for a restored Jewish temple."

"He was just nuts—"

"Yes, but ideas like yours encouraged him. He said so himself." Daniel paused. "I can't speak for this whole motley crew"—a few chuckles—"but I suspect one thing most of us object to is your certainty." He could sense people nodding. "It must be nice to be so certain, to put such faith in your reading of biblical prophecies, but to a group like ours it feels arrogant. As I told you coming in, I'm a seminary professor, and the way you read scripture is not how I have learned to read it."

Tim had been gathering his notes and brochures while Daniel was speaking. He now looked up. "We have professors like you who come here from time to time," he said brusquely. "Professors who think more people will like them if they tiptoe around the hard truths of God's word. Here we don't pick and choose what parts of the Bible to accept."

These words gnawed at Daniel as they exited the building. Maybe Christians are supposed to be more certain than he often felt. Was "hearing both sides" just another way of saying "wishy-washy"? The rest of the group, however, was clearly pumped up by the meeting. "At least we weren't at odds with each other," Devorah exclaimed, "because we were all against him!"

Back on the bus, Daniel was surprised when Ghazala sat down beside him. "It was good to go there," she told him, her voice soft and affirming. "Saeed and I agree it was good to hear him. And Daniel, don't worry. None of us thinks he represents all Christians." She smiled. "It just proves that Muslims aren't the only ones who have crazy ideas."

Daniel had reserved a private room for lunch in a hotel restaurant because that made it possible to squeeze in yet another presentation. Liz and Jim, the two Catholics in the group, had once heard a French priest named Laurent, who served the Church of Saint Anne in Jerusalem, speak about the Holy Land, and they thought he was great. In fact, his talk in their Columbus parish, while on a speaking tour in North America, was the reason they signed up for this interfaith trip.

Daniel followed up on their recommendation and invited Father Laurent to join them for lunch, talk about his thirty years of living in the Old City. Daniel expected a description of how the city had changed, perhaps some comment on Christian shrines. A relaxing conversation after a heavy morning. But Father Laurent, clearly not one for small talk, had other things on his mind.

"You should know, if you don't know it, that the so-called 'historical sites' are to be questioned because history is written for the purpose of politics. As we say in French, *la politique est toute importante*. And it is happening today, *la même chose*. The PLO has said to Palestinian historians that they cannot say there ever was a Jewish temple in Jerusalem. And the Israelis pretend they did no *atrocité* in '48, when we know that is not the truth."

Layla looked like she was ready to speak, but Daniel beat her to it. "This is territory we've covered as a group, at least part of it."

"*Très bien*," said the priest. "Very good. Listen to everything, as you Americans say, with a taste of salt."

"What about the Christians?" asked Jon, smiling. "You've mentioned the rest of us, but—"

"Oh, we are the worst of them all! You must remember that so-called Christian countries divided the Middle East, drawing lines on a map like they were playing a game. And now they say *tsk-tsk* when people they stuck together do not get along. There are no innocents here, and do not trust any people who say there are." He looked around the group. "*Mais malheureusement*, there are not so many Christians left in Jerusalem. In 1948, yes, but now just enough of us to open the doors of the places you come to see, *portiers* in a big museum."

As Father Laurent continued, Daniel could see that Liz looked increasingly distressed. Finally she said, "I don't remember you being so . . . so negative, Father, when my husband and I heard you speak in Columbus. Is there anything good you can tell us, something our group can take back that's positive?"

"If you want beautiful things and peace," said the priest, "go to Paris." He took a deep breath. "*D'accord*. Many people come here and leave and never learn anything. You are asking questions, and that is, as you put it, a positive."

The bells of the Holy Sepulchre had just struck two when the group plunged into the Old City for what Daniel called "a three-hour highlights tour," and a break from all the politics. They went, of course, to the Western Wall where he recounted his meeting with Reb Shlomo (to the envy of the Jews in the group). "It's past the hour when the general public can go up on the Temple Mount, the Haram al-Sharif. So you can go there tomorrow, if you want. I know Ghazala wants to," he said, smiling in her direction. "To be honest, I think it's better we not all go at the same time."

He took them, of course, to the Holy Sepulchre where he recounted spending the night (to the slight envy of a couple of the Christians). He also told them the story of how Caliph Umar, when he took control of Jerusalem in 637, declined an invitation to pray in the church lest his followers then turn it into a mosque (a story that greatly pleased the Muslims).

The day had turned hot, the sun nearly blinding as it bounced off the ubiquitous limestone. After a stop for cold drinks, they made one more visit: to the Tomb of David and the Room of the Last Supper on Mount Zion. Daniel did not, however, take them to the Rooftop or talk about his experience on it. As Devorah had said at

Yad Vashem, some things are too significant, too personal, to be just another stop on a tour. While some were still in the shrines—Saeed, Ghazala, Alan, Sandra, and Liz collapsed on nearby benches—Daniel said, "I'll meet you in a minute," and ran up the rickety staircase for a daytime glimpse.

While Daniel liked the holy places, he loved the alleys of the souk, where you saw Franciscan priests in their brown cassocks brushing past uniformed Israeli soldiers, old men in jackets and keffiyehs alongside dust-covered masons, Arab women in abayas next to Americans in jeans. As he had told Shoshana, this mixture of differences was one of the first things that attracted him. But when the group met that evening after dinner to debrief, he quickly learned that such love was not shared by most of the Bridge Builders. For everyone who spoke, the alleyways were too crowded, almost claustrophobic. People had stumbled into Liz's bad ankle. Barbara said she had practically been shoved into a shop, which was embarrassing because she didn't want to buy anything. Sandra told of nearly being knocked over by boys pushing overloaded carts. "At my age, I can't afford to fall, not on those stone pavements."

That was just the beginning of the complaints. "There is so much death there," Liz grumbled. "It feels creepy to think of what you're walking on, all the people who were slaughtered wherever you stand."

Sarah had a different gripe. "Like you say, Daniel, there is diversity, but it's all walled off—Muslim Quarter here, Christian Quarter here, Jewish Quarter over here. What's the other one? There might as well be walls inside the walls."

"The history is what it is," said Daniel. "But as far as the crowds are concerned, it will be easier if we don't try to move through those streets as a group of twenty-five. You see that tomorrow is open on our schedule. What I propose is that you do what you want. You have guidebooks, and you've now seen a few highlights. Tomorrow, just wander a little, go places that you want to see, spend part of the day resting if you need to. Have dinner in the hotel, or somewhere else if you prefer. We have tickets for tomorrow night's light show at the Tower of David, which starts at eight thirty. So let's plan to meet here at seven thirty and go together."

Chapter Eighteen

Once the travel group agreed with Daniel's plan for Thursday the 17th, he called Shoshana. Her morning was packed with appointments she couldn't reschedule, but she could meet him at half past two on the terrace of the Golden Walls Hotel, not far outside the Damascus Gate.

Daniel left the Baruch Haba early in order to have coffee and his breakfast pizza in the Old City. Shoshana had told him in one of her letters that Al-Kamal was gone, replaced by a shop that sold shoes and cheap clothing. He intended to ask Ibrahim at breakfast what had happened to the hotel, and to Bassam, but Ibrahim's bakery was dark and empty. The man who owned the jewelry store across the alleyway from Al-Kamal was still there, however, and from him Daniel learned that Bassam now worked at the Hotel Shukran just down the souk.

Sure enough, Bassam was behind the reception desk in the nicely furnished lobby, with framed Palestinian embroidery on the stone walls. "Bassam, you have moved up in the world! This sure beats the Al-Kamal." But while Bassam smiled and nodded, it was soon clear he had no real recollection of Daniel. Between people leaving or asking for keys, Daniel tried to jog his memory. "I used to buy tea for the old men who sat there in the evenings. I'm the student who was staying there when that idiot from Australia set fire to Al-Aqsa."

Bassam smiled but shook his head. "Lots of students stayed at Al-Kamal." Although Daniel couldn't recall any others.

One last try. "You told me I had a choice, either go where all the tourists go or stay there and experience Arab hospitality."

"Yes," said Bassam, as he moved to answer the phone, "that is what I said when I saw someone like you."

Daniel left the hotel with a mix of irritation and unease. Was Bassam just playing with him? The times at Al-Kamal loomed large in his memory. Was his memory accurate? Had he blown that experience, and others, out of all proportion?

Musa, on the other hand, was delighted to see him after all these years. They drank a cup of Arabic coffee, Daniel's third of the morning. Then, since his head was buzzing, he switched to tea while Musa waited on the few customers and, once they were gone, turned his attention to a pair of earrings made of Ottoman coins. At one point in their rambling conversation, Musa asked if Daniel had gotten married. And before Daniel could explain that his marriage was probably on its last legs, Musa had given him a necklace and a set of earrings.

"Your wife's ears are pierced?"

"Yes," said Daniel, somewhat embarrassed—or maybe amused—to realize he was thinking of Shoshana.

Musa closed the shop not long after noon so they could eat falafel at Samir's tiny café, Daniel keeping an eye on the clock. Before his friends could insist on another cup of coffee, he excused himself and headed through the market and out the Damascus Gate. Even with a stop at the bathroom in the hotel lobby, he was on the terrace by two fifteen—only to find that Shoshana was already there, seated at a corner table. Her hat was off, hair pulled back on one side, and he thought she looked amazing.

Shoshana stood as Daniel approached, moving around the table, and they embraced—longer than he had expected, much as he had hoped. When they were seated, he said, "Because of our letters, I feel as if we can just pick up in mid-sentence."

That smile. "So what's the sentence?"

"That it's incredible how much I think about a woman I haven't seen for almost ten years." They ordered glasses of orange juice before he added, "I hoped you might visit family in the US at some point. Don't you have a cousin—"

"An aunt, my mother's younger sister. She's still in Boston." She took a drink. "To be completely honest, which we should be, I did come once, a year or two after you were last here and we met at the King David. I went to Boston with Ofra and Yossi."

Daniel had raised his eyebrows and Shoshana smiled. "Yes, of course I wanted to see you, but you were in Ohio. And what would I have said to Yossi? 'You stay here with our kid and my relatives while I take off for a few days to see an old lover'?"

"I would have come to Boston."

"Daniel, *ahuvi*, you were—are—married, too. What was the point of telling you when it couldn't happen?" His hand was resting on the table, and she now reached across and took it. "I sometimes think we are like this damn peace process. There are always complications that get in the way."

They talked about Ofra the teenager—bright, headstrong, on the swim team, too popular with boys for her mother's peace of mind.

"I would love to meet her. She sounds like a young you."

"Someday." That smile.

They talked about her work, which had been part-time for years. "You know from my letters that I'm helping new immigrants find housing and jobs. What I haven't told you is that I've just switched to full-time. That's why I couldn't meet you this morning; we had a new group of Russian Jews. As I remember, I almost lost my job in 1970 because I was spending so much time with you."

She asked about his teaching and his interfaith work, and they both laughed when he told how pleased his Jewish friends were that he knew all the prayers and ritual for lighting the Sabbath candles. "I tell them how I learned from a great friend in Jerusalem, but I don't tell them what else we did on the Sabbath."

But when he asked about living at Neve Ya'akov, her smile faded. "Actually, I may not be there much longer." She paused and Daniel remained silent. "I haven't told you the whole story in my letters. But full honesty now, right?" She didn't wait for a response. "I've already filed for divorce, which isn't so easy in Israel since those awful Orthodox control it. Yossi has moved out for now, but eventually he can have the apartment. He's the one who wanted to live there, who fancied himself a settler. As long as he agrees to help Ofra pay for university." She shook her head. "Naturally, he demanded to talk about this after he was off work on Tuesday. That's why I couldn't meet you."

Since the waiter came by, they ordered another juice and then sat quietly for a moment, gazing at each other across the table. This time he took her hand.

"I'm sorry," he said softly.

"What are you sorry for?"

"That your life hasn't gone quite the way you wanted."

She smiled. "It is what it is." She looked down and fiddled with her hat before saying, "I never told you why things were so messy when you came to Jerusalem in 1975, just as we were moving to Neve Ya'akov. Yossi was married when he and I first met, which I didn't know right away. Well, I knew he'd been married, but not that he was still technically married. That was bad enough, and then it wasn't clear when he could finalize the divorce." She paused. "That evening when he acted so badly, his problem wasn't so much with you as it was with me. He knew I had doubts, about how he had rushed the wedding once the divorce was final, about moving to a settlement, even, I suppose, about whether we were right for each other. And he could tell that you meant more to me than any others."

Her greater honesty now prompted his. "I think inertia has kept Peg and me together this long," he admitted. "She has her life, I have mine. It's not unpleasant. Neither of us has been unfaithful, as far as I know." He paused. "At least not yet."

On impulse, he leaned across the small table, intending to kiss her cheek, but she moved, or maybe he did, and they kissed on the lips. "This hotel is used to Westerners," she said, smiling, as they settled back in their seats, "but it's still an Arab hotel, so we had better be a little more discreet." Daniel nodded, his body tingling.

While they didn't touch, the conversation became, in a way, even more intimate. Yes, he had thought about coming back to Israel for a visit. Often. But the trips he took with Peg always cost more than he had planned. And he traveled so much, speaking to various groups and at various schools, that the idea of another trip, even to Jerusalem, lost some of its appeal. Except to see her . . . and she was married . . . and so was he.

Yes, she was going to stay in Jerusalem, find an apartment, perhaps in the area where she used to live back when they were young. Rahel wanted her to move north, be closer to family. She could always get a job as a social worker, her sister assured her. But Jerusalem was where she and Ofra felt at home. Besides, most of her friends were here. And, no, none of them even potentially romantic.

Yes, he still considered himself to be religious, but it was sometimes more routine than passion: going to church whenever he was in Columbus, bringing a sack of groceries for the monthly food drive, serving on committees when asked, trying to pray, although not often on his own. "I guess it's always hard," he concluded, "to hold on to Rooftop experiences . . . of any sort."

No, she didn't still observe the Sabbath as faithfully as she once had. Yossi wasn't into it, made it feel awkward. But maybe it wasn't too late to reclaim things from her past that she regretted losing.

And, yes, she missed working for environmental causes, just being outdoors for that matter. Planting trees for Israel had felt like a mission. Her current work was good and important in its own way, but it was just a job.

"Why," she asked him, "do you think you fell for two women who are big into nature?"

It was several seconds before Daniel said, "Maybe I was looking for the one in the other."

At a quarter to five, he called the hotel, leaving word that those who were having dinner there should go ahead and eat without him. He would be back just in time to leave for the light show. Shoshana called Ofra with a similar message.

They headed for the American Colony Hotel, only five minutes by car, finding a table under mulberry trees in its courtyard restaurant. More than he expected, all that he had hoped. Here he didn't have to hide holding her hand or pressing his leg against hers. At one point, she gently ran her fingers along his temple, only a fleeting touch, but one that sent tremors through his body and so many memories through his mind. That was when he told her that he meant the word he used at the end of his letters, and she nodded and smiled. The waiter brought their food and a bottle of fine Israeli wine, and then stayed away until, reluctantly, Daniel summoned him for the bill.

The next day, soon after breakfast, the Bridge Builders boarded the familiar bus and set out east to Jericho, then north to Nablus and back through Ramallah. It was a long, tiring day even though the plates on their bus allowed them to pass quickly through the checkpoints, including Qalandia, where all traffic from the northern part of the West Bank funneled into Jerusalem.

"Do you think there will ever be an end to this conflict and all these checkpoints?" asked Liz as they neared the city. Daniel could tell that, despite their fatigue, most of the group were listening.

"From what I hear, the Norwegians are serious about their offer to mediate, maybe even get Israel and the PLO in the same room. So this could be a decade when things start looking up. I'm always hopeful that new relationships—and renewed ones, for that matter—are possible."

Since it was Friday, they made sure to be back before sunset. Having eaten a big lunch, the members of the group seemed happy to eat a light Shabbat dinner in the hotel, complete with kiddush cup and candles. Daniel, however, was more than wide awake, excusing himself as soon as he could do so politely.

It would not be good to meet at Neve Ya'akov, Shoshana had told him. Ofra was staying with a friend, but neighbors might see them and gossip to Yossi. So he had made a reservation at the Polis Hotel, just inside the Jaffa Gate. As he was leaving the Baruch Haba, he ran into Ghazala, who said with a gentle smile, "I think you, too, have a special love for something in Jerusalem."

This was their only night together because the group was leaving for the airport the next day—and it was glorious. More than twenty years had passed since they had been lovers, but her body felt thrillingly familiar. The way she touched him with her hands, her legs, her lips; the way her smile put him at ease, making him feel that, somehow, he alone was right for her; the way she let him pretend that only he had kissed her scar, knew her secrets. He remembered, with a clarity that astonished him, the shape of the birthmark on her neck, the curve of her hips, the scent of her hair and the way it fell on her shoulders. The question crossed his mind: What if home isn't a place?

After making love for the second time, he raised the obvious topic. "Ofra would really like it in the United States. You know she would. All the opportunities. You said she's interested in languages, maybe something like diplomatic work. There are any number of schools . . ."

Shoshana raised up on her elbow and looked at him, tenderly. "You know, Daniel, I can't do that. This is where her friends are. It's what she knows, where she wants to be."

"She'll be out of the home soon, in the army, going to university. Maybe then—"

She touched her finger to his lips in a way that flooded him with images of the past. "This is likely where she'll be. How could I be there?" They were quiet for a minute before she added softly, "But you don't have children."

"Shoshana, my love, I'm not fluent in Hebrew. What would I do? Certainly not be a professor. If I taught aeronautical engineering or biomedicine maybe, but not religion. This country already has too many religion scholars, those 'awful Orthodox.'" They both smiled, looking at each other. "Your job is more . . . Like Rahel said, you can find something easily . . ." But he could tell the discussion was essentially over.

For the next hour, he held her, nestled against her back. And although neither spoke, he knew that she, too, wasn't sleeping.

PART FOUR

ROADBLOCKS
(2003)

Chapter Nineteen

It was Daniel's idea to combine a morning trip to Qumran and the Dead Sea with an afternoon visit to Hebron, even though getting from one to the other meant going back through Jerusalem. And it was his idea to hire an Israeli guide for the day. His friend, Caleb, the Middle East secretary for Daniel's denomination, had been invaluable in arranging and helping lead this student tour, a January course at the seminary where Daniel taught. But Caleb was decidedly pro-Palestinian, and Daniel thought it would be good for his students to hear another voice, get another perspective.

As their bus skirted Bethlehem on the way to Hebron, Daniel, not the guide, gave a short introduction to the Tomb of the Patriarchs. "We will visit both the area where Jews are allowed to pray and the mosque", he told the sixteen students, ranging in age from Jen, who was twenty-two, to Julia, one of several second-career students, who was sixty. "On the way there, we will walk through a market that has netting above it to catch garbage dumped by Israeli settlers from their apartments. When I was here with an interfaith group, I even saw—"

The guide, Yaniv, had swiveled around in his seat at the front of the bus and now cut in. "The settlers can be a problem, that is true. But they also have been threatened. You need to hear the two sides of the story and not exaggerations. I've heard people say that the trash, some of it, is put there to make Jews look like they are bad." Daniel could see Caleb biting his tongue, and several of the students were shaking their heads—particularly Ian, who had been to Israel before and knew more than the rest of the group about the region.

The visit to the tomb went smoothly, although Daniel noticed several of the students wandered off whenever Yaniv began his explanations. But when they gathered afterward, standing in front of the mosque, Ian said, "Baruch Goldstein." He was looking directly at Yaniv. "Were you going to mention him or just pretend it didn't happen?" He turned to the other students. "Goldstein was a zealot who, about ten years ago, burst in here with his army assault rifle and killed, I think it was thirty, Muslims praying in the mosque. Wounded a hundred more. Right here! I showed Andrea the bullet holes."

The guide glared at Ian. "I was going to tell about that." He paused. "Since you know so much about history, you must know about the massacre of Jews here in Hebron in 1929. Someone started telling lies about Jews taking over Al-Aqsa Mosque in Jerusalem, and that was the excuse for killing, for raping women. They burned people alive! Hebron was a town where Jews lived during all the years of exile, but an Arab mob destroyed the houses and the Abraham synagogue. Five hundred years it was here, and they made it a place for donkeys and goats."

Ian shook his head. "I'm talking about something that just happened—well, just ten years ago—and you bring up something from a whole different era, as if that justifies anything. Jews are killing Palestinians every day, right now!"

"Be accurate," said Daniel. "Some members of the Israeli military and a few extremist settlers have, at times, killed Palestinians. And Israelis, too, have been killed in this intifada."

"Thank you," said Yaniv. Caleb started to speak, but the guide wasn't finished. "You talk about what is happening now"—looking at Ian—"but have you ever seen what it's like after a terrorist blows himself up in the middle of other people? I have. I was there when a terrorist, a woman terrorist that time, blew up a bus in Jerusalem.

Pieces of the bodies here and there, all over the street. A leg was ripped off and laying there right in front of me. Sometimes I still hear a person screaming and screaming . . . You wash and wash and wash and still it is like you have blood and little pieces of flesh all over you, in your hair and on your clothes." He stopped, and then said in a softer voice, "There is an organization called Zaka, Orthodox Jews that pick up these pieces of body. They look for them, down on their knees, all over the streets, scrape them off walls and put them in sacks so at least something, even the smallest part, even a fingernail, can be buried."

The wind was picking up, the sky a January gray, as the group stood, somber and silent. *We should get back to the bus*, Daniel thought. It was three thirty and had already been a tiring day. Besides, he was hoping to see Shoshana. On the other hand, wasn't this the kind of dialogue he hoped for as a professor? Wasn't this when learning really happened?

Julia broke the silence, almost in a whisper. "Do they only do this for Jews?"

"How would they do that? Who can tell if a foot or an ear belongs to a Jew or a Muslim or a Christian? Yes, some of the settlers, we should say it, are crazy in the head. And Goldstein was a murderer. *Yimakh shemo!* May his name be forgotten! But most Israelis don't want all this death and violence. Who would want this?" He looked around the semicircle of students. "This barrier you don't like that Israel is building, who can like it? But we need to stop the bombings."

Yaniv shook his head several times, his expression a cross between anger and sorrow. "I did not know anyone on that bus in Jerusalem, *alechem hashalom*, but a friend . . . a very good friend was killed in a bombing at the market in Netanya. She"—his voice cracked and he paused—"She and I, we sometimes argued because she was a big supporter of Palestinians. And she is the one killed. It makes everyone afraid, and then things are very dangerous."

Ian looked as if he was about to speak, but Daniel beat him to it. "I am sorry for the death of your friend."

He looked around the circle to see how all of this was being received. Jen, who rarely said anything in their public discussions, looked especially agitated. *Try to sit with her on the bus*, he told himself. But to his surprise, it was Jen who now spoke. "All this hatred! Is there anybody in Hebron who is working to make peace?"

Daniel thought immediately of the two older men—one a Christian, one a Muslim—who had met with the interfaith group eleven years before. While he was wondering if they might still be alive, Caleb answered. "The Christian Friendship Team is in Hebron, and their office isn't far from here." He looked at Daniel. "Shall I try to reach them?"

As Daniel nodded, Yaniv said, "They aren't as neutral as they pretend," but Caleb ignored him. He used his mobile phone to make sure someone was in the office, and within ten minutes the nineteen of them were climbing a rickety outside staircase and squeezing into a single room. The CFT volunteers—an older woman and a younger, robust-looking man, both Americans—apologized for not having enough cups for tea, and then explained their program as trying to be a go-between, to promote more mutual understanding here in the city they called Al-Khalil. Daniel thought he saw the Israeli guide roll his eyes at one point and exhale sharply, but he didn't interrupt.

The woman ended her part of the story by saying, "After the Goldstein massacre . . . Have you heard about—"

"Yes," said Daniel quickly, "we're familiar with it."

"After that happened, with all the blood splattered on the walls and carpets of the mosque—I've seen pictures, and it was horrible—after that there were riots. What would you expect after something like that? Anyway, Israel closed down some streets, including the main market, Shuhada Street. It's two minutes from here." She pointed toward the wall behind her. "Palestinians are forbidden to go there, but we sometimes take visitors so they can get a feel of what's going on." She glanced at her colleague. "Barry had some trouble last week, but it's usually okay. Would you like to see it?" The students thought this was a grand idea; Yaniv thought it was a terrible one; Caleb said he thought it could be an important part of their trip; and although he had mental reservations, Daniel said, "Okay, let's do it."

On the way there, the robust man, Barry, told them that *Shuhada* means "martyrs." "Martyrs Street. It would be like shutting down Broadway in New York or the Champs-Élysées in Paris."

"This," said Yaniv, "is what I mean when I say there are exaggerations."

Barry continued as if the other man hadn't spoken. "This wasn't only the main market for Palestinians in Al-Khalil, it was the main road leading to the Tomb of the Patriarchs. You used to see tour buses all along here. There are regular demonstrations demanding that the Israelis open Shuhada. And that's no exaggeration."

"Maybe not," said the guide, "but until the Jordanians took over and turned it into a market, this street was the center of life for Jews in Hebron. Why do people forget this? Why do they forget the massacre of 1929? You can't just remember yesterday and call it history."

They reached the street and, since there was no vehicle traffic, moved to the middle of the pavement, Hebron's old city to their right, a Muslim cemetery to their left. Many of the shops lining the street had metal awnings that were once green but now spotted with rust. All were closed, large padlocks attached to doors covered in graffiti. "This one," Caleb translated, "says 'Welcome to Apartheid Street,' which is what Palestinians sometimes call it."

They had walked no more than fifty yards when four heavily armed Israeli soldiers—in flak jackets, plastic face guards pulled up on top of their helmets—walked slowly from the side of the street and stood, stone-faced, in front of the group. One, who seemed slightly older than the others, said in English, "This road is closed. Why are you here?" Images of soldiers on an Old City street all those years ago flashed through Daniel's mind.

He wasn't sure whether he or one of the Christian Friendship Team should respond, but to his surprise, it was Yaniv who stepped forward, speaking to the soldier in Hebrew. At first, he was smiling, but soon it was clear that there was nothing lighthearted about their exchange. The guide turned to Daniel. "I told him who you—who we—are, but he says it is too late in the day for a group like ours to be walking here."

"Too late in the day?" Caleb said loudly. "It's not much after four o'clock. Tell him that US tax money funded the project that paved this street. We paid for it, we should be able to walk on it. Tell him that."

"I speak English," said the soldier, sounding testy. He muttered something quickly to the other three, who stayed where they were while he moved several feet away, now speaking on a two-way radio. When the soldier returned, he gestured toward Barry. "You cannot be here. You caused trouble before, so you leave." He looked back at Yaniv and said nonchalantly, "The rest of you can go ahead, as far as that tall building." He gestured down the empty pavement.

By now, Daniel had decided it was better for all of them to get off the street; but before he could say this to Caleb, Barry set off down Shuhada, walking slowly, almost a swagger. "I'm not breaking any laws," he yelled over his shoulder. "What are you going to do, shoot an American in front of twenty witnesses?"

The Israelis' guns were now raised, two pointed at Barry, two at the group. Daniel could see fear in the eyes of the students nearest him, but also in the eyes of the younger soldiers. Although it was January, a trickle of sweat ran from under the helmet of one, while another repeatedly squeezed the butt of his assault rifle. *Do something!* said a voice in Daniel's head, and before he could think further, he was shouting, "Stop!" He walked rapidly toward Barry, grabbing him by the arm. "What the hell are you doing?"—his voice low but strident. "I have sixteen students here who are my responsibility, and you just put them in danger."

"They won't dare shoot. It would cause an international incident. Don't let 'em push you around." Barry's tone was almost casual, which increased Daniel's irritation.

"Even if they don't shoot you—or, accidentally, one of us—they can hold us here for hours." He let go of Barry's arm. "This isn't peacemaking! It's provocation, with us in the middle."

"Americans *are* in the middle, whether—"

"Well, these students aren't, not today." He turned to the Israeli in charge. "If he goes back, we can go on down the street, no more trouble?" The soldier shrugged but then nodded. And after a few tense seconds, Barry also shrugged and headed back the way they had come.

As he passed the group, he said to Caleb, "This is why they get away with shit; no one stands up to them. You need to set your friend straight."

It was after five when they got back to their bus. Since this was clearly a tourist group, the minibus breezed through the Israeli checkpoints, reaching Jerusalem in less than an hour. The mood was unusually subdued, with only low conversations here and there. Daniel couldn't tell whether the students were processing what had happened or were just exhausted. Rather than find out, he spent the time staring out the window at the rocky hillsides, resolving never to take another group to Hebron.

Chapter Twenty

The years following the interfaith trip in 1992 were for Daniel the best and worst of times. His professional career flourished. He was now a tenured professor whose courses were generally well received, especially the long-running course on Jewish-Christian dialogue with Rabbi Eisen. He published three books in the century's last decade, the most popular being *Sacred City: The Problem of Jerusalem in Israeli-Palestinian Relations*.

He was also frequently invited to give public lectures, including on his favorite topic: "Jerusalem: Why It is Holy to Three Religions—and to Me." Jerusalem, he told audiences, has been far more imagined than experienced. Often he would have pictures projected while describing how idealized paintings of the Holy City proliferated in medieval Europe. "Meanwhile, Jews have continued to pray at Passover, 'Next year in Jerusalem!' The city has been an object of longing for both Jews and Christians, frequently depicted as a woman: Jerusalem the widow, Jerusalem the harlot, Jerusalem the daughter of Zion, Jerusalem the bride of Christ. The problem," he would add, "is that many have thought the real Jerusalem must be destroyed in order that the ideal might come to pass."

Daniel was also interviewed by *The Columbus Dispatch* and the local PBS and NBC stations regarding the Oslo Accords. The establishment of the Palestinian Authority and the commitment to peace negotiations are encouraging, he told each of them, but the devil will be in the details. And those included the status of Jerusalem.

"What do *you* think should happen with Jerusalem?" the newspaper reporter asked him.

Daniel tried to dodge the question. "Let's see what the negotiators come up with."

But the reporter persisted.

"I think," said Daniel, after a pause, "that the predominantly Jewish areas of the city should be Israeli, the rest part of a future Palestine. This likely means that Jerusalem will be the capital of both countries. The Palestinians should have sovereignty over the Dome of the Rock and the Al-Aqsa Mosque, the Israelis over the Western Wall. And the UN should be asked to guarantee that the Old City and surrounding holy sites will be open to everyone. But I don't expect any of the parties would be satisfied with such a proposal."

At the same time that Daniel's career was coming together, his marriage was falling apart. His success actually added to Peg's resentment, or so it seemed to him. His increased travel and church involvement meant less time together, which may have been part of the point, or so it seemed to her. With no children to raise, with few shared interests or commitments, and with Shoshana always in the back of his mind, the relationship deteriorated until divorce was the obvious option. He moved out in June of 1993, and it became official by the end of the year.

He wrote about all of this to Shoshana. In fact, he now told her things he didn't say to anyone else. It was safe to pour out his fluctuating emotions to someone six thousand miles away. But more than that, since his last trip to Jerusalem, they had a bond he had trouble putting into words. She didn't know him as a teacher or scholar. She only knew him as the Daniel he was with her, and she seemed to like—no, more than like—that Daniel. She demanded nothing of him, expected nothing from him. She was clearly delighted when he was happy, sad when he was distressed. She remembered him as someone willing to put himself in new situations, which encouraged him to hold on to this trait. She remembered him as a young man who listened more than he talked, which encouraged him to keep this characteristic as he aged. Maybe they couldn't be together physically, but wasn't there a genuine intimacy to what they now shared? Could it even be, he wondered, that they were better together when they were physically apart? Wasn't he a better, more understanding person on paper than he was ever likely to be in the flesh?

Until Daniel moved out of the house he shared with Peg, Shoshana sent her letters to the seminary's address. Maggie, who sorted the mail, may have raised her eyebrows at the number of envelopes with Israeli stamps, but she made no comment to Daniel, not even when he couldn't hide his excitement at receiving a letter or his disappointment when four or five days passed without one.

He read some of her letters over and over until the words permeated his thoughts. Some relationships, she told him more than once, just run their course, like hers with Yossi. You love one another, are important to one another, have special, even irreplaceable, times together, but gradually you both change. It was her regular refrain: Don't beat yourself up, don't be a martyr. You deserve to be happy, and so does Peg.

Are you happy? he asked her, but it was the one question she never answered directly. She liked her work with new immigrants, although government regulations could be a pain. She had a good circle of friends, never suggesting any of them were more than that. She enjoyed seeing her sister Rahel and family for holidays, although her father's death left a hole. Above all, she loved her daughter. She was proud when Ofra began her service in Tzahal, the Israel Defense Forces, she worried when Ofra was stationed on the Lebanese border, and she rejoiced when Ofra finished her regular military service and entered Hebrew University in the fall of 1996. Since the university was in Jerusalem, they spent lots of time together, which Shoshana wrote about at length in her letters. She also sent pictures: she and Ofra at a café near her apartment, the two of them on a day trip to the Dead Sea and at Rahel's for Passover, even mother and daughter in front of the Western Wall.

Then came word that Ofra had been accepted for a semester of study at Georgetown University in Washington, DC, scheduled to arrive at the end of August 1997.

I didn't tell you she'd applied, Shoshana wrote, *in case she wasn't accepted, or changed her mind, which she often does. But it now seems to be a go. I can't believe the two of you have never met. How can that be? I know you're busy, but I would love it if you could go see her.*

As it happened, Daniel was scheduled to speak at a conference in Philadelphia the first week in October. He made plans to take a train from Philly to DC, and arranged through Shoshana to meet Ofra at a restaurant just off Dupont Circle.

Shoshana said her daughter might be late, and she was, more than twenty minutes. When she finally entered the restaurant, Daniel recognized her immediately, not only from the pictures, but because she reminded him so much of a younger Shoshana. Solid, but not overweight, like her mother. Thick, dark hair, like her mother. That slightly protruding upper lip. Even the way she tilted her head when she looked at him.

The dinner, however, was awkward. Ofra answered his questions without elaboration, showing enthusiasm only when speaking of the university's pool where she swam daily. She declined dessert, even though he highly recommended the cheesecake.

But she did agree to coffee, and while they were waiting for it, finally said what he suspected was on her mind all along. "I don't get it. What are you to *Ema*, to my mother?"

The coffee arrived, and Daniel waited until the server was gone before he asked, "What does she say?"

A slight smile. "That's what she would do, answer with a question. She says you are good friends, but people who are just friends don't write each other two or three times a week. And now that you have email, I bet it's every day. She even has a picture of you two in her bedroom," a revelation that pleased Daniel greatly, though he tried not to show it.

He studied her face. The same deep-set eyes, which made them look even darker. "Yes, we have been more than just friends." Then, before he could overthink it, he added, "I have been in love with your mother since 1969." He paused, but she was silent. "Actually, I'm hoping you might want to transfer here so maybe she would join you."

A smile, and again he could see Shoshana across the table. "She said you might say that. But I still don't get it. What kind of . . . love affair is it when you only see each other once a decade or something?"

"This one, I guess."

Ofra shook her head. "You know, she has a life. She isn't just sitting around waiting for you."

"No, I don't suppose she is." He could feel his stomach tighten as he said, "I take it there's someone there you think she should be with."

"My father, but that's not going to happen."

"Look, I'm not trying—"

"I don't even mean that. They weren't right for each other, especially . . . I don't know about that part of her life. But I can't see how writing to you can be enough. I don't get it."

Daniel finished his coffee, realizing the conversation was beginning to get on his nerves. "Why does this bother you? That's what *I* don't get. If your mother is happy, why not just be happy for her, for us? Is there some book that says two people can't love each other, *really* love each other, long distance?"

"I've got homework to do," she said abruptly. "Thanks for dinner." She extended her hand for a formal shake and then was gone, leaving Daniel to berate himself for what he'd said.

Ofra was right about one thing: They now emailed almost every day, sometimes more. Daniel didn't tell Shoshana much about the dinner with her daughter, and he noticed that, after an initial inquiry, she didn't ask. As she would say, it was what it was.

So he was surprised when Shoshana wrote that Ofra would like to see him one more time before she returned to Israel. Could he come sometime the week of December 7, preferably at the beginning of the week? As it happened, his courses were over on the 5th, final papers not due until the 12th. He booked a flight, arriving in Washington on the afternoon of Monday, December 8, and when he came out into the main terminal, there was Shoshana.

He held her long enough that when they finally let go, she said, "It's a good thing I left Ofra in the restaurant, or we would have embarrassed her." That wonderful smile. As they made their way to where Ofra was waiting, Shoshana added, "I want you to know that it was her idea I come. My thoughtful daughter told me that coming here was more important than my work." She let go of his hand and turned to face him. "And she brought up the idea of inviting you to come, although she knew that's what I wanted. She said that as long as we're in love we ought to spend time in the same city, even if it's not Jerusalem."

Daniel changed his return flight, extended his hotel reservation, and stayed until Friday evening. He would have made it longer, but Shoshana was clear that she needed to spend the weekend with Ofra. "Let her show me her Washington before we both fly back on Sunday evening. But she still has courses to finish until then, so the week is pretty much ours."

It was one of the greatest weeks of his life. Shoshana, of course, stayed at the hotel, which meant intimate nights and mornings that conjured memories of the spring of 1970 when they were young—and Israel, having reclaimed the Wall, was still hopeful. Since Shoshana had never been to the city, they visited the National Gallery, toured the Capitol, and strolled, bundled up, on the Mall. But much of their time was spent talking in coffee shops and neighborhood cafés: about the people she worked with and the students he taught, about Jerusalem and how it was changing, about new settlements that were sprouting across the West Bank, about the future. "Let's see what Ofra decides to do," she told him. "I might end up here, after all."

On Wednesday, they had dinner with Ofra, who was far more

relaxed and friendly than she had been when she and Daniel met in October. She spoke with enthusiasm about her courses at Georgetown and laughed in a pleasant way as her mother told of Daniel's attempt to speak Hebrew at Passover, and how gently he tapped people with his plastic hammer on Purim. "You know," said Shoshana, no longer smiling, "that square where we were on Purim is where Yitzhak Rabin was assassinated. It's hard to think of it now as a place to celebrate. As if Israel has anything to celebrate."

Ofra threw her head back, smiling. "Ema, you are always so negative! Israel survives when no one expects it to, when all the world is against it. It always does what it has to do." She paused, looking at her mother. "But maybe living there is getting to you a little." Another pause. "You know, I don't understand why the two of you don't just go ahead and live in the same place. You seem pretty happy together."

Daniel began to say, "Because your mother wants to be near you," but decided against it.

Chapter Twenty-One

Small-scale violence had continued to roil the Jerusalem area in the final years of the century, including the bludgeoning deaths of an Israeli couple in the settlement next to Neve Ya'akov. Then everything escalated in the year 2000. In July, Israeli Prime Minister Ehud Barak, Palestinian Authority Chairman Yasser Arafat, and President Bill Clinton met at Camp David for a peace summit, trying to revive momentum lost in the years since the Oslo Accords. Ultimately, the effort stumbled over four seemingly intractable issues: the amount of territory under Palestinian sovereignty; the rights of Palestinian refugees who fled, or were expelled, from Israel during the fighting in 1948; the steps Israel could take to preserve its security; and what to do with Jerusalem. Daniel followed these developments closely, informed by materials sent to him by his denomination's Middle East expert, Caleb Sadek.

On September 28, three weeks into Daniel's fall semester, Ariel Sharon, leader of the main opposition party in Israel, made an in-your-face visit to Haram al-Sharif, the Temple Mount. Guarded by hundreds of armed Israeli riot police, he posed for pictures in front of Al-Aqsa. Predictably, the Old City erupted the next day following prayers. Palestinians threw stones over the Western Wall at Jewish worshippers, the Israelis responding with live ammunition after the chief of police was knocked unconscious by a stone. As the protests spread across the West Bank and Gaza, Daniel thought often of the day Al-Aqsa burned. He could feel the crush of the crowd on El-Wad, hear again the pain and anger in the chanting. And these memories made the current events seem even more immediate.

"What do you think about the uproar in Jerusalem?" he asked the seminary's president. "I'm having a hard time keeping to my syllabus because it feels like we should be talking about what's happening now."

"I have to admit," the president told him, "I haven't really been following it."

On October 12, Palestinian Authority police arrested two Israeli reservists who had accidentally strayed into the outskirts of Ramallah. A crowd—angered by Sharon's hour of arrogance, by weeks of tear gas and bullets, by years of occupation—stormed the police station where they beat, stabbed, and hideously disemboweled the hapless reservists, all of it captured on video by an Italian television crew. Israel responded with air strikes at targets in the West Bank and Gaza, and the second intifada, often called the Al-Aqsa Intifada because of where it all began, was well underway.

The following year witnessed a wave of suicide bombings in Israeli cities, including Jerusalem. One on a crowded bus Daniel had ridden with Shoshana. One in front of a pizza parlor where they had eaten with friends. One near the gates of a school he had often walked past, the head of the bomber thudding into the schoolyard as children played.

In response, "Stand with Israel" rallies were organized across the United States. Daniel was asked by the Jewish Federation to speak at the one in Columbus, which he agreed to do against the advice of several faculty colleagues. "Standing with Israel," he said in his remarks, "does not mean standing against the Palestinian people and their legitimate aspirations for peace and security. But it does mean saying 'No!' emphatically to suicide bombings and other acts of terror against civilians. The time when friends stand with friends is not simply when it is easy to do so, but precisely when it isn't. Now is such a time to stand with Israel."

He received lots of gratifying affirmation from the local Jewish community. Devorah sent a note that read *You are a mensch!* But as Israel began building its separation barrier, in some places a cement wall, twenty-six feet high, he began to have second thoughts. Was this the Israel he had known in 1969? Did standing with Israel mean endorsing a repressive government? And such thoughts multiplied after a phone call from his friend Caleb.

"Royce sent me a copy of your remarks at the pro-Israel rally. He said you shared it with him and others on the faculty."

"Yeah, I thought it was important to say something given what's going on, the bombings and all. And I've had some indication that even seminary faculty don't follow the situation very closely."

"I get it," said Caleb. "But, you know, Israel is also killing civilians."

"Of course I know. It's all bad. If there's a 'Stand with Palestinians' rally, I'll be willing to speak at it, too."

"That's part of the problem. Israel has a big lobby that organizes rallies. But who stands up for Palestine?"

Through all of this, Daniel was in daily email contact with Shoshana. Was she being careful? Why was she still riding buses? What was the mood among her friends and colleagues? And every few days, they talked by phone, including after the pizza parlor bombing.

"I'm safe," she told him, "but of course I worry about Ofra. She's out around the city more than I am. Out with her new friend, Adam."

"Do you think this separation barrier will help?"

Shoshana laughed, but with an edge of bitterness. "'Separation barrier.' As if we don't have enough walls."

"I thought it might help people feel less afraid."

"Or make us more afraid. From what I read, the Western press makes it seem that Israelis and Palestinians live in completely separate worlds. But that's not how it's been, at least not for me. I told you, I had Palestinian clients when I did social work for the government. When I lived at Neve Ya'akov, I bought vegetables at a Palestinian market. I can't remember his name, but I can picture the man who used to repair our car. Now they're just going to be those scary people we can't see on the other side of the wall." She took a deep breath. "But maybe it will stop some of the bombings. I don't know what to think anymore."

It felt to Daniel as if they, too, were separated by a wall, a wide wall of water. But it was not impenetrable. In 1999, Daniel accepted an invitation to speak at an October conference hosted by the Vatican. The minute it was over, he told Shoshana, he would come to Jerusalem. She had a better idea, one that involved traveling on her part. And so, while it wasn't Jerusalem, they had four spectacular days in Rome, strolling through museums without the hassle of summertime crowds, lingering in cafés around the Pantheon and the Campo de' Fiori, and, of course, enjoying one another.

By this time, Daniel had already begun speaking with the seminary's dean about making his three-week course in January of 2001 a study tour of Israel-Palestine. Plans were on track when the intifada derailed them. "It's just too risky," the dean announced, as if Daniel wasn't well aware of the risks. "And there are too many places you would want to go that are off-limits, at least for now."

So that summer Shoshana spent two weeks in Columbus—"at the urging of my daughter"—which for Daniel was wonderful, but also heightened the frustration of not being together more often.

The travel seminar, rescheduled for January of 2002, was again postponed due to the violence of the intifada. Daniel resolved to go on his own in June of that year, but then his mother had a debilitating stroke and the plans were shelved. "We have a harder time getting together than Israelis and Palestinians," he lamented to Shoshana on one of their regular phone calls.

This feeling was reinforced when a visit Shoshana was planning for the fall was scuttled after Ofra was in an automobile accident. "Her leg will heal, but it's not a good time for me to be gone."

So he stepped up his plans for a travel seminar in January 2003. Caleb agreed to help set up the itinerary, even go with him and the students as long as Daniel agreed to meet Palestinian leaders and truly expose the students to life under occupation. "Yes," Daniel assured him, "I want this trip to focus on the West Bank, using Jerusalem as our base. A political focus. No side excursions to places like Eilat." Enrollment for the seminar was capped at sixteen, and the slots were immediately filled.

Chapter Twenty-Two

The student group had arrived at Ben Gurion Airport on Monday, January 12, and despite Daniel's resolve, spent the first five days in the Galilee. "These are Christian seminarians," the dean pointed out when Daniel presented him with a proposed itinerary. "They need to visit the places where Jesus lived and preached. This travel seminar shouldn't be all about politics, not if the seminary is going to sponsor it."

So it wasn't until Saturday the 17th that the group of sixteen students, Caleb, and Daniel boarded their twenty-five person minibus, just as Shabbat was ending, for the hour-and-a-half drive from Nazareth to Jerusalem. Their lodging for the remainder of the trip was the guesthouse of St. George's Cathedral, an Anglican church only eight minutes on foot from the Damascus Gate. It was nearly seven o'clock by the time they arrived, and most of the group were happy for a quick dinner in the cathedral dining hall before turning in.

Daniel, of course, left immediately to see Shoshana, who was living in the Rehavia neighborhood of new Jerusalem. "Come whenever you can get away from your students," she told him. "Just don't bring any of them with you." As if the thought had crossed his mind.

Although Rehavia is fairly near the Old City, it was too far for Daniel to walk. He found a taxi and within minutes was at her apartment, where she met him at the door, arms outstretched, wearing a turban instead of her usual hat. They kissed even before entering the apartment, but it was soon apparent that Shoshana wanted to talk before anything else transpired. She pointed him toward an armchair and pulled its twin until they were facing one another, knees almost touching, which is when he saw her missing eyebrows. Before he could ask, she said, "You need to see something, or maybe I should say there is something I need to tell you, and this is one way to do it." She pulled off the one-piece turban to reveal her baldness.

For the next few minutes, Daniel held her hand while she answered his barrage of questions. Breast cancer, diagnosed early in December . . . The results of the chemotherapy will determine the extent of the surgery . . . Here in Jerusalem at Hadassah . . . Yes, they think they caught it fairly early . . .

"Why would I tell you this in a letter or a phone call when I could tell you face-to-face in a month or so? You didn't need to be worried about me while you were finishing a semester and getting ready for this trip."

And then the question she seemed to be expecting: "Why don't you come to the US for treatment? There's a cancer center associated with the big university in Columbus. A colleague was a patient there and said it's first-rate. I can—"

"Daniel, my love, listen to yourself. We have great health care in Israel, including an oncologist I really like. We export doctors to America, for God's sake! And besides, my treatment here is basically free."

"I have full health coverage through the seminary."

His grip tightened, and she now pulled her hands away. "Yes, I'm sure, for you . . . and your wife." They sat looking at each other, Shoshana smiling slightly. "Daniel Jacobs, are you proposing to me?"

"Who else could I marry? You already know all my secrets." The silence was intense until he said, "Shoshana Broder, I have been proposing to you for years. I just didn't do it quite like an Israeli."

They were both smiling, but he could see tears in her eyes and feel them in his. She took his hand. "We both know . . ." She stopped mid-sentence and sat quietly for a moment, looking down. "There was a time when Ofra might have moved. All she could talk about was Mariah Carey and Janet Evans and Amy what's-her-name because she was such a swimmer. After I left Yossi, she wanted us to live in Tel Aviv where she could swim in the sea and live more like an American. But now she's almost thirty. She has a job, a job she likes. She has a husband who has a good job in Israel. She's not leaving, no matter how insane things get here."

Shoshana had been sitting on the edge of the chair, but now leaned back. "Do you know what I fear the most?" She didn't wait for an answer. "I've thought about this a lot. It's not the cancer, though that's scary. My mother 'disappeared' when I was eight, you know about all that, and I have always been afraid that, for some reason, I wouldn't be there for Ofra. Now that she's older, this may sound a little silly, but that's been my biggest fear." She smiled. "Sometime you can tell me yours."

She stood up abruptly and walked toward the small kitchen, motioning for him to follow. "It's been long enough since my last chemo, so I declare that I am eligible for a glass of wine. Besides, this is a special occasion, a celebration. But if I get sick to my stomach, I'm blaming you!" That smile. "And I bet you're hungry."

Daniel opened the wine while she scooped hummus onto a plate. As she was cutting pita in half, he said softly, "I am willing—I *want*—to marry you, even if we don't live in the same place."

Her back was to him, and she didn't turn around. But she did nod, as if this, too, was not unexpected. "Why would you want to make a long-term commitment when I may not have . . ." He started to protest, but she added quickly, "Let me get through the treatment, and then we'll see what happens." She turned. "Okay?"

He pulled her to him, but gently, and they stood that way until Shoshana stepped back, wiping her eyes. "It really is crazy, isn't it? How long were we together, if you can call weekends being together? Maybe four months, thirty years ago?" She smiled. "You've actually been in love with different women; you know that, don't you? Not just that I've begun to wrinkle and have gray hair, when I had hair. I've been a daughter and a student, a wife and a settler, sort of, then a mother. And to think that no matter how much I change, there is this crazy American"— she was crying harder—"who says . . ."

Daniel stepped toward her, but her look stopped him. "Have you been thinking about all this, or just when you heard about the cancer?" Now her expression was almost fierce. "If you wanted to be with me, Daniel, why didn't you come more often, or move here? Why were you still married when Ofra might have been willing to move? Why has this been so fucking *hard*!"

Even though he now held her too tightly, she didn't protest.

Daniel was back at St. George's before the others were up in order to shower and change clothes. The strain of the previous evening must have been evident, however, because as they were getting coffee Caleb asked, "You okay?" Daniel beckoned for Caleb to walk with him down a hallway, apart from where students were beginning to gather.

"The friend I went to see yesterday, she isn't well. I'll tell you the details later, but can you cover for me if I need to slip away again this evening, and also later in the week?" Caleb nodded, and after shaking hands they returned to the dining hall.

Since it was Sunday, the group worshipped with the cathedral's congregation, the service conducted in both Arabic and English. Daniel spent the first few minutes praying silently that God would heal Shoshana (although he usually didn't believe that's how God worked), his attention returning to the worship at hand just in time for the sermon.

The biblical texts were taken from the lectionary, but the sermon itself, preached by the priest of the cathedral, felt as if it were aimed at the seminary visitors. "'Come and see' Jesus told the two disciples who followed him. It was an invitation that echoed Psalm 34: 'O taste and see that the Lord is good.' Come and see for yourself, with your own eyes, what good things God is doing through his Son. It is a calling at the heart of Christian faith." The sanctuary's vaulted ceiling and rough limestone walls made his deep voice even more resonant. "But 'come and see' is also the message we Palestinian Christians give to the world. Don't rely on the press or on the word of friends or, God forbid, on travel brochures. Come and see with your own eyes the reality of our lives. Come and see the faces of people living under occupation. Come and see that God upholds us and sees us, even when the world turns its back."

Students were still talking about the sermon that afternoon when the priest and the bishop, both Palestinians, met with the group for a time of welcome and orientation. "We hope," said the priest in his Oxford-inflected English, "that you have come to see, not just the monumental stones of history, but the living stones of our present community." When he sat down, the students applauded.

The jovial-looking bishop began his remarks by asking, "Have you heard that we have a little conflict in this part of the world?" The students dutifully chuckled. But then his tone changed abruptly. "When people think of this as a fight between Jews and Muslims, they have missed something essential, because Christians are essential to Palestine. The followers of Jesus have lived in the land of Jesus for two thousand years. But today, there are more Christian Palestinians living in Chile than in Palestine. At the time of the Nakba—independence for Israel, catastrophe for us—at that time, there were more than thirty thousand Christians living in Jerusalem. Now there are ten thousand."

"Not even that many," said the priest, and the bishop nodded.

"Because the occupation makes it too difficult to live—to find a job, to find a house, to get health care, to travel. People must leave this place they love, this place that for them is home."

"See for yourself," the priest added. "That's what I was saying this morning. We are glad you have come to see for yourself."

While the two church leaders were speaking, a middle-aged woman, wearing a baggy sweater, had slipped quietly into the back of the room. Once the bishop sat down, also to warm applause, Caleb introduced the woman as a spokesperson for the mayor's office. Why,

Daniel wondered, had Caleb included her on the itinerary when what they were likely to get was a boilerplate "welcome to our city" speech?

He let his mind drift to thoughts of Shoshana, until he heard the woman say "Come and see"—she nodded toward the priest—"that your ideas about Israel may not all be true. You may have heard that where there are three Jews, there are four opinions, and that *is* true." No chuckles, but the students seemed attentive. "In America, you have two political parties. Here in Israel, we have thirteen parties in what we call the Knesset because we have many—how do you say it?—points of view. That means many disagreements about the conflict with Palestinians. As our friends here in this church know, there are Israeli organizations that protest against home demolitions and others that protest because they think we are too weak on terrorists. There are settlers who think the whole land, from the Mediterranean Sea to the Jordan River, is ours, and there are Israelis like my cousin who think the Palestinians should have their own country, with its capital in Jerusalem." She smiled. "Being the mayor of Jerusalem is a very hard job."

There was a glass of water on the table near where she was standing, and she paused to take a drink. "I heard the priest say 'come and see.' Yes, come and see all the differences, but please keep this in your minds: Israel, tiny Israel with not seven million people, is surrounded by nations, with more than two hundred million people, that have tried to destroy it. More than once. In Gaza, the strongest party says it wants to drive all Jews out of the land. We have many points of view, but all of us—Orthodox and not religious, Ashkenazi and Sephardi— we all want, like any people must want, to have security and to live in peace." Tough questions followed, but when the mayor's spokesperson left, there was applause and a handshake from the bishop.

Although it wasn't on the schedule, Caleb offered to take the students for dinner at a restaurant near the Jaffa Gate. "We can talk about what we heard this afternoon, and going inside the walls will be an appetizer for the banquet later in the week when we explore the whole Old City." He pointed toward Daniel. "Your professor, who is the one in charge, has to take care of some trip-related business, so we will see him tomorrow."

Shoshana was more like her old self that evening: happy, talkative, sexy. They even took a walk in her leafy neighborhood, his arm around her as she pointed out her grocery store and favorite bakery. For the first time since he saw the missing eyebrows, the knot in his stomach began to unravel.

As a result, Daniel was in a better frame of mind when he greeted Caleb and the students on Monday morning. Over breakfast, with the students clustered around two tables, he gave a short presentation on the history of Jerusalem, emphasizing that the religious identity of the city's rulers had changed no fewer than eleven times. He found this interesting, but the students clearly had other things in mind.

"I heard that Dean Frazier wants this trip to be about religion," said Corey, a former teacher in his thirties. "But some of us were talking, and we're hoping to focus more on the political situation, like we did yesterday."

"Your mini lectures on religious things are good," added Julia quickly, "but now maybe we're ready for something else."

Daniel smiled. "Well, you're in luck. This week, thanks in large part to Caleb, you'll get a real taste of how Palestinians, and a few Israelis, experience what's going on."

"But also," said Caleb, "how it relates to the church. Religion and politics in this part of the world . . ." He held up his hands with his fingers interlaced.

They began their investigation that morning by meeting with mission workers and local doctors at the Augusta Victoria Hospital, which sits prominently on the ridge of the Mount of Olives. Daniel and Caleb had scheduled this stop on the itinerary to show how church mission dollars are spent providing health care, but it quickly became political when a doctor described how dialysis patients must pass through as many as five checkpoints, three times a week, for treatment. "Navigating Israeli security," he told them, "makes dialysis a full-time occupation." He then recounted the story of a patient who had a heart attack and died on the way to the hospital after a two-hour delay at a checkpoint. "I know this is the truth," said the doctor, his face grim, "because he was my father."

Most of the students were visibly upset as they left Augusta Victoria—especially Donna, a former nurse—and this attitude was reinforced by an afternoon visit to Bethlehem.

Daniel had intended for their time, in what had once been a predominantly Christian town, to highlight the work of local churches in promoting Palestinian art and culture. Maybe culture could be a bridge. He even considered inviting Shoshana to see the work of Palestinian artists. Would that be possible? Would she do it?

But this visit, too, became political as soon as their bus had to pass through the massive gray wall that now encircled much of the town. Once inside, the students insisted on stopping to take photos of the graffiti adorning the concrete barrier: *Free Palestine! Make hummus not walls. Don't forget the struggle!* Several had their picture taken in front of a painting of Israeli soldiers, their rifles aimed at a woman waving a Palestinian flag, others in front of the painting of a small Palestinian girl frisking an Israeli soldier as he stands facing the wall.

The Lutheran pastor did show them his church's art gallery and studio, but he was also more than ready to point out damage to the church building caused by an Israeli tank during fighting in 2002, and to answer questions about the wall. "You have seen it, how our whole town is like a prison. If *you* want to go to Jerusalem, you just go. But for us, it is often not possible." After three or four questions, all having to do with the political situation, he stood up. "Come," he said. "I will show you something."

They loaded into the bus and drove to a small house that seemed to rest against the wall that loomed behind it. The pastor led them around the house to where the wall was no more than eight feet from the back door, the face of a child appearing at a window. "The Muslehs are members of our church, so I am welcome to bring you here. Mr. Musleh owned an orchard where his children played. It is now on the other side." He made a fist and hit the wall lightly. "This man did not do anything against the law or the military," said the pastor. "His 'crime' was being Palestinian."

There were several seconds of silence before Jen asked softly, "Is there any hope?"

"Oh, yes!" said the pastor with surprising exuberance. "Israel has won military victories with all its weapons, but you saw the pictures on the wall. When the image of Palestinians in the eyes of the world is not guerillas with guns but children throwing rocks, then we have won the bigger battle."

Chapter Twenty-Three

Daniel called Shoshana as soon as the group arrived back at the cathedral. "It was a tough day," he told her. "More so than I expected."

She didn't ask him for specifics. Instead, she said, "You should stay with your students this evening. I will rest and see you tomorrow."

Caleb agreed with Daniel that a relaxing, upbeat dinner was in order, so they reserved tables for eighteen in the courtyard restaurant of the nearby Jerusalem Hotel, an old Arab mansion with wooden latticework, rough limestone walls, and painted tiles. It was cool when they arrived at half past seven, but not cold, despite being the middle of January. While they ate, a trio of musicians—playing oud, flute, and riq—provided background music, and partway through the evening, an older man began the rhythmic dancing, which brought several of the seminarians to their feet. Water pipes were available, and some took the opportunity to try them. The mood of the group, which had been heavy, grew lighter.

Daniel's comments were consistent across various conversations: Life for Palestinians could be grueling, they saw that today. But there is also joy, as they saw that evening. Tomorrow, they would hear from other Christian leaders, visit a Palestinian village, get still more perspectives. They should take it all in. Keep an open mind.

The next morning, however, got off to a rocky start when the first meeting of the day was canceled. "I thought we were going to have a conversation with a Presbyterian aid worker from the US," Caleb told the group at breakfast, "but something came up, and she's still in a town north of here."

"Let's have another cup of coffee," said Daniel, "then go into the Old City. We can wander for a few minutes in the Christian Quarter before our meeting with the Orthodox patriarch at ten thirty. By the way, the proper way to address him is 'Your Beatitude.'"

"That may stick in the throat of a low-church Protestant like me," said Andrea, and everyone laughed, including Daniel.

At 10:55 they were ushered by a priest, who wore a black cassock, into an ornately furnished room and directed to chairs lining the two long walls, portraits of bishops staring solemnly above their heads. After a few minutes of subdued conversation among themselves, they were served tea and pastries; and sometime after eleven thirty, the white-bearded patriarch entered, flanked by priests, and took his place in a large gilded chair. Speaking through an interpreter, he welcomed the group to "the Holy City where our Lord and Savior suffered, died, was buried, and on the third day rose from the dead. We are the keepers of his blessed memory, the preservers of the true faith that is the hope of the world."

Daniel responded by thanking His Beatitude for his gracious hospitality, explaining (since the patriarch didn't seem to have been briefed) that they were from a school of theology in America. "We know your time is valuable, but we would be honored if you would entertain a few of our questions." Out of the corner of his eye, he could see that some of the students were barely suppressing smiles.

The first question came from Heather, a seminarian not long out of college, who skipped the formal salutation. "What's the biggest problem you face as a church?"

The patriarch murmured several sentences to the interpreter, who cleared his throat before saying, "His Beatitude would like you to know that our biggest problem is the Christians moving out of the Holy Land to countries like yours." The patriarch murmured again. "The problem is that, with less people, we cannot repair our churches, and some are in bad repair." He looked at the patriarch, who nodded.

Two questions followed about the Israeli occupation of the West Bank and Gaza. Doesn't your church see *this* as a major problem? *The* major problem? The interpreter nodded slowly after listening to the patriarch. "His Beatitude wants me to remind you that your country is very young. The church here has survived many wars and conflicts. It will be here, giving praise and witness to our Lord, when all politicians are returned to dust."

The final question came from Julia. "Your Beatitude," she began, glaring at other students, "I realize and appreciate that the church is not a political organization, but Christians are still called in scripture to be peacemakers. I would like to know if the division of the various churches makes it hard to work for peace."

The patriarch smiled as Julia was speaking. "There are no divisions," he replied in heavily accented English. "The Body of Christ is . . ."

He spoke softly to the interpreter, who finished the sentence. ". . . is like a cloth with no seams or tears."

The students were still buzzing about this encounter as they ate falafel sandwiches at Samir's hole-in-the-wall café on Christian Quarter Road. Once everyone had food, Samir stood on a chair to announce that "Daniel is my good, good friend from long ago. Friends of him are friends of me!" He smiled, wiping his hands on his Penn State T-shirt, while the group applauded.

It was already after one o'clock when they boarded their bus and headed south toward the West Bank village of Fadal. But unbeknownst to Caleb, the unpaved road to the village had been made impassable by piles of dirt and rock. They were forced to abandon their minibus just off the highway between Bethlehem and Hebron and walk the final half mile. Many of the students were wearing tennis shoes, but that didn't keep them from slipping and sliding over the mounds of dirt. Those in dressier shoes had an even harder time, so Corey, Heather, and Eric moved back and forth, offering a hand to those who needed it. As they rounded a corner, the village now in sight, a massive bulldozer, with CATERPILLAR emblazoned on its side, sat like some monstrous creature across much of the road. At Ian's suggestion, they took a group picture in front of it, several students making a V sign with their fingers.

As soon as they had passed the first building, the group was welcomed by the head of the village council—a man Caleb had met on previous visits—who escorted them to his home. The concrete block house had a surprisingly large room obviously meant for entertaining; instead of chairs, a wooden bench with cushions was built into three of the walls. "Sit, sit," the man told them when Jen and Eric offered to stand. But no sooner were they all seated than he invited them to lift the bench seats, where, to their delight, they discovered several plates of Palestinian sweets, and soon his wife and daughter began serving tea.

"We call this tea *maramia*," the older woman said to the group. "I don't know your word for it."

"Sage," Caleb told her.

"I hope you gave them money for all of this," Daniel whispered to him.

While they were sipping the hot tea, the man who had welcomed them made introductions. "I am Naeem, my wife is named Maryam. And this is our daughter, Aisha. Aisha has a sister, she studies in Nablus, and a brother, he has work in Amman. Someday soon, Aisha also will leave us." The girl smiled. "It is not our will, but it is, perhaps, the will of Allah. There is nothing in Fadal for young people."

He had sounded wistful, but his tone now changed abruptly. "You have seen our trees with so many oranges? *Alhamdu lillah*. It means 'praise to God.' You are too late by a little for the harvest of olives." He paused. "Caleb knows we are a small village with only ten families to work in the fields and in the orchards."

"Extended families," said Caleb. "Everybody's related to the others, in some fashion."

Naeem nodded and smiled, then looked around the room. "You will wish to ask, 'Why is the road made so you cannot drive a car on it?' The Israelis will say they are building a road to the settlement, the one you can see from the edge of the village. But the real reason is that we make a protest."

"Some boys from Fadal," Caleb clarified, "have been arrested during the intifada."

"Yes, so the Israelis play these little games."

"We are better than some villages," said Maryam, who was standing in the doorway to the kitchen. "A village close to here has no electric."

"It's true," said Naeem. "It has been a promise for years, but nothing."

"All they have is . . ." She asked her husband a question in Arabic.

"Generators," he told her.

She nodded. "They have two generators. That is all. Here our children can read and study in the night."

Following a few questions, the students were invited to wander in the village. "Go in small groups, three or four, so you can all talk," Naeem urged them. "Go in our store. The young people and some of the others speak English." Daniel was about to join one of the groups when Naeem tapped him on the shoulder. "Perhaps you will come with me."

As they walked toward the east edge of the village, Naeem said, "I learn from Caleb that you once study in Tel Aviv."

"One year, many years ago. But even then, I spent a lot of time in old Jerusalem."

Naeem nodded. "That is good, but Jerusalem is like another world. There is no place like Jerusalem."

They had reached a spot where the land dropped off sharply. Below them was a new road, under construction, leading to the settlement that was off to their right. Ahead of them—not two hundred yards away, but on the other side of the ravine—was a man with a donkey, plowing a small plot of land. "That land," said Naeem with a sweep of his hand, "that land will be taken soon. The Israelis have not told us yet, but I am sure of it."

"Then why is he plowing?" They stood for a minute in silence before Naeem turned and they headed back toward the center of the village.

It was not a long ride back to Jerusalem, once they had climbed over the piles of dirt on the way to their bus, but long enough for Jen, Heather, and Eric to tell Daniel about their encounter with a very angry woman. "She's about my age," said Jen. "Her English was not great—"

"Better than our Arabic," said Eric.

Jen ignored him. "But we could get the point. Her brother and one of his friends from another village—I think that's what she said—are in prison for throwing stones."

"She wanted to know what we could do about it," said Heather. "I think she knew we couldn't do anything, but she kept asking and asking until I just wanted to get away."

After dinner in the cathedral, Daniel took a taxi to Shoshana's apartment where they spent a quiet evening, much of it with her head in his lap as he talked about the students, the fun time they had at the Jerusalem Hotel, and their meeting, such as it was, with the patriarch. He said almost nothing about the village.

He was back early to the cathedral guesthouse in order to prepare for what he hoped would be a fun trip to Qumran, the Dead Sea, and Hebron. There was no way he could have prepared for the encounter with the soldiers on Shuhada Street.

Chapter Twenty-Four

Daniel was fatigued, mentally and physically, following the incident in Hebron. The image of the soldiers, their guns pointed in the direction of his students, was imprinted on his brain. But despite the fatigue, he was looking forward to another evening with Shoshana. Maybe she would even feel up to making love. But as Daniel, Caleb, and the students were entering the St. George's compound, a member of the staff handed him a note that turned out to be from Shoshana's daughter, Ofra: *Ema wants me to tell you she is feeling sick, so maybe you can see her tomorrow, not tonight. It's good she has an appointment with her doctor in the morning.*

Daniel caught Caleb in the hallway as they were headed to dinner in the cathedral's dining hall. "I know we're supposed to go to Ramallah in the morning, but I think the students are worn out. Bethlehem, the village, Hebron . . . it's been a lot. What if we stayed in Jerusalem tomorrow, then went to Ramallah on Friday?"

"I've scheduled meetings with two Palestinian Authority officials for tomorrow."

"Do you think you can change them?"

Caleb looked closely at Daniel. "You seem . . . Yeah, I can surely find a couple of people in the PA, especially Christians, who will speak with us on Friday. They want outsiders to pay attention." He paused.

"Do you need me to lead the tour here in Jerusalem tomorrow?"

Daniel smiled slightly and nodded. "You are a great friend, you know that? If you could take them in the morning to Yad Vashem and the other places we talked about in the new part of the city, that would be a real gift. We're supposed to meet the priest I told you about at one o'clock, in that restaurant in the Muristan. I can meet you there."

He immediately called Shoshana, who sounded groggy. "Did Ofra give you my message?"

"Yes. I won't come over this evening, but I'm going to go with you to your doctor's appointment."

There was silence on the other end before she said, "Are you sure? It's just a checkup with the oncologist now that I've had one round of chemo. I probably won't learn anything new."

"I won't take no for an answer."

He could imagine her smile. "Okay. Meet me here at . . . Just come as soon as you can, seven thirty or eight, and we'll have coffee before we go."

The next morning, as he looked back on it, was extraordinary for its wonderful ordinariness: driving together in her car, talking about the weather ("rain tomorrow"), complaining about the traffic, discussing what to expect when the chemo resumed, holding hands as they walked into the office—like a regular couple.

The receptionist knew Shoshana from previous appointments, and they chatted and smiled as she checked in, occasionally glancing at Daniel, who had taken a seat.

"She wanted to know if you're my husband," Shoshana told him as she sat down.

"What did you tell her?"

"No, but it wasn't out of the realm of possibility." That familiar smile.

Shoshana looked ready for a nap when Daniel kissed her goodbye and headed for his rendezvous with the group at the rooftop restaurant where he had once stood with Ghazala. Father Laurent arrived shortly after one o'clock, and Daniel introduced him to the students.

"I cannot go with you all afternoon," the priest informed them, "but we can talk now." He moved closer to the students, most of whom had gathered around adjoining tables. "I have lived here so long I am like one of the stones"—and they all laughed. "So, you have questions for an old stone?"

There was a pause, no one wanting to go first, before Julia said, "Yesterday, I asked Patriarch Jacobus about divisions in the church here in Jerusalem, and he said there aren't any. But I'd like to hear your perspective."

"*Il est un idiot*," said the priest, more under his breath than to the group. "You will go from here to the Holy Sepulchre, *n'est-ce pas?*" He said this looking at Daniel, who nodded. He turned back to the students. "When you go, look at the ladder, our famous ladder. Your professor knows about it. It is there on the front of the Holy Sepulchre since more than two hundred years, but if a Greek or Latin or Armenian dares to remove it, the others will start a war. They fight over where a chair is put or if someone sweeps dust on their piece of floor. I don't mention the Protestants because they have invented their own place, the Garden Tomb, as a competition to the Catholics and Orthodox. No divisions! The church in Jerusalem is filled with divisions. 'A house divided against itself.'"

"But the churches are now making statements together about the conflict, like their Christmas message this past month." Daniel knew how this sounded as soon as the words left his mouth.

"Statements! *Oui*, they make statements and send messages, but where are the actions? They talk, talk, talk of unity and then keep others from the Eucharist, from their celebrations."

Daniel started to ask who "they" were, but decided against it. Instead, he said, "We will go to a few of the religious sites, but also swing by the archaeology dig, the excavation, to the south of the Temple Mount. You have seen a lot of new archaeological discoveries in your time here."

Father Laurent shrugged. "The past"—he said in his matter-of-fact way—"everyone fights over the past in Jerusalem." He paused as if searching for the right words. "I will tell you something of myself. I was born a year after the war, in Strasbourg, in the region called Alsace. I was born in France. My father was born in the same city, but in Germany. When his parents were born there, the same city, it was France. Should it belong to France? Should it belong to Germany? It is a matter of when you start to tell *l'histoire*. The Jews dig up part of David's city and say, 'Jerusalem belongs to us because we were here three thousand years ago.' The Palestinians say they come from the Jebusites who were here before King David, so it belongs to them. But, yes, see the archaeology. It is interesting." He took a drink of water. "Excavation . . . it is a good image for Jerusalem. People here think that history is a *carrière*—you say 'quarry'?—where they dig up arguments that are of use in their battles."

By five o'clock, as the whirlwind tour concluded at the Western Wall, most of the students were dragging and ready to head to the cathedral. Daniel knew, however, that this was likely his only opportunity to see Musa. "Why don't you all go back to St. George's with Caleb. I want to make one more stop in the Old City before I meet you there for dinner." To his surprise, Julia asked if he would like company.

As the two of them made their way through the fading light toward the shop, Daniel described his friend. "Don't expect an orderly store, like you see in the souk. It will look pretty chaotic."

"Are you sure he'll be there?"

"No. Of course the shop will be there. It's the ground floor of his home, and the house has been in his family for a few hundred years. I hope he's there. Musa is the antidote to Father Laurent's pessimism."

Musa was, indeed, in the shop, but his previous exuberance wasn't. There was warmth in his greeting of Daniel, and he welcomed Julia by giving her a pendant he had made out of old glass; but he responded to Daniel's questions—Have you found more Palestinian materials from the time of the Mandate? Are you making lots of jewelry? How is your uncle in Detroit?—with little enthusiasm. The shop was even more disorderly than Daniel remembered, filled with what looked more like junk than merchandise or raw materials, and the bright *Visit Palestine* poster that had hung over Musa's workspace had been replaced with a battered poster showing the Dome of the Rock through a hole in Israel's separation wall.

When they had arrived at the shop, Daniel had explained that Julia was one of sixteen students on a study seminar he was leading, but Musa had asked no questions about it. Finally, after an awkward gap in the conversation, he asked, "What are you teaching the students?"

Daniel glanced at Julia. "Well, Julia can tell you what she has learned, but my primary goal is to give them some sense of the Palestinian-Israeli conflict."

"We're getting different perspectives," Julia added.

"That's good," said Musa. "That's good." He looked absently at the wall behind Daniel. "But when I hear these words 'Palestinian-Israeli conflict,' sometimes it sounds to my ears like a problem of mathematics: 'The Palestinian-Israeli conflict,' 'the Israel-Palestine conflict' . . . Like a box with a lock, and we only need to find the key." He raised his hands as if in prayer. "There is no key. That is what I have learned: there is no key."

Chapter Twenty-Five

It was overcast and chilly the next morning as Daniel, Caleb, and the students boarded their bus for the short trip to Ramallah. Corey managed to make it, although he had been up much of the night with stomach problems; and, in general, the energy level on the bus was not high. Their overseas trip was coming to an end.

They left in what seemed like plenty of time for a nine o'clock meeting with the head of the Quaker community, to be followed by meetings with Palestinian officials. "I pulled a few strings yesterday," Caleb told Daniel, "and got us time with a spokesperson for the Palestinian Authority. She's a Christian who knows how to talk to groups like ours."

It proved harder than expected, however, to negotiate the Qalandia checkpoint just north of Jerusalem. The students were mostly silent as they watched, from the safety of the bus, as dozens of Palestinians lined up on foot to pass through metal detectors and turnstiles. Daniel's attention was particularly drawn to an old man in a black-checked keffiyeh, supported by a younger companion, and to an obviously pregnant woman dragging two small children. It was also impossible to miss the heavy equipment used in constructing the wall that snaked, gray and forbidding, next to the roadway.

Eventually, an Israeli soldier, rifle slung over her shoulder, boarded the bus and glanced at a half-dozen passports. She took her time, however, with Caleb's, flipping slowly through the stamped pages, asking questions in Arabic that he answered in English. "I am an American who works for a church . . . They are students. I'm helping lead the group . . . Because there are churches in Ramallah. We are visiting churches."

Once the soldier was gone, Caleb turned to the students. "The yellow license plates on this bus indicate that we're probably tourists, so they usually would just wave us through, like they did when we went to Hebron. But apparently there's been some sort of *incident*"—he said the word sarcastically—"not far from here, so we might run into a temporary checkpoint."

Sure enough, within five minutes all traffic was stopped at a crossroads on the edge of the Qalandia refugee camp, which over the course of a half century had morphed into a small city, sprouting antennae and rebar from the roofs of drab concrete buildings. Two minarets completed the skyline.

Through the bus's front window, spotted by occasional raindrops, Daniel could see several soldiers in olive-green uniforms, one of them motioning with one hand, a submachine gun in the other. Even though it was January, another soldier was wearing only a shirt with the sleeves rolled up to the elbow. A group of men—most of them young, as far as Daniel could tell—was gathering on the corner nearest Qalandia. Diagonally across the intersection was the wooden cart of a fruit vendor, unhitched from an old pickup parked nearby.

Since it looked as if they might be there a while, and it was barely drizzling, students asked if they could get off the bus. "Yes," said Daniel, "but stay close in case things start to move, and don't try to speak with the soldiers. They seem pretty agitated about something." Several of the seminarians scrambled up a hillock that overlooked the crossroads. Others—including Julia, an older student named Frank, and Heather—stood by the side of the road or leaned against the bus.

When Daniel joined the leaners, Heather asked, "What do you think's going on?"

"Your guess is as good as mine. Maybe the Israelis got word that somebody on their wanted list was seen around here. Or maybe some kid just threw a rock at one of them. I appreciate the need for security, but . . ." His voice trailed off as a car ahead of them moved a few feet.

"From what I've seen," said Frank, "they go out of their way to make things miserable. Like what we saw in Hebron." Daniel nodded as the others voiced their agreement.

"I hope we have more time to talk about all this," said Julia. "What we've seen is really disturbing. I don't know what I thought we'd see, but I wasn't ready for Hebron or that checkpoint back there."

A couple of cars ahead of them passed through the crossroads. It seemed like their driver was about to restart the bus when soldiers began to shout at the man selling fruit. Caleb was walking toward the intersection so he could better hear the exchange, and Daniel fell in beside him. "What are they saying?"

Caleb held up his hand to indicate he was still listening to the fruit vendor, who was now also shouting and gesturing. "They're telling him he doesn't have permission, some kind of official permit, to put his cart here, and he's saying, from what I can make out, that he's been doing it for months. He said 'years,' but that apparently pissed them off—they're calling him a liar—so now he's saying 'months.'"

All sixteen students had gathered near them, trying to overhear the conversation, so Daniel repeated what Caleb had told him. While he was speaking, an army Humvee pulled into the intersection. Daniel turned to look as the driver got out hurriedly, spoke to one of the soldiers, got back in, gunned the engine, and then, without apparent warning, rammed the vehicle into the vendor's cart, collapsing one corner of it and sending oranges, lemons, apples, grapefruit, avocados, and pomelos spilling across the roadway. A few drivers honked their horns, whether in protest or support Daniel couldn't tell. Before he realized what was happening, Ian and Andrea were dashing about, picking up the rolling fruit for the vendor, and most of the other students, even older ones such as Julia and Frank, quickly joined them.

While some of the soldiers yelled at the students, in Hebrew and English, to leave the fruit alone, the soldier with rolled-up sleeves approached Daniel and Caleb. "This man," he said loudly, pointing toward the wrecked cart, "he has been warned not to sell here. He doesn't listen."

"Why?" Caleb's voice was as loud and sharp as the soldier's. "*He* is not blocking traffic. *You* are the ones doing that!"

The soldier acted as if Caleb hadn't spoken. "Tell your people to stop and get them on the bus."

Daniel had been nervous about the students getting involved, but now he found himself saying, "No! They're helping clean up the mess, a mess you made."

By now, there was more honking and shouting in Arabic. The soldier with the rolled-up sleeves had begun to reply when a rock struck the open-sided Humvee that was idling in the middle of the intersection, followed by two more, one of them perilously close to the head of a soldier in the passenger seat. The handful of young men standing on the corner had swollen to a good-sized crowd, with more people pouring out of Qalandia.

The shouting grew louder, and Daniel could tell it was difficult for some of the seminarians to hear him as he yelled, "Get back on the bus!" He was waving to get the attention of the stragglers when he heard the first shot, just a single pop, then another. Now people were screaming as he shoved the last of his flock onto the bus. Through the wide front window, he could see the chaotic scene of running youth and pleading women, soldiers with weapons pointing in all directions. But for all the chaos, there was no missing the boy, clutching his bloodied head, by the side of the road.

That evening, the bishop made an appearance while they were eating in the cathedral's dining hall. He made a half-hearted joke about Anglican food being more than bread and wine, before saying, "I heard what happened today at the checkpoint. Unfortunately, incidents like this aren't unusual. What's unusual is that you were there to see it. I wish that someday someone will be there with a video camera."

Once the bishop finished, Daniel thanked him for the church's hospitality. "But we have another favor to ask. The students, and I agree with them, think we should spend some time this evening talking together about what we have experienced, especially in Hebron and then today at Qalandia."

"Stay right here," said the bishop. "We'll leave the fruit and pastries in case you get hungry while you discuss."

Daniel had called Shoshana as soon as the bus arrived back at the cathedral. They had tentatively planned to spend the evening together, light the Sabbath candles as they had done thirty-four years before. "But I really need to be here," he told her. "The students want to talk, need to talk, and since I'm the professor—"

"Daniel, *motek sheli*, you don't need to explain. And it's just as well. It will give me a chance to rest up for our time tomorrow."

After the dishes were cleared and the chairs rearranged, Caleb, who had been gone for part of the dinner, started the conversation. "I found out a few minutes ago that the boy we saw is fourteen years old, from Kfar Aqab, which is next to Qalandia. There have been lots of rumors, but I'm told by someone I trust that he's going to be okay. He was apparently hit in the head by one of the rubber-coated bullets, which can kill you, but not in this case. I don't know how badly he was hurt, but from what I learned he is being treated at Al-Istishari Arab Hospital in Ramallah."

Donna spoke next, standing so she could look around the room. "Some of you know I was a nurse in another life, a large part of it in pediatrics, and I want to tell you that was the most helpless I have ever felt, seeing that boy bleeding there, slumped over, and not being able to do anything about it."

"What I intend to do," said Frank, "is go back home and talk about all this. People back home don't know the real situation." Several nodded their agreement.

"How about others of you?" asked Daniel. "What are you thinking and feeling about what we've seen the past few days?"

"When we first saw the boy, he wasn't moving, and I thought he might be dead," said Eric, a military kid who had grown up overseas. "And the question that kept going through my mind was 'Who will remember him?' Yesterday, we saw all these memorials to Jesus and David and Muhammad. We heard two or three times that Jerusalem is a city of memory. But who remembers the little people killed in all the sieges and battles, or in putting up all these grand buildings?" He paused, but no one interrupted. "I was looking forward to seeing all the holy places; that's a big reason I wanted to take this course. But to be honest, the past few days have made me incredibly sad. And today just made it worse."

"The image I have isn't the boy," said Matt, a student in his late twenties. "By the time I got to that side of the bus, there was a crowd around him, and then we were being waved through the intersection. I don't know how anybody writes history because you miss things even when you're right there. Anyway, the image I'll carry with me is this old man being helped through the checkpoint with all the turnstiles. He looked like somebody's great-grandfather, and here he was having to hobble through a degrading obstacle course just to get from one city to another."

Corey, sitting next to Matt, was shaking his head. "Surely not all Israelis agree with this. I mean, we can't be getting a complete picture."

"No, of course not," said Caleb. "But like Frank said, what you're seeing on this trip needs to be better known."

"That's true," said Daniel, "but let me give an indication of this more complete picture. There is a suburb of Jerusalem, a wealthy suburb, called Mevaseret Zion where some residents actually petitioned the High Court asking for an amendment to the route of the separation barrier. The original route would have cut off the neighboring Palestinian village—I forget its name—from its olive and fig orchards, and the

Israelis in Mevaseret Zion said that hurting the village would create tension, and this would be bad for them as well as the Palestinians. If you don't keep messing things up, they told the government, we can live together in peace." He paused. "When you go home, you'll find there are lots of people who know little about the conflict and don't care to know. But there will be others, pro-Palestinian or pro-Israeli, who will try to tell you how it is, even if they haven't been here. I hope you will resist simplistic pronouncements."

The next student recounted the fear she had felt on Shuhada Street in Hebron, which was echoed by two others who added that they also had felt afraid at the crossroads. "I never expected," said Heather, "to be afraid on a trip to Israel." Daniel wanted to comment, but he wasn't sure how to phrase his thoughts graciously.

After several more had spoken, Julia raised her hand. "Jen said something to me that I told her she should share with everyone."

Jen looked slightly embarrassed. "I was just telling Julia that my brother married a Jewish woman and he converted, so they're a Jewish family. She—that is, my sister-in-law—spent a summer or semester in Israel when she was younger, and my brother has been here with her a couple of times. They're the ones who encouraged me to take this trip." She cleared her throat. "But they, especially her, don't even want to talk about the Palestinians, the whole situation. It's like it's off-limits. The one time we did talk about it, she said there will never be peace, so Israel might as well build a wall—she doesn't call it that—to protect itself."

"I told Jen there has to be some answer," said Julia. "People can't continue to live like this, decade after decade, on either side."

A couple of students asked questions—Had the wall actually reduced suicide bombings? Were there checkpoints like this all over the West Bank? Were church leaders of any use in peace negotiations? Caleb answered these, Daniel adding a brief observation or two. Another asked where God was in all this, which left Daniel wondering why he hadn't invited them to think about that question. With all parties claiming God's sanction, what could they possibly say about divine will and presence?

He had been anticipating comments from Ian, and they finally came, the student looking directly at his professor. "I know you studied in Israel and have lots of dialogue with Jews. I understand and appreciate that. But how can you defend this country? A nation that occupies the land of another people, treats them like shit. It doesn't have any legitimacy—none—as far as I'm concerned."

"That would make most countries illegitimate," said Daniel, "including ours." It seemed that Ian was about to speak, so he quickly continued. "Look, I'm not here to defend Israel." He glanced at Eric. "And I'm not here as a tour guide to the holy sites. As your professor, my responsibility is to show you at least some of the complexity of this situation—conflict, tragedy, call it what you want—so you can make up your own minds about it. For example, Hamas, a Palestinian party that is very strong in Gaza, says in its charter that its goal is the elimination of Israel. Complete elimination. We may not like how the Israeli army acts sometimes. I certainly don't. But unless you think Israel shouldn't exist, it needs a strong military. As a good Israeli friend once said to me, nothing here is black and white."

"Yes, sure," said Ian. "I respect your knowledge of this place. And most of the time, I appreciate the way you see both sides of things, your 'bridge building.' It's good. But maybe that time is over as far as this struggle is concerned. Maybe it's time to take sides. That," he added, "is what Caleb has done."

Caleb stood up, and all eyes were now on him. "Since I have been mentioned . . . Do you know what my last name, *Sadek*, means in Arabic? It means 'honest,' so let me be completely honest. You have exactly the right professor for this trip. Yes, I have probably been more outspoken than Daniel about Palestinians, but he's been more outspoken than me about how Christians have treated Jews for two thousand years. One of these seems more immediate, but can we say one is more important than the other?"

"Okay," said Ian, "but can't we make some distinctions when talking about what's going on here? We can acknowledge that there are reasons why Israel should exist and still say that the settlements shouldn't, that they are wrong, that they're a violation of international law, which they are. And the language we use shows our bias." He looked again at Daniel. "One of the readings you had us do for this trip talked about 'Palestinian terrorists.' Aren't the settlers also terrorists?"

"You can condemn the settlements," said Daniel, an angry edge to his voice, "but not all settlers! Some are fanatics, I agree, but I have a good friend, a very close friend, who lived for years in a settlement, and she is not and never was a fanatic or a terrorist."

Chapter Twenty-Six

Saturday the 24th had always been marked as a free day on the travel seminar's itinerary. West Jerusalem, the Jewish part of the city, would be shut down for the Sabbath, but there was still plenty for the students to do, including shop for presents and souvenirs in the Old City markets. "There are also lots of sites we didn't see," Daniel told them at breakfast, "and this is your chance. Like the Garden Tomb, even if Father Laurent doesn't appreciate it, and the Armenian Cathedral of Saint James, and the Room of the Last Supper on Mount Zion. If you go to Mount Zion you might . . ." He stopped mid-sentence. "Or just hang out in a tea shop and people watch. Let this amazing place, this one square kilometer, capture your imagination. The day is yours."

As he was leaving the guesthouse, he ran into Caleb. "I'll be back early tomorrow, although we don't need to leave for the airport until around nine."

Caleb smiled. "If we take another of these trips together, maybe I'll have a reason to be gone and you can cover for me."

When Daniel arrived at Shoshana's apartment, he found she was feeling better, so much so that she suggested they walk the two-thirds of a mile to the botanical gardens. The day was chilly and overcast, but not raining, and they took their time. When it was clear Shoshana was getting tired, Daniel suggested they sit for a while on a bench in the gardens.

Once they were seated, Daniel's arm around her shoulders, Shoshana asked, "What happened yesterday that the students were so hot to talk about?" So he told her about the incident at the crossroads, including how the military vehicle rammed the cart of the fruit vendor. He wasn't going to mention the boy by the side of the road, but then she asked, "Was anyone hurt?" and he told her.

"We learned later that the boy should be okay," he concluded. "Caleb is checking on him again this morning." Pause. "I really don't want to spoil our time together by talking about Palestinians versus Israelis."

Shoshana had been staring at a bed of winter-blooming cyclamen, but now shifted to face him. "There is no way to avoid it, my love. It infects everything, like a virus." She leaned back against his arm. "What happened right before the gunfire?"

"Some rocks were thrown at the Humvee."

She nodded, her eyes on the flowers. "It's quite a cycle, isn't it? Our soldiers get attacked, they defend themselves, and are condemned as brutal."

"Do you really want to talk about this?"

"Isn't that what couples do, talk about things?"

"All right. The Palestinians we spoke with yesterday would also say there's a cycle: Israel takes their land, they respond, and are called terrorists."

The only sound was a motor in the distance until Shoshana said, "Let's walk some more. I just needed to rest for a minute."

As they wandered slowly through a grove of eucalyptus trees, she said, "When I was a child—and I know I'm older than you, but not that much older!—Israel was seen as David in this story. Now we've become Goliath, and Palestinians are the darlings of people who care about justice. Strange, isn't it? We don't murder collaborators, at least I don't think we do. We don't go in for—what do they call them?—'honor killings.' Some of their leaders say the Holocaust is a lie invented by Zionists and cheer when Jews are killed in Istanbul or wherever."

She stopped walking and let go of his hand. "Do you remember Rahel's little boy? He must have been two, no more than three, when you and I were at their house for the Seder, the time we made you read the child's questions." She smiled at the memory. "Now he's a *Rav Seren* in the military. I don't know what rank you call that in English. I talk to him often, so I know he hates the occupation as much as I do, as much as you do, probably more. Sending young men to places that seethe with hostility. Their fear makes them edgy, callous, sometimes cruel; that's what he says." She was now looking directly at him. "But Daniel, what are we supposed to do? You tell me, what are we supposed to do?"

He knew enough not to respond, and soon they resumed their walk. As they approached a pond, Shoshana seemed to pick up her thought. "This intifada . . . if I were a Palestinian, I suppose I would support it, too. But I'm not, I'm an Israeli who lives with the nagging fear of losing . . . everything, the way Jews have often lost everything. And pretty soon you have less compassion, and you support politicians who say they will make you safe."

They returned to the apartment, Ofra arriving around five. With a little direction from her mother, she began digging in a cupboard and putting something on a plate. "I know you wanted to welcome in the Sabbath together," Shoshana told Daniel, "but since that wasn't possible, we can usher it out and welcome the new week."

She stood up, steadying herself on the arm of the chair. "Have you ever participated in the Havdalah ceremony?" When Daniel shook his head, she took his hand and led him to the table where Ofra had set a braided candle with two wicks, a small plate of cinnamon, and the familiar, slightly tarnished kiddush cup. "It's very brief. We drink wine from the cup, the one you gave me, to remember the joy of Shabbat. We smell the spice to remember the sweetness of Shabbat. And the candle, woven like that, reminds us of how we came together on the Sabbath, which we did!" That glorious smile. "Once we've said the blessings, we say *Shavua tov*. And it *will* be a good week." She paused, continuing to smile even though her eyes were blurry. "*Havdalah* means separation, but temporary separation, because the Sabbath always returns." She looked down. "Well, you see how it might apply to us."

When they were finished, Ofra said, "I told Ema I would join you for dinner, but I didn't want her cooking."

"She doesn't like my cooking!"

Ofra ignored her joke. "She thought you would probably like to eat in the Old City, and that sounds good to me. Then I will leave the two of you alone."

They took a taxi to the Jaffa Gate, walking the short distance from there to the Armenian restaurant on the street leading to the Zion Gate. The dinner conversation was lively and, for Daniel, refreshingly superficial. Shoshana reported to her daughter on the doctor's appointment, emphasizing the question from the receptionist.

"Maybe," said Ofra, "she was being prophetic."

Daniel described some of the seminarians, and they all laughed when he told how twenty-two-year-old Jen complained about the fickleness of her boyfriends while sitting next to fifty-five-year-old Frank, who was on his third marriage.

Ofra responded to a question from Daniel by confirming that she still loved to swim but now was only able to do so a couple of times a week. "I'm learning that it takes a lot of time to have a husband."

The two women asked Daniel about his teaching load for the spring and feigned interest while he outlined the remodeling he had in mind for his house.

The conversation also included the ordinary back and forth of a mother and her adult daughter: Were Ofra and Adam still planning to come for dinner next week? She promised to pick up food rather than cook. Since Shoshana insisted on going to the store, would she pick up an extra face cream for her daughter? Had Ema remembered to save her that soup recipe? Daniel both soaked it in and felt a twinge of envy at their intimacy. "I hope we didn't bore you," said Ofra as she excused herself. She hugged him warmly and kissed him on both cheeks.

It was nearly seven thirty when Daniel and Shoshana exited the restaurant. Instead of turning right, back toward Jaffa Gate, she turned left toward Mount Zion, and he gladly followed. They said little as they walked, arm in arm, through the bullet-pocked gate, past the Dormition Abbey to the staircase that was now shrouded in darkness. Shoshana labored a bit on the stairs. "We don't have to do this," Daniel told her when she stopped to rest, but once on top, she led him to the familiar railing, looking east, where they stood without speaking. He put his arm around her, and she leaned against him in a way he wished would never end. As he tried to pray, a simple line repeated in his head: "God, whatever you are, heal this woman and give us time together."

Back in the apartment, they began to make love, but once it was clear she was in pain, they simply lay together propped against the headboard. At some point, she suggested he pour them a glass of wine, and when he returned from the kitchen, he asked, "Do you leave the turban on all the time?"

"It hides the scar, which really shows without hair. But I guess I know by now it doesn't bother you." She took the turban off before resting again against the headboard. Then, as if intuiting a question he didn't ask, she said, "I got this scar long before Yossi. Well, you know that because I had it when you and I first met. Yossi could be a hothead, as you saw, but he wasn't violent."

She paused, sipping from her glass of wine. "Before I met you, I had a boyfriend, pretty serious I thought, although I knew he had a temper. Then, one night he got really drunk. Something I said set him off, I have no idea what, and he hit me, several times. Enough that it loosened a tooth." She opened her mouth and pointed to the incisor on the upper left. "I threw something at him and that's when he hit me with a vase, so there was blood all over and I ended up with eighteen stitches, which they didn't do very cosmetically"—all of this said without emotion. "It's crazy, I survived the war without a scratch and then get wounded in my own apartment." Another pause. "That's why I wasn't dating anyone when I met you. Good timing, huh?" A slight smile. "I told myself, just friends, no deep relationships, at least for a while. Make lots of flippant remarks, keep men at arm's length. But part of it was that I didn't feel very attractive. Sort of like now. Then it was the scar, now it's the cancer."

Daniel reached out, intending to hold her, but she sat straight up in the bed and faced him. "That first night, sitting there on the log, I could tell you wouldn't hurt me—couldn't. It's not who you are. So that's why I decided seeing each other would be okay, would be good, because you were in Tel Aviv, not right here. I could stop it whenever. But then . . . Anyway, I knew you were going to leave, go back home, so it couldn't get too heavy. That's what I told myself." She smiled. "We see how that worked out."

They sat in silence, occasionally sipping the wine, until Daniel said, "After I came here and found out you were married, I thought we'd probably lose touch."

"Well, I'm glad you were wrong." They clinked their glasses together.

"It's strange," he said softly. "We haven't lived together, but when I look back on my life, I see that so much of it revolves around you."

"And Jerusalem."

"And Jerusalem." They smiled.

"I'll tell you what's strange. There must have been, must be, women who have far more in common with you than I have. Living in the same country, for one thing." He started to speak, but she cut him off. "At first, I thought you were gone, and that was that. Then I began to think you really would find a way to get back to Israel in a year, maybe two. But when that didn't happen . . ."

"I love you, Shoshana. I have always loved you."

"Look at me crying! And I'm supposed to be the tough Israeli. Maybe it's the drugs." She smiled, without opening her lips, and wiped her eyes. "You know I love you, Daniel, although how is this possible when for years you just made guest appearances in my life?" She shook her head. "I've got to get through these treatments, quit feeling so sick, so unattractive. And then let's see . . . You remember how I used to say 'it is what it is'? Well, maybe it doesn't have to be how it's been."

PART FIVE

ROOFTOPS
(2010)

Chapter Twenty-Seven

The rusted iron handrail that dated from the British Mandate had been replaced by a solid wooden banister, and in place of narrow metal steps with holes for drainage were wooden ones, wide and nicely stained to match the railing. The dome still took up one end of the small rooftop, as there was no changing the architecture of the building, but instead of being plastered with posters, it was now sheathed in metal.

Daniel was ambivalent about bringing Valerie to the Rooftop. How could he not share with his wife something so special to him? He had shared it with the other great love of his life. But what if it wasn't all that special to her? He knew it was absurd to expect another person to experience what he had experienced, to feel what he had felt four decades ago. *He* wasn't even the same person he had been in 1969. He was determined, if they went, not to treat this as some sort of test or rite of passage. Still, he knew he ran the risk of being disappointed, and so he hesitated. Then, ten days after their arrival in Jerusalem, Valerie said, "You've never shown me what's on Mount Zion." She said this while they were eating lunch on a Friday, and Daniel took it as a sign. Erev Shabbat was the right time to go.

He had started to tell her about the place as they made their way at twilight out the Zion Gate, on the southwest corner of the Old City, but then decided not to. Let Valerie feel whatever she felt without putting his thumb on the scale. Instead, once they were outside the gate, he turned to show her the bullet holes, barely visible in the fading light, from the day in 1948 when Palmach fighters broke through this entrance.

"It's tragic how many people have been killed fighting over this city," said Valerie.

"Yes, fighting over a place that has no oil, no major source of water, and isn't on any trade route. Jerusalem's value seems to be that more than one group thinks it's valuable." He gestured toward the austere gate. "I hate war, but it's moving to me to imagine the risks they took trying to rescue other Jews trapped just down the hill"—he motioned to his right—"there in the Jewish Quarter. That must have been when your friend's uncle was evacuated."

Since Holy Week and Passover had come and gone, the city was no longer swarming with tourists and worshippers. The booths selling trinkets on Mount Zion were closed for the evening, and there was no one on the walkway ahead of them as they ambled toward a cluster of buildings beside the Dormition Abbey, its distinctive pointed dome outlined against the nearly dark sky. When they'd reached the buildings, parts of which were from the Crusaders, Valerie used the light on her cell phone to read the signs: *David's Tomb* (in Hebrew and English) and *Upper Room*.

"So *this* is the site of the Last Supper?"

"Tradition has it. What I want to show you, however, is on the roof. Actually, it's the roof I want to show you. I know you don't like rooftops as much as I do, but I hope you'll like this one, and I think it's best to see it after dark."

The bells of the Holy Sepulchre rang seven o'clock as they ascended the outside staircase with its new wooden banister and steps, Valerie urging Daniel to go slowly, perhaps because he now seemed to be in a hurry. "Remember, sweetheart, you are still recovering."

Once on top, the first thing they saw, slightly illuminated by lights on the adjacent abbey, was a tiny stone room in a corner of the rooftop. "Surely nobody lives here," she said, slightly out of breath.

"No. They call it the President's Room, but I guess you could say it's a miniature synagogue. This rooftop was the closest Jews could come to the Western Wall from 1948 until Israel captured the Old City in '67. It would be like keeping Muslims out of Mecca or Catholics away from Lourdes or the Vatican."

He took her hand as they turned east, squeezing past the metal-wrapped dome, plastic cups and bottles littering the ledge surrounding it. They stood in silence at the railing on the other side of the dome, watching lights blink on in the village at the foot of Mount Zion, before Valerie said, "You're right, it's . . . *beautiful*. That's not even the word for it. Tell me what I'm seeing."

Daniel smiled as he looked at her, although she may not have been able to see his face clearly. "The hill on the other side of the valley is the Mount of Olives; you can see the outline of it. And these lights"—he pointed to the bottom of the hill—"are in the Palestinian village of Silwan, which is on the original site of David's city." He paused. "The City of David, three thousand years ago . . . amazing." Another pause. "But that means the Israelis have destroyed Palestinian homes to uncover the layers of Jewish ruins. I suppose Palestinians might do the same, if things were reversed." He turned toward her. "We've walked around a lot in the last week and a half, so you probably know what you're looking at."

She shook her head. "I like you to show me."

He turned back to the scene in front of them. "Well, the open space with all the lights—down there to the left, beyond the wall of the Old City—that's the plaza in front of the Western Wall. Just imagine, there above the plaza was the most magnificent religious sanctuary in the ancient world; but the Wall is all that's left of the great temple Herod built, the temple Jesus knew. The Romans tore it down, toppled all the huge blocks of stone, when they conquered the city." He glanced at Valerie before adding, "I feel like I'm rambling on. You probably know all of this already."

"Sometimes, sweetheart, I'm not sure you know me very well. I love hearing you talk about the things you love to talk about," which made Daniel smile.

"Okay." He pointed toward the lighted plaza. "You saw how people write prayers on slips of paper and stick them in crevices between the stones? I've done it, several times. Twice a year, before Passover and Rosh Hashanah, a rabbi clears out all those pieces of paper and buries them on the Mount of Olives. Like they're sacred, which I guess they are in a way." They stood, silently gazing, until he added, "Sometimes it's called the Wailing Wall. You hear that low droning sound? That's the Orthodox Jews *davening*—praying, not wailing—in front of it. Some Jews, some I've known, don't much like the Orthodox, but they are part of the city."

Daniel put his arm around his wife, and they stood listening for a minute to the faint hum of prayer. Finally, he said, "From the top of the Mount of Olives, you can really see that other wall . . . that scar on Jerusalem. As an Israeli friend said to me, it's a wall that makes people more afraid of what's on the other side." He cleared his throat. "At the foot of the Mount of Olives is the Garden of Gethsemane, where we were on Wednesday. It's possible—nobody knows for sure because different groups claim their place is the real one—but, anyway, it's possible that Jesus ate his last supper with his disciples somewhere around here, somewhere on Mount Zion, and then they all headed down the hill toward the garden. You see the outline of the church right below us? Next to it, archaeologists have uncovered a stepped street that Jesus might have walked on. Who knows? If you look . . ."

But he now could tell, even in the darkness, that Valerie wasn't looking where he was pointing; she was looking at him. Her voice was little more than a whisper as she said, "This rooftop is sacred for you, isn't it?"

He could feel tears welling. "How do you know that?"

"Because," she said softly, "your heart has been racing since we got here, and I know it's not just from the climb."

He kissed her, and before long the muezzin's call rang out from multiple minarets in unintended syncopation, echoing off the ancient stones. When the sound finally faded, he told her of his experience, all those years ago, and how it had redirected his life. "I think of it now as a religious experience, but at the time I didn't have the vocabulary for that." Valerie nodded and smiled—not that other smile, but wonderfully her own.

"To be honest," he continued, "I don't really remember what I felt forty years ago. It's all buried under layers of experience. But since then, whenever I come here, I'm moved by the mental image of people, standing right here, longing for something they can't yet reach. There are so many walls in this city. From up here, I feel like I can see beyond them, even if I can't get there."

More silence. "I tried to imagine what this trip would be like," she said at last, "but never realized I would be coming here with a pilgrim."

She was right, he thought. This is what pilgrimage looks like in this new century: longing for mystery and holiness in a world that has less and less space for either, mixing religion with politics until they seem inseparable, recognizing that places like this Rooftop can, indeed, be sacred—when they are connected with people you love.

Chapter Twenty-Eight

For Daniel, 2008 had been a year of significant changes. The first one came in January when he suffered his initial heart attack while rushing to catch a plane in Columbus. "If you have to have one of these," he told friends, "there are worse places than an airport." Medical personnel arrived quickly as he slumped forward in a seat in the terminal, trying to find a position that would ease the pressure in his chest. He was transported immediately to the nearest hospital where surgeons inserted two stents. "And I had great pastoral care because so many ministers in the area are my students!"

It turned out that one of the pastoral caregivers was Ian, and they spent hours in Daniel's hospital room reliving the travel seminar—the confrontation on Shuhada Street, the reception in the Palestinian village, the hostility at Qalandia—and all that had happened since in that violence-plagued part of the world. Perhaps because Ian was trying to be gentle with his sick professor, they found they now agreed on many things, including that there is no military solution to despair. That only feeds it.

A second change was evident at the end of the year when Daniel took part in a Palestinian-organized demonstration against Israel's bombardment of Gaza. In fact, he was invited to speak. "Israel has a right to defend itself," he told the crowd gathered at Riverfront Park, "but there can be no justification for such extensive bombing of civilian targets. Terrorism, which I hope we all condemn, is often a weapon of the weak, but it can also be a weapon of the strong. Israel, for its own sake as well as that of innocent Palestinians, should stop its terrorizing bombing campaign and seek to understand the causes of Palestinian anger and despair."

As expected, he got pushback from Jewish friends, including Devorah. "You know they use human shields," she said to him over the phone after reading a newspaper account of the protest. "How is Israel supposed to avoid hitting civilians when the rockets are fired from schools and apartment buildings?"

To his surprise, however, he got a somewhat supportive email from Ben and Sarah. "I don't know whether you spoke out against Hamas's rocket attacks," Ben wrote. "You may have, and I just missed it. But I hope you did, because then Jews will listen to what you have to say about Israel's response. In any case, you are right that something has to change. Israel is just making things worse for itself. Pretty soon, it's not going to have any friends left."

Between the heart attack and the protest, on Saturday, September 20—ten days before Rosh Hashanah and twelve days before Eid al-Fitr, which marked the end of Ramadan—Daniel got married. It was an evening wedding in order not to exclude any of his religious friends.

Valerie was also a professor, not of religion but of psychology, at Ohio State. They met through mutual friends soon after his heart attack, had coffee, went to dinner, discovered how much they enjoyed each other's company, joked about romance at their age, and six months after they met, made the decision to marry. Daniel had waited before and resolved not to do that again.

They also joked about not being an obvious couple. While he listened mainly to classical music, occasionally reminiscing to music of the oud, Valerie's tastes were astonishingly eclectic.

"It's fun," she explained, "to see if I can come to appreciate what at first just sounds weird."

Daniel's house (always neat) had numerous photos and paintings of Jerusalem, while Valerie's (usually messy) was filled with pictures of her two sons and three grandchildren.

"Where does 'husband' rank on your list of priorities?" he asked her, only half joking.

She smiled broadly. "It's a six-way tie."

While Daniel was over six feet tall and rode his exercise bike religiously, especially after the heart attack, Valerie was five foot four, if she stretched, and seemed to care little about being in shape. And while Daniel was a consistent churchgoer who spent much time with things religious, Valerie was a long-lapsed Lutheran. She had no objection to being married in a church ("my mother would have approved"), but likely would not have done so if not for Daniel.

For him, however, the attraction was deep and immediate. People often talked about how accepting Daniel was of differences, but he had to work at it, while Valerie was just wired that way. Psychologists were supposed to be good listeners, but Valerie would have been one regardless of her profession. She had a curiosity about people that was anything but forced or artificial. He marveled at these traits and how, whenever he was with her, he felt like a better version of himself. "I have come to believe," Daniel told friends, "that having a lot in common is overrated. There are other things that are much more important."

Daniel expected some hard bargaining over where they would live, but Valerie surprised him. "I think I should move into your place. I'm less likely than you are to lose touch with friends in the old neighborhood. But," she said smiling, "it will take a while to get used to all these pictures of walls. You have a real thing for walls!"

She was looking, as she said this, at a woodblock print of the Western Wall and, next to it, a painting of the Damascus Gate. "I suppose this is my favorite," said Daniel. He gestured toward a photograph of a group standing in front of a cement wall covered in graffiti. "I remember the day I took that in Bethlehem." He pointed to an older woman in the front row. "This is Julia, the student I told you about. The man at the end of the front row is Ian, who kept me company in the hospital, standing next to Andrea. They're married now. The tall young woman in the back is Jen, and next to her is Eric. The man on the left end in the back is Caleb, who helped me organize the trip. It was a good group, but the trip was hard for lots of reasons, including that damn wall."

Valerie had stopped smiling but now started again. "You know, psychologists like me also deal with walls. Only mine are the walls we build inside ourselves to keep from seeing what we don't want to see."

"And walls between people."

She nodded. "That too. I guess, if you look at it that way, walls are one thing we have in common."

Daniel's love for Jerusalem wasn't only reflected in his home decor. His most recent book was on how to maintain Jewish-Christian relations when disagreeing about the Israeli-Palestinian struggle, and Jerusalem figured prominently in the discussion. It was Valerie who raised the idea of going there together, perhaps research another book, but Daniel surprised her by suggesting they go other places. "I've been there a lot," he told his new wife, "and in the last couple of years it has lost some of its attraction." Their honeymoon, delayed until the December break, was to Japan, a country new to both of them.

But then, on January 2, 2010, Daniel had a second heart attack, along with four more stents and a recommendation from his cardiologist that he consider retiring or, at least, cutting back. "We have enough money," said Valerie. "Why don't you talk it over with the powers that be at the seminary?"

So he did, and they agreed on a plan for him to slide into retirement. While he would still teach a course or two each year, the seminary would throw a party in February to celebrate his thirty years of full-time teaching at United School of Theology.

The celebration was a grand affair. The seminary's gift was an original painting, done by a local artist, of the Tower of David and a section of the Old City wall, which made Valerie smile and roll her eyes. There were

Muslim, Buddhist, Baha'i, and, of course, Jewish speakers. "Professor Jacobs is a *moreh*," said Rabbi Eisner in his remarks. "If you aren't Jewish or haven't studied Hebrew, you'll have to look it up. But suffice it to say that 'teacher' doesn't capture the full Hebrew meaning. We Jews would like to claim him as our special friend and teacher, but one of the things he has taught all of us is the danger of being exclusive. So we gladly acknowledge that he is a friend to people of other religions as well."

Such words were gratifying, but the speeches also made Daniel uncomfortable. Three of the speakers emphasized his capacity to see all sides of an argument, to the point that it began to grate on him. What if this alleged strength was at times a weakness? What if his penchant for saying "both-and" made him an untrustworthy friend in situations that demanded "either-or"? Ian's words that evening in St. George's Cathedral rang in his ears: "Maybe it's time to take sides."

On the way home from the party, he tried to express all of this to Valerie, who immediately disagreed. "I love your 'both-and'! In my experience, once you see different people up close, it is hard to say one is entirely right and the other entirely wrong."

Daniel's doctor had insisted he take a month or two just to relax and recuperate. "Do something fun, and that doesn't mean sitting at your desk doing research on a new book. You probably teach about the Sabbath, so take a long one. I heard Valerie say she's on sabbatical this spring, so go someplace where the two of you can get outdoors, do a lot of walking. But also rest. This second attack caused some real damage to your heart."

"I think I know just the place for you to heal," said Valerie, and after they talked it over, Daniel agreed. They made plans to arrive in Jerusalem the week after Easter.

Chapter Twenty-Nine

Daniel assumed he would line up the accommodations, but Valerie had been doing her own research. "What about staying at the Polis Hotel? Their website says it's in a nineteenth-century building just inside the Jaffa Gate. I'm sure you know it. Have you stayed there?"

Images from eighteen years earlier flashed through his brain before he suppressed them. "Not really. One time I . . . It will be fine."

The hotel—which Valerie assessed as "comfortable, if a little past its prime"—included access to the rooftop, and they headed there soon after checking in. Once they squeezed past stacks of plastic chairs and a collection of empty planters, there in front of them was the unmistakable skyline: to the north, the two domes of the Holy Sepulchre; to the east, the golden Dome of the Rock next to the less conspicuous Al-Aqsa; turning south, the rounded dome of the reconstructed Hurva Synagogue and the pointed dome of the Dormition Abbey.

"This gives you a general orientation," he said after identifying the various landmarks.

Valerie nodded. "It really is wonderful." She breathed deeply. "I like views from up here, but to be honest, I suppose street level is where I feel more at home."

They saw plenty of the streets. Each morning, after coffee and breakfast in the hotel, they walked downhill through the markets to where El-Wad intersects with the Via Dolorosa. "Climbing steps is good for you," she reminded him, "just not too fast." So once they were confident that Daniel's breakfast was digested, they began the slow ascent—231 stone steps, an outdoor staircase of sorts—past souvenir shops adjacent to the various stations of the cross, past Christian Quarter Road, past the Saint Saviour monastery, until they reached the New Gate, where they rested and drank a glass of lemonade garnished with mint leaves.

Since the holidays were behind them, the alleyways weren't packed, but that only increased the aggressiveness of freelance tour guides wanting to show them around. "They're just trying to make a living," Valerie pointed out. "Maybe we should hire one, see what he might show us."

Daniel wouldn't hear of it. "I know my way around the Old City," he snapped at one of them.

"That's what everybody says," the guide mumbled before finally leaving them alone.

The truth was Daniel wanted to be the tour guide for Valerie, show her the wonders of Jerusalem, impress her with his knowledge of the city's fabulous, tragic past. But he soon realized that, while she listened to his descriptions attentively, she was less interested in seeing religious sites and hearing historical anecdotes than in speaking with people who lived and worked in the midst of all that history and religion. She showed such interest in a spice merchant—behind his tower of green oregano, cream-colored sesame, and red sumac—that he began to greet her by name and made a point of showing her pictures of his grandfather who had sold spices at that same location.

Since the shop was on Khan al-Zeit, Daniel asked if the spice merchant remembered a small hotel near there called Al-Kamal. "I'm sure my father would have known it," said the merchant. "He told me stories of things that happened on this street, like the soldiers chasing him on the day the Israelis set a fire in Al-Aqsa."

One day, Valerie spent nearly a half hour in a five-by-eight-foot shop with a haggard woman who sewed purses and shoulder bags. Valerie examined all the merchandise, somehow communicating her admiration to the woman who spoke no English, before buying three pieces.

"They aren't very well made," Daniel commented when they finally left the shop. "You can find better—" He stopped mid-sentence as Valerie rolled her eyes.

Their daily trek up the 231 steps took them past a store that sold old photographs of Jerusalem, some from the 1920s. Daniel had walked past the store often during previous visits, but it was Valerie who learned that the pictures were taken by the proprietor's Armenian grandfather. "He was a kid in Turkey who survived the genocide, came to Palestine as a refugee, and ended up apprenticed to a photographer," she informed Daniel. "Isn't that an *amazing* story?" And after a week, she was having coffee with a woman in the Jewish Quarter whose shop specialized in silver jewelry. "Her uncle," she reported, "was one of the defenders of the Jewish Quarter in 1948 when the Jordanians fired mortars into the Old City. He would have died for sure if they hadn't been evacuated when they were."

When Daniel went back to their room for an afternoon rest, something his cardiologist had recommended, Valerie often spent time with the old man whose daughter now ran the hotel. "We have lots of history without stepping out the door," she reported. "They say Kaiser Wilhelm stayed here, although that sounds a little hazy, and the opening in the wall was made so his carriage would fit through. I'm sure you knew that. But you may not know there's a cistern under the hotel and part of an ancient wall that protected the city. Mr. Barakat's family has run this hotel for I forget how long, and he tells me there used to be a café next door called the Vagabond. Isn't that a great name? He says it was quite bohemian for its day. Can you imagine, a literary coffeehouse kind of place nearly a century ago in Jerusalem! There's great history all around here."

Naturally, they ate falafel at Samir's stand, where Valerie complimented him on his fresh pomegranate juice and laughed loudly when he wiggled his red-stained fingers. She quickly learned all about his children and grandchildren and asked questions that Daniel, for some reason, had never thought to ask. Like "what's your opinion of Israel and the conflict?"

Samir shook his head. "It is not important."

"What you think is important to me," said Valerie, sounding to Daniel very much like the psychologist she was.

"No, I mean the conflict, as you call it, is not important. It is important, but not the way people think it is important." He looked at Daniel. "You know what the Bible says. We are in the last days. What is happening is part of God's plan. The Muslim and Jewish leaders talk and talk about this and that like it matters. But God is in charge. Since you are a minister, you know about this."

Daniel started to protest that this was not at all how he read scripture. In fact, as far as he was concerned, it was dangerous nonsense. But then Valerie kicked him under the wobbly metal table, perhaps harder than she intended, and he remained silent.

"That may be true," she said. "I'll leave it for you and Daniel to talk about some other time. But meanwhile, people are suffering because of this conflict here and now, at least from what I've read and what my husband tells me. I'm sure, Samir, that you as a Christian care about people suffering."

Samir smiled but said no more while making them tea.

The person Daniel most wanted Valerie to meet was Musa. He took her to the out-of-the-way shop on their second day in Jerusalem, but the door was locked. There had never been a sign identifying the place, and there had always been junk in the windows, so it was hard to tell if Musa was still in business. They went back two more times with the same result. "I'm sorry," said Valerie. "Your friend sounds interesting; I would like to meet him. But things change, whether we want them to or not."

They were, however, able to meet with Father Laurent, bumping into him in the souk. Daniel introduced Valerie, after reintroducing himself, and suggested they have dinner together that very evening.

It quickly became evident that the priest was as blunt as ever. "When were you last here?" he asked Daniel as soon as they were seated at an outdoor restaurant, gravel underfoot, potted plants all around them.

"It was 2003. I made a couple of other quick trips, but I last saw you when I was with students in 2003."

"Seven years. So much has changed *pour le pire*. People here live in different realities, even more than in 2003. Secular Jews hate the *Haredim* because they avoid the military, don't pay taxes, and have big families. The *Haredi* Jews throw stones at Jews that drive on the Sabbath and dress like they're at the beach. Both of them fear the Arabs, who fear all Israelis. You cannot even walk in someone else's neighborhood as you could before." He adjusted his cassock. "Your country is made paralyzed by divisions. Why would here be different?"

"I thought the Christians, at least, were getting along better," said Daniel, glancing at Valerie to see how she was reacting. "I read somewhere—"

"Oh, it is a little better, on the top. More of the church leaders are from here, not somewhere in Europe." He snorted. "But beneath, they still are convinced, all of them, that they are doing God's will." His voice rose. "I hate those words: 'God's will'! Every *fanatique* in the history of religion said he was doing God's will. Now we have Jewish *zélotes* moving into Silwan because God told them to recapture David's city, and Muslim *zélotes* blowing themselves up on buses in the name of Allah, and Christian *zélotes* that think they should burn down or blow up Al-Aqsa so Jesus will return. They all act like hatred is a form of prayer."

They were quiet for a minute, Valerie clearly taken aback by the torrent of pessimism. Finally, she broke the silence. "I heard someone talking about a group, Palestinian and Israeli parents of children killed in the conflict. That sounds pretty hopeful, at least to me. Well, not that young people were killed, but that their parents . . . are crossing those barriers."

The priest took a bite of food and a sip of water before he spoke.

"It may help them to share *leur chagrin*. But do the politicians take notice?" He let the question hang unanswered.

Valerie tried again. "I'm not very religious myself"—she smiled in Daniel's direction—"but it is moving to me to see people showing such devotion, I guess you'd call it, at places like the Western Wall. You surely aren't saying they're all zealots."

"No," said Father Laurent, "*c'est vrai*. There are real believers, but also much politics. The Wall has been a place of prayer in history, but it is more important today because the government has made it a symbol of Israel being born again. It is what Americans call civil religion."

Daniel started to speak, but the priest was not to be interrupted. "The Christians, we are no better. When in history the Greeks and the Armenians and the Latins and the Copts fought over inches of the Holy Sepulchre, they were really going to war for their governments. And Al-Aqsa is important to Muslims, but do not say it is *as important* as Mecca or you will be in a war with the Saudis."

By the time the meal was over, Daniel wasn't at all sure that meeting with friends was a good idea.

On the seventh day of their stay in Jerusalem, Valerie and Daniel bought tickets to walk along the top of the ramparts surrounding the Old City, something Daniel remembered doing years ago for free. They took their time, stopping periodically to gaze at the jumble of TV antennae and tangle of wires; at domed stone buildings, minarets and spires; at washed clothing hanging on rooftops strewn with abandoned toys. Valerie took particular delight in small incongruities, such as a soccer ball resting against the wall of an ancient-looking mosque or a satellite dish perched atop an Ottoman-era building.

"I can still picture soldiers with Uzis standing on this wall the day of the fire," Daniel told her as they looked at the walkway ahead of them.

"It's strange," said Valerie. "You said that was in 1969? I would have been twenty-two and pretty aware of the world. But I don't recall reading about that fire at all."

It was a beautiful April day, not yet hot but warm enough that they didn't need a jacket or sweater. The walkway was too narrow to walk side by side, especially when people wanted to pass. But whenever he and Valerie reached a tower where the passage widened, Daniel put his arm around her, moments he wanted to preserve in temporal amber.

Why, he asked himself, had he never come here with Peg? She professed to dislike long flights and to have little interest in the Middle East, but she might have come if he had insisted. The interfaith group wanted her to join them, would have paid her way. But the answer to his question was obvious, even as he mentally asked it. When in the past he had come to Jerusalem, he had wanted to spend time with Shoshana. And that was no longer an option.

After the student trip, when Daniel first learned of Shoshana's cancer, they had exchanged emails daily, hers ending *love always*. They talked on the phone at least weekly, often two or three times a week, conversations that both lifted his spirits and left him wistful. Being together, which had seemed possible, even likely, was, at best, on hold. She was sick and getting excellent care; those were the important facts. How could he press her to change continents? How could he entreat her to move away from Ofra when she was already feeling so unsettled?

So he traveled to Jerusalem as often as his teaching schedule and finances allowed. The first of these trips came in April 2003 when, following completion of chemotherapy, Shoshana had a mastectomy. "Now," she told him, "I will have an even bigger scar for you to pretend not to notice."

"You are still as beautiful as ever to me."

"Daniel, my love, I was never beautiful. With my big front teeth and ugly birthmark. Other people said I was cute or pretty, but beautiful . . . only you."

He returned in August and again during the seminary's fall break in October, when they walked hand in hand in Bloomfield Garden and had dinner with Ofra and Adam at the Sabra Restaurant. As dessert was being served, Shoshana pressed her leg against his, and he knew they were both remembering their first dinner together.

He was back in January and June of 2004. During the latter trip, they spent time with Rahel and Yaron at their home in Nahariyya, a coastal town just north of Haifa. The two of them slipped away from family long enough to stroll along the Mediterranean as the sun was setting, the sea smelling slightly of sulphur, and it was there he told her of his plan to take early retirement—in a year and a half, when he could make it work financially—and move to Jerusalem. Once and for all. To be with her. Other strollers may have stared or looked discreetly away as they stood embracing.

The last day of Hanukkah 2004 was Wednesday, December 15. Daniel planned to finish grading papers from the fall semester as quickly as possible and fly to Israel on Tuesday the 14th. The thought was glorious! He would spend Hanukkah and Christmas in Jerusalem with the woman he loved.

But on November 18, Ofra phoned to say her mother was back in the hospital. He asked the question that caused his jaw to clench even as he said the words. There was a pause before Ofra answered: "Yes, they say the cancer has spread." Another pause. "Of course she wanted you to know, but she also said I was to tell you not to rush over here like some madman. She said you should finish your semester and then come when you have planned, later in December."

He immediately called the dean, who agreed that Daniel could cancel his classes until after Thanksgiving. He managed to get an airline reservation, with an open return date, and was in Jerusalem at the Hadassah Hospital by the evening of the 21st.

He had, of course, let her know he was on his way, and when he entered the room, he half expected her to say again that he shouldn't have come. But, instead, her first words touched his soul: "I am glad you are here, *neshama*. I am so glad you are here."

He spent much of the days sitting by her bed, talking quietly when she was awake, reading when she wasn't. "You should take a break," she urged him periodically. "Go see Musa and Samir, walk in the Old City."

But he resisted. "I'm here to be with you." He did have to sleep, spending the nights, restless as they were, in her apartment, amid things that reminded him of what they had shared: a brochure from the National Gallery she kept as a memento of their week together in Washington; a picture of the two of them, Ofra in between, the Tower of David in the background; a book he had given her of *The Gardens of Jerusalem*; the old print of Chagall's *The Praying Jew*; the kiddush cup, badly in need of polish.

Twice, while she was sleeping, he wandered in the hospital's synagogue with its famous windows by Chagall. Twelve stained glass masterpieces, one for each of Israel's tribes. Twelve gates, according to a booklet he found in the synagogue, through which prayers can reach to heaven. He moved slowly around the room, thankful he was alone, fingering the prayer beads in one pocket, the key chain in another.

On his second time there, he lingered in front of the brilliantly red Judah window. After all, the biblical Daniel was supposed to be a descendant of David, and David came from the tribe of Judah. So this window, he silently declared, was meant for him, and he stared at it intently. After a while, he consulted the booklet, which told him the lion, depicted in the glass, was a symbol of the strength of the Jewish people, and the buildings behind it were Jerusalem. He prayed that God would give Shoshana, a woman of Jerusalem, the strength she needed now.

Daniel had been in Jerusalem just over a week when Shoshana learned she would be going home. Good, he told her. He could stay there and take care of her, make her a cake for her birthday like she did for him thirty-five years ago. But she was firm: Ofra could do the caregiving. He should go back, finish his semester, and come in December as he had planned. They would have a grand Hanukkah-Christmas celebration!

"Okay," he said, "but I'm not teaching in January, so you will have to put up with me here for a month. Maybe more."

That evening, with Shoshana not yet released from the hospital, Daniel finally went to the Old City, entering through the Damascus Gate, walking slowly down Khan al-Zeit, ending up on the Rooftop, where his mind inevitably drifted back. The fire at Al-Aqsa, the night in the Holy Sepulchre, the experience on this very rooftop, meeting Shoshana . . . Peg had accused him of fixating on his year abroad the way a football player replays his high school heroics. But why not? That miraculous year had outlined the narrative of his life. How amazing! A city where he had never lived, a faith that for him was never secure, a conflict to which he would always be an outsider, a woman to whom he had never been married. *God,* he prayed, *you who may be there in the darkness, protect this woman I love.*

He looked around the dome to make sure he was alone, then rested his arms on the railing. It would be easy, he knew, to play "what could have been." This whole region of the world was filled with what-could-have-beens. But standing there now, with the familiar landmarks spread out before him, he could honestly say he did not for a second regret falling in love with Shoshana. *Only let us have more time with one another.*

It was not to be. On December 12, two weeks after Daniel left Jerusalem, and two days before his scheduled return, the call came from Ofra.

"My Ema has died. It was so fast. Some of her last words were to tell you"—her voice cracked—"that you were the love of her life."

Chapter Thirty

Valerie's presence, and Shoshana's absence, made this trip to Jerusalem dramatically unlike any of Daniel's previous ones. And the Old City itself had changed. He had warned Valerie to expect piles of trash and the smell of urine, mixed with that of spices and fruit, but the alleyways were now quite clean, with even an occasional bin for garbage. There were still butchers, but no fly-covered carcasses hanging in front of their shops. You could still see jumbles of electrical cables on some walls, but the streets were well lit. This, he realized, couldn't have happened overnight. He must have been so preoccupied with Shoshana's illness that he hadn't noticed the improvements the last few times he was there. One change (Daniel wasn't inclined to call it an improvement) that was impossible to miss was the construction of a light-rail system in new Jerusalem, with a stop near the Damascus Gate. "Next," he fumed, "there will be a cable car to the Western Wall."

The real question was whether the biggest change was in the Old City or in himself. In 1969, it had all felt wildly exotic and vaguely frightening. Did it feel that way now to Valerie? he wondered. Forty years ago, the maze of streets made the Old City seem expansive; now it felt remarkably small. Even their slow climb from El-Wad to the New Gate took less than fifteen minutes, assuming they didn't stop for tea or a conversation with the Armenian in his photography shop.

Daniel *was* glad he didn't have to worry if Valerie was in danger when she went alone to meet her new friend in the Jewish Quarter or just stretch her legs while he was immersed in some book about the city. But along with danger, the area inside the walls seemed stripped of its mystery. The robed figures of different faiths were simply people in religious garb, the churches and excavated religious sites just stops on a tour group agenda. And God knew the place was filled with tour groups! He shuddered to think what the streets were like in July.

"I'm sorry Jerusalem has lost some of its charm for you," Valerie said after one of his frequent laments, "but being safer and cleaner is a good thing for the people who live here. And all the digging makes it more interesting for people who are into history and archaeology. That's not a bad thing either. Change happens. You don't want the Old City to be a museum, do you?"

Daniel couldn't help but smile. "No, you're right. I just wish it wasn't so . . . modern, with these mini tractors zipping around. I won't be surprised if soon there's a McDonald's by the Tower of David."

They were having tea in the courtyard of a hotel not far from their own. As Valerie sipped hers, she said, "I doubt many people think they visited their favorite city at the perfect time. It's always 'You should have seen Paris when the real artists were here,' or 'Rome was much better before the restaurants began catering to the tastes of Americans.'" He could see her smile over the rim of her cup. "You, my dear, have an image from the 1960s in your mind, but there are probably still a few persons around who would say, 'You should have been here in the '40s when this was a real Arab city.' It seems to me that a city isn't only a place, it's a combination of who you are and who you're with when you go there."

That evening he took her to the Rooftop on Mount Zion.

———

Since Valerie wasn't a regular churchgoer, Daniel had not intended for this trip to emphasize religion; but in Jerusalem some religion is inevitable, including a visit to the Holy Sepulchre. "It won't be what you expect," he told her.

"That won't be hard. I have no idea what to expect."

It was only a four-minute walk from their hotel to the unprepossessing basilica, so they went there on their second day. "It's no Notre Dame," he said as they stood facing the church, "but at least it looks better than it did in 1969 when there was scaffolding all over the front."

Valerie was quiet as they weaved past tour groups toward the twin-door entrance, the right-hand door completely sealed with medieval bricks. Finally, he asked, "What do you think?"

She paused, looking back around the constricted courtyard. "I am imagining all the millions of people who have thought of this as holy ground. And I'm glad it doesn't feel at all like a museum."

Once inside, Daniel pointed out different areas of the church—the place of the crucifixion, the stone on which Jesus's body was laid, the tomb in its own enclosure—emphasizing that all of this was according to tradition more than history. Valerie's favorite part, however, was the staircase down to the crypt of Saint Helena where ancient pilgrims had carved crosses into the stone walls. She traced one of them with her finger, the rock cool and damp to the touch. While they sat on a bench in the dimly lit crypt, watching groups mill in front of them, Daniel told her more about spending the night there, listening to the chanting monks. She slid closer to him, looping her arm through his, and rested her head on his shoulder.

That evening they walked out the Jaffa Gate to a restaurant in the nearby Mamilla Mall, but only after Daniel promised Valerie he wouldn't grouse about there being a shopping center so close to the Old City. Once they were seated and eating *baba ghanouj*, she said, "I know this is Jerusalem where religion is in the air, but there must have been other things that contributed to your religious 'conversion,' I guess you'd call it, when you were here as a student. I mean, you changed your major, your whole career. That's a big deal! That really is a conversion. And I think it's very interesting that your identity as a

Christian developed when you were surrounded by Jews and Muslims."

She waited patiently while he scooped some of the eggplant dip with a piece of pita. "I remember," he said when he stopped chewing, "waking up in the middle of the night in my dorm in Tel Aviv and feeling—I don't know how to explain it—empty, I guess, but a panicked emptiness. This was early in my time at the university. Nothing was particularly wrong, but I didn't feel like I belonged anywhere. The men at the Al-Kamal asked where I was home, and I wasn't sure. They took being Muslim for granted in the same way the Jews at the university took being Jewish for granted, as something they were from birth, and I wasn't either of those. But I wanted to be *something*." He paused, but Valerie, true to form, didn't interrupt. "The courses I was taking were okay, but I no longer could imagine spending my life focused on politics. It just seemed like there must be something more, so I suppose you could say I was primed to have religious experiences."

"You had all of these experiences on your own?"

Again he paused. "Yeah, at first. But I had a friend in Jerusalem who was experimenting with being religious, so that helped later on. Yes, that made a real difference, now that I look back on it."

"Does that friend still live here? I would like to meet him."

"Her, actually. And she no longer lives here." Their meal arrived at that moment, and after they were served, he changed the subject.

Daniel had also intended for this trip to steer clear of politics. When he mentioned this one morning over breakfast, however, Valerie informed him that their very hotel was caught up in the conflict. She had been talking again with Mr. Barakat, who had filled her in on the controversy. "It turns out that he doesn't actually own the building, he leases it from the Greek Orthodox Church. And in 2004, the church, someone in the church, sold the property to a right-wing Jewish group." Daniel raised his eyebrows as Valerie continued. "He claims it's a settlers' organization that is trying to buy up everything they can in East Jerusalem. The patriarch, I forget his name, said he knew nothing about the sale, blamed it on the church's finance guy, but I guess the church members didn't believe him and ran him out of office. This is all from Mr. Barakat, who seems trustworthy to me. Anyway, it's all been tied up since then in Israeli courts, with talk of bribes and I-don't-know-what-all. So," she concluded, "you can't escape politics here any more than you can avoid religion."

Daniel also hadn't intended to talk much about Shoshana. He had told Valerie, when they first got together, that he'd had a good friend in Jerusalem who died two years ago, but not much more. He knew Valerie wouldn't be jealous, even if Shoshana were still alive; jealousy wasn't in her nature. But she would want to know all about her, and what was the point? They hadn't been married, so was there need to say more? Valerie would see right through him, would sense the lingering pain, would want to grieve his loss. And he was through grieving.

He did, however, tell Valerie about Ofra, with whom he had kept in touch, and her response was predictable: "Let's meet her for dinner! I want to meet friends of yours. And a real Israeli at that."

They met at a not-too-noisy vegetarian restaurant in new Jerusalem, an easy walk from their hotel. Ofra greeted Daniel with a quick hug and shook hands with Valerie. "I'm afraid it must be a fast meal," she told them, even before they were seated. "My husband, Adam, isn't so good at getting kids in bed." This led Valerie to ask about Ofra's children (How many? How old? What do they like to do?) and her husband (What was his profession? Was he from Jerusalem?). Daniel could feel the initial unease sloughing off.

After they had ordered, Valerie asking Ofra for suggestions, Ofra said, "There was a terrible suicide bombing in a bar just across the street." She pointed out the window. "It was in 2001. I remember because it was just before my twenty-fifth birthday, and friends had plans for us to go there." That led to a discussion of trauma survivors. It was clear that Ofra and Valerie had common interests, which pleased Daniel, who sat listening. At one point, Valerie suggested that not only Israelis but Palestinians were undoubtedly suffering from collective PTSD. Ofra readily agreed, which pleased Daniel even more.

Then the conversation took a turn he hadn't expected. "Daniel had a traumatic experience in the Old City," said Valerie, "years ago when he was a student. He was there when the Al-Aqsa Mosque was set on fire and was in danger of being arrested for it." She turned toward her husband. "I imagine that having such a dramatic moment in your life happen here is part of what kept drawing you back to Jerusalem."

"I didn't know about that," said Ofra. She paused. "But there was something else that kept him coming back." She glanced at Daniel, and when he didn't shake his head, she continued. "He and my mother were very close."

Valerie smiled. "I've had some inkling of that." Pause. "And I think you have more you want to say about it."

"Yeah, I guess." Ofra fumbled with her large shoulder bag, finally pulling out a greeting-card-sized envelope. She looked at Daniel. "I found a letter Ema wrote to you when she was in the hospital at the end. It got mixed up with her stuff so I didn't see it until . . . Anyway, I was going to send it, but you said you were coming back to Jerusalem, so I thought I'd just give it to you, if we had a chance to meet."

Back in the hotel, Valerie said, "I think you should read the letter." While she busied herself in the bathroom, Daniel sat on the edge of the bed, staring at the envelope. He had read somewhere that it's hard to remember voices, but he could hear Shoshana's voice in his head as clearly as if she were in the room, just as he could see in his mind's eye the birthmark on her neck, her many hats, hair flowing from underneath, and, of course, her smile. Finally, he opened the envelope to find a card with Chagall's *Green Violinist* on the front. Inside was her handwriting—so familiar, though somewhat shaky—words crossed out as she apparently searched for the right ones.

My dear Daniel, ahuvi,

Even though it has been almost 40 years, I remember so clearly when we first met and those special months when I had the pleasure of helping you learn to be a lover. You were so naive that sometimes I felt 10 years older, not 3. There was something deeper than sex between us (much deeper), but I had no illusions. You were a visiting student. Your real love was Jerusalem, and I was part of the experience.

But it didn't work out that way, did it? You didn't forget me, wouldn't let go of me even when I thought I wanted you to. I knew of course that the Shoshana you said you loved was a Shoshana of your imagination. But isn't this true for lots of people? And isn't it possible to love someone more and more through the words they write, through the person (you would probably call it the "soul") they show you without being present? Even now I know you will not forget me in death just as you did not forget me in life, and I love you for it—more than I managed to tell you. [these last words written in the margins]

My friends said I was crazy to have a relationship with a guy who showed up every few years! Maybe yours did too. One guy I was dating saw one of your letters and told me he couldn't compete with some ideal man who wasn't even here. He was right.

The last two paragraphs were written in a different-colored ink, the handwriting even more erratic.

Would we have made a good couple? I don't know. I chose to be an Israeli rather than an American. That is a crucial part of who I am. While you, my love, for all your love of the Old City, are an American through and through. You have always been a visitor in the place that is the home of my heart. You study what I live.

So would we have made a good couple? I don't know. But propped up here in this hospital room reviewing my life, I can now say that I wish we had tried.

My love always,
Shoshana

Daniel sat silently weeping, head down, almost feeling as though he couldn't breathe. After a minute, Valerie sat next to him on the bed and said, gently, "I think you loved Ofra's mother very much."

He nodded slightly. "But you are—"

She put her finger to his lips, the way Shoshana had often done, which made him cry harder. Finally, she said, "I know you love me now. And I am glad you have loved deeply before."

Chapter Thirty-One

On their last day in Jerusalem, Valerie suggested that Daniel walk the alleyways of the Old City by himself. "You might not get back," she told him, "at least for a while, so you should spend as long as you want at your favorite spots. You, sweetheart, are the only person I know whose life story revolves around a city where he's never lived. Go breathe it in. I'll stay here and see if Mr. Barakat has any more gossip to share with me."

They had a cup of coffee together in the hotel dining room before he headed out around seven thirty. A book he once read called this the time of day when the Old City is naked, before the scarves and jewelry and purses, put there by vendors, cover its stones. Valerie had taught him to appreciate the vendors; he had always loved the stones.

Daniel could smell fresh bread as he exited the hotel, the Jaffa Gate to his right, the Citadel looming across the open space in front of him. He turned left and headed east down the familiar steps of David Street, past the bead shop where he had purchased earrings for Shoshana. At Jewish Quarter Road, he turned right into the part of the Old City rebuilt since Israel's victory in the war of 1967. Past shop windows with menorahs made of brass and silver, with paintings of rabbis wearing prayer shawls and tefillin, with intricately decorated kiddush cups, like the one he had bought for Shoshana. But also past a shop with T-shirts reading *Jerusalem: Ours Now and Always*. He could practically hear Shoshana ranting about how "everyone thinks this place belongs to them!" What, he wondered, accounts for this desire to have exclusive possession? Was he, in his own way, guilty of it?

He zigzagged through the Jewish Quarter, from the Cardo with its columns from Byzantine Jerusalem, to the excavation of the "Broad Wall" built in the time of King Hezekiah, seven centuries before the birth of Jesus, to Hurva Square with its grand, newly rebuilt synagogue. He sat for a minute on a bench at the edge of the square, remembering how he and Shoshana . . .

Enough of this! he told himself. This was also where Valerie had tea with the woman who owned the jewelry shop. Although why not think of them both? Loving Valerie did not require forgetting Shoshana, did it? Even Valerie agreed, didn't she?

He walked quickly through the rest of the small Jewish Quarter, coming out on the plaza in front of the Western Wall, where a handful of Orthodox Jews were already at prayer. He strolled toward the spot where forty years ago he had watched the students dance and received the yarmulke from Reb Shlomo. But now his recollection was colored by the knowledge that this very spot had been home to an eight-hundred-year-old community of Moroccan Muslims whose houses were razed soon after Israel captured the Old City. In Ohio, he reflected, you might be standing on the site of a Native American village, your home might mark the spot where a once-famous chief died in battle, but you would likely never know it. Here history forced itself on you. Here history fed the imagination with images of Israelites and Babylonians, Romans, Crusaders, Mamluks, and Ottomans.

Just beyond the Wall was the gray dome of Al-Aqsa, a building that had played a surprisingly prominent role in his life, even though he couldn't recall ever being inside it. Maybe once as a student the week before the fire, but then he had paid little attention to the carpets or the soon-to-be-destroyed pulpit or the ornate ceiling. Now, he would know how to see what he was looking at. Now, he would know to value each sight—each experience, each person—because there may not be another chance. A sign indicated that Haram al-Sharif was closed to visitors because it was a Muslim holiday, and that was okay. It was already part of his memories and imagination.

Daniel donned his red velvet yarmulke, musty from years in a trunk, and put a paper prayer between stones in the Wall, a six-word prayer of thanksgiving, and then left the plaza by way of the stairs on the northwest corner. He went left on the Street of the Chain, then right into one of the three parallel streets at the heart of the souk, streets that converged to become Khan al-Zeit. Now his memory was in high gear, especially at the location—he knew it precisely—where he had encountered the Palestinian youths and the Israeli soldiers, who were little more than youths, on the morning of the fire. And here, maybe, was the shop where he dropped the knife. What if the soldiers had discovered it on him? Valerie called it a traumatic event in his life. Had it been?

He paused in front of the cheap clothing store where he thought Al-Kamal had been. Either there or in what was now a candy store, its bins of sweets already on display. He was no longer sure. When he reached the steps that descended from the Damascus Gate, he stopped for an orange juice, shaking his head when an older woman—a woman his age, he realized—tried to sell him a calendar with two sets of dates. Then, remembering the lobby of Al-Kamal, he changed his mind and bought one. Instead of bargaining, as she no doubt expected, he gave her more than she asked.

Turning back, he took the left fork onto El-Wad where he had been caught in the furious, grieving crowd. He went left again at the Austrian Hostel and was soon standing in front of the Sisters of Zion convent. Memories of Sister Mary. She likely had no idea of her influence on his life, just as he was unaware of people he may have touched through his lectures and books. He said a prayer of thanksgiving for Sister Mary and for her steering him to the Rooftop.

He continued straight, toward the Lions' Gate, past the Church of Saint Anne and the building next to it that was home to Father Laurent.

Although the priest was nowhere to be seen, Daniel acknowledged him with a wave of his hand. Out the gate and down the long hill to the Garden of Gethsemane, where he prayed again, giving thanks this time for peacemakers he had known, including Musa, Ghazala, Abu Yusef, Reb Shlomo, Julia, Mr. Khoury, and Mr. Shehadeh. And, he added, Valerie.

He plodded back up the hill and through the gate, this time following the Via Dolorosa and the by-now-familiar climb toward the New Gate. The sun was growing warmer and the alleyways more crowded with tour groups led by guides with identifying flags or umbrellas, their voices raised in order to be heard. Just beyond the Armenian photo shop, he turned left on Christian Quarter Road and left again, down a flight of steps to the pinched courtyard in front of the Holy Sepulchre.

For a minute, he simply stood, taking in the familiar facade, the lock so high on the battered doors that a ladder was needed to unlock them. He was mentally plotting how to use his time—spend a few minutes in the church, then go to Mount Zion—when a balding man about his age asked, "Are you, by any chance, a tour guide?" His tone was tentative, clearly not wanting to offend.

Daniel laughed. "No, I'm afraid not. But I'm flattered you don't think I look like a tourist."

A cluster of folks had gathered around, trying to hear the exchange. "We're part of a larger group from Des Moines," said the man who had spoken to him. "We're staying at a hotel, a nice place near the sea in Tel Aviv, and it's our last day in Israel. So they gave us a choice: spend the day on the beach or come back here, where we had less than a full day early in the trip. Most of the group stayed in Tel Aviv—"

"We don't have beaches in Des Moines," said another man, and several of them chuckled along with him.

The first man completed his explanation. "But ten of us—is that right?—ten of us said we wanted to come back to Jerusalem."

"Well, as far as I'm concerned," said Daniel, "you made the better choice."

"The problem," said the first man, "is that one of our group got a bug of some sort—"

"Or it was something she ate," said the woman next to him.

"Yes, or something she ate, and she threw up right as we were walking down those steps, not fifteen minutes ago."

"It wasn't pretty," said the woman. "Somebody came out and threw water but that didn't take care of all of it."

"So the guide who was with us took her to a clinic or someplace like that. We couldn't really understand what he was telling us. We did understand that he will meet us by the Jaffa Gate, which I think we can find, at two o'clock. And he said there would be lots of guides looking for work that we could hire to show us around. So that's why I asked—"

"If he says he's not a guide, he's not a guide," said a tall man with bushy white hair. "He probably didn't need all that explanation."

The first man smiled at Daniel and shrugged his shoulders. "Well, thanks."

Daniel looked at the group, people who now struck him as worn out and a little worried, but also eager. Good people, like ones he had known growing up in Ohio. The kind of people Valerie would love talking to, and who would love talking to her.

"I'm certainly not an official guide," he told them, "but I do know my way around. So, sure, I can give you a tour of the Holy Sepulchre, if that sounds satisfactory."

The Iowans nodded enthusiastically, after which they all introduced themselves and were impressed to learn he was a professor—of religion, at that. "Where's your home?" one of them asked, and they were delighted when he revealed he was from a state near their own.

He turned their attention to the front of the church, moving them back far enough to see the multiple domes. But before he could speak about the history of the basilica, one of them said, "I didn't expect it to be so ugly."

Daniel smiled. "A wise person has urged me not just to look at the outside, but to imagine all the people, the pilgrims, who have regarded this place as holy." He saw that most of them were nodding. "Before I tell you about the church, turn around and look at the mosque behind you." And so he told them the story of Caliph Umar refusing the invitation to pray inside the Holy Sepulchre lest his followers insist on transforming it into a mosque. "This mosque marks where he prayed instead."

"This," said the first man, "is the kind of thing I hoped we could learn." More nods.

After they finished their tour and were leaving the church, Daniel recounted his adventure of spending the night there. "Back then, I thought it was some kind of daring transgression. I've since learned that people do it all the time. You just make a reservation with the Franciscan friars." He laughed and so did the group, the gentle laughing-with of friends.

"Say, would you all like the best pomegranate juice in the whole Old City?" Affirmation all around, so he took them to Samir's café, one minute away on Christian Quarter Road, where they fit only if three of the larger men stood outside.

Samir, of course, stood on a chair and announced that "friends of Daniel are friends to me."

As they were leaving Samir's, one of the women said to Daniel, "He's a Palestinian, right? I should have asked him what he thinks about all the fighting and the settlements."

"To be honest," Daniel told her, "Samir isn't a typical Palestinian when it comes to the conflict." He chuckled, more to himself than to her. "I'm not sure what 'typical' means, but what you need to do is make another trip. Come and see, come and meet Palestinians as well as Israelis."

The group walked slowly down Christian Quarter Road, Daniel pointing out the huge grooved pavement stones dating back to the Romans. Then, remembering Musa, he took them to the shop of the textile merchant and, after promising they would buy something, got him to move a display case so they could glimpse the Crusader church buried beneath it.

"That's Jerusalem," Daniel told the group. "There are always things beneath what you see."

"Let us take you to lunch," said the first man as they were exiting the shop. "Everyone is saying how lucky we were to bump into someone who is so much more than a tour guide."

Why not? he thought. Valerie would love it that he was sharing his love for the city. They were right at the Muristan, so he led them to the restaurant with rooftop tables, the place where he and Ghazala had stood gazing at Al-Aqsa. While they were waiting for their food, Daniel pointed out various landmarks, including the onion-shaped domes of the Russian Church of Mary Magdalene on the side of the Mount of Olives. "Pilgrims go past there on Palm Sunday, following the path Jesus took into the city."

"Do you think it's true?" asked the tall man.

Is it true? How, Daniel wondered, can you answer such a question in Jerusalem?

"I have no idea whether a particular event or site is historical," he told the man. "But many people testify that God has touched earth *here*. Right here. That I do know."

"This is such a wonderful view," said one of the women. "What is it, one o'clock? I could stay here until it's time to get on the van."

Daniel turned to look at these new friends gathered near him, half wishing he could again experience this city as they were—for the first time.

"This *is* a great view," he assured them. "But since you've got time, let me show you an even better one."

Acknowledgments

A Rooftop in Jerusalem is a work of fiction; the plot, characters, and dialogues are products of my imagination. The scenes that begin the first four parts of the book, however, are heavily informed by my personal experience. With that in mind, I want to acknowledge with appreciation the Eden Theological Seminary students who took part in a travel seminar course to Israel and Palestine in January 2007, and the St. Louis–based participants in an interfaith study tour to that region later the same year. I was the professor in charge of the student seminar, assisted by the Rev. Dr. Peter Makari, the executive minister responsible for relations with the Middle East in the United Church of Christ and the Christian Church (Disciples of Christ). And I was coleader of the interfaith tour, along with Rabbi Mark Shook, rabbi emeritus at Congregation Temple Israel in St. Louis. The experience of traveling with these groups, and working with these colleagues, influenced the shaping of this novel. I learned every bit as much as I taught!

Peter Makari also provided valuable help with the Arabic used in the novel, although I am responsible for decisions about transliteration.

www.ingramcontent.com/pod-product-compliance
Lightning Source LLC
LaVergne TN
LVHW041916070526
838199LV00051BA/2630